ZANE

Books by Madeline Baker

A Whisper in the Wind
Apache Flame
Apache Runaway
Beneath a Midnight Moon
Callie's Cowboy
Chase the Lightning
Chase The Wind
Cheyenne Surrender
Comanche Flame
Dakota Dreams
Dude Ranch Bride
Every Inch a Cowboy
Feather in the Wind
First Love, Wild Love
Forbidden Fires
Hawk's Woman
Kade
Lacey's Way
Lakota Love Song
Lakota Renegade
Love Forevermore

Love in the Wind
Midnight Fire
Prairie Heat
Reckless Desire
Reckless Destiny
Reckless Embrace
Reckless Heart
Reckless Love
Renegade Heart
Shadows Through Time
Spirit's Song
The Angel and the Outlaw
The Reckless Series
The Spirit Path
Under a Prairie Moon
Under Apache Skies
Unforgettable
Warrior's Lady
West Texas Bride
Wolf Shadow
Zane

About the Publisher

This book is published on behalf of the author by the Ethan Ellenberg Literary Agency.

https://ethanellenberg.com
Email: agent@ethanellenberg.com
Facebook: https://www.facebook.com/EthanEllenberg LiteraryAgency/

Books by Amanda Ashley

"Born of the Night" in
  Stroke of Midnight
"Midnight Pleasures"
  in *Darkfest*
"Music of the Night"
  in *Mammoth Book of*
  Vampire Romance
A Darker Dream
A Fire in the Blood
A Whisper of Eternity
After Sundown
As Twilight Falls
Beauty's Beast
Beneath a Midnight
  Moon
Bound by Blood
Bound by Night
Dark of the Moon
Dead Perfect
Dead Sexy
Deeper Than the Night
Desire After Dark
Desire the Night
Donovan's Woman
Embrace the Night
Everlasting Collection
Everlasting Desire
Everlasting Embrace

Everlasting Kiss
His Dark Embrace
Immortal Sins
In the Dark of the Night
Jessie's Girl
Maiden's Song
Masquerade
Midnight and Moonlight
Midnight Embrace
Night's Kiss
Night's Master
Night's Mistress
Night's Pleasure
Night's Promise
Night's Surrender
Night's Touch
Quinn's Lady
Quinn's Revenge
Sandy's Angel
Seasons of the Night
Secrets in the Night
Shades of Gray
Sunlight Moonlight
Surrender the Dawn
The Captive
The Music of the Night
Twilight Desires
Twilight Dreams

Zane

Madeline Baker

Zane

ISBN: 978-1-68068-292-2

You can reach the author at:
Email: darkwritr@aol.com
Websites: www.amandaashley.net and www.madelinebaker.net

Dedication

To Austyn Madeline
The newest member of our family
Wishing you much love and happiness.

Chapter One

Wyoming Territory
1874

He'd been on the run all his life. Running from the bru-
tality of the white man who had been his father. Running
from the stigma of being called "half-breed." He had run for
years until he got tired of running, tired of backing down,
tired of pretending he was less than everyone else because
his mother had been a Cheyenne medicine woman.

His mother. She had been the only good thing in his
life. Kind, caring. She had loved him more than her own
life and had died at the hands of his father rather than let
the bastard hit him again. In a move that had become habit
whenever he thought of her, his hand caressed the butt of
the .44 Colt on his hip.

The same Colt that had killed his old man twelve
years ago.

Zane Two Shadows smiled faintly. He had killed other
men since that night but none had given him the same
sense of satisfaction as firing six .44 slugs into his father.

He had met a priest once who had told him he was surely
bound for hell. Zane had nodded, thinking he wouldn't
mind spending eternity tormenting his old man.

Throwing the dregs of his coffee on the fire, he kicked
dirt over the ashes then swung onto the back of his horse.

With luck, he would make it to town before dark. He'd had enough of his own company, enough of sleeping under the stars. It was time to treat himself to a bed, a bath, and a bottle. And maybe spend an hour or two with one of the whores at Sally's Saloon.

Not long ago, Cross Creek had been little more than a wide spot in the road. If it hadn't been for the three large ranches in the area, the town would have died long ago. The place had grown some through the years.

Zane tended to head in this direction whenever he felt the need for a taste of civilization.

Sally's Saloon was the largest of the trio that lined the dusty street. Sandwiched between the saloons were a combination barbershop and bathhouse, the Cross Creek Bank, a hotel with a small restaurant, and a smithy run by a big bear of a man named Karl Powers, who'd been acting as the sheriff since the last one up and quit six months ago and no one else was willing to take the job.

As he rode further down the road, Zane noticed two new, false-fronted buildings, one on either side of the street at the north end of town.

He snorted softly when he read the sign on the first establishment. *J.J. Lee. Attorney at Law.* A lawyer? Here, in Cross Creek? Unbelievable. The population of the town, not counting cowboys and ranch hands, was less than a hundred people. To his knowledge, none of them had ever needed any legal advice.

Zane perused the second sign. *Grant's General Store.* That made a hell of a lot more sense. He was in bad need of a new shirt. And maybe a pair of socks. The doctor's office resided in a single-story house at the end of the block, identified by a small, hand-lettered sign that read *Doctor Joseph Fontaine, M.D.*

He drew rein in front of Sally's. Dismounting, he tethered his mare to the hitch rail, settled his Colt on his hip, and strode into the saloon.

Zane paused inside the door for a moment, letting his eyes adjust to the dim light. The place hadn't changed since he'd been there last—the same long bar stood opposite the batwing doors. The same faded painting of a voluptuous nude hung on the wall behind the bar. Sawdust on the floor. Round tables scattered at intervals. Three men sat at one, engaged in a desultory game of poker. Two cowboys stood hipshot at the bar, arguing over which of them was going to spend an hour or two with Sally's favorite whore, French Lil. Ed, the bartender, stood nearby, idly polishing a glass, ready to step in if it looked like words were going to turn into action.

Zane took a chair at one of the empty tables. He noted French Lil looked bored by the argument going on. He grinned when she looked around the room, her eyes lighting up when she saw him. Pushing the two men aside, she hurried toward him.

"When did you get into town?" Lil asked as she plopped down on his lap. "I'm so glad to see you!" She was a pretty thing, with a mass of curly hair that was too red to be natural and flashing brown eyes wise beyond their years.

"Here now!" the taller of the two cowboys at the bar exclaimed, glaring at Zane. "Get your own whore."

"I did."

The two men exchanged glances, their former animosity apparently forgotten as they strode stiff-legged toward him, eyes narrowed.

"Better move out of the way," Zane advised Lil. "They look angry."

"Damn right, we're angry!" The tall man grabbed Lil by the arm and pulled her off Zane's lap. "She's ours."

"Let her go," Zane said, his voice deceptively mild.

"And if I don't?"

Zane unfolded from his chair in a single, fluid movement.

The tall man and his companion exchanged glances again. The shorter one nodded almost imperceptivity.

The move wasn't lost on Zane.

As the tall man backed up, dragging French Lil with him, the other man reached for his gun.

He never cleared leather.

The tall man's eyes grew wide as his friend sprawled face down in the sawdust. Releasing Lil as if her skin had suddenly scorched his hand, he backed away and then darted out the side door.

"Is he dead?" Lil asked.

Zane nodded. "Get me a drink, will ya?"

With a last look at the dead man, she hurried toward the bar.

Zane holstered his Colt then turned toward the door as it swung open.

Karl Powers stood there, rifle in hand. He took in the scene in a single glance. "You kill him, Zane?"

"He didn't give me much choice."

"Did you see what happened, Ed?" the acting sheriff asked.

The bartender nodded. "It was self-defense, just like he said."

"I'll send Henry to pick up the body. Zane, I'll need you to come down to the office and sign a statement."

"Yeah."

"You, too, Ed."

"Sure thing, sheriff."

After giving Zane a stern look, Karl Powers took his leave.

Zane strode toward the bar. "Thanks for backing me up, Ed."

"I owed you one," he said, handing him a drink.

"I guess we're square now."

"Are you staying in town long?" Lil asked, sashaying up beside him.

Zane shrugged. "I haven't decided."

She leaned against him, her thigh brushing his. "I wish you would."

"Any of the ranches hiring?" He didn't care much for herding cattle, but he was damn near broke.

"The T Bar K is looking for a few men," Ed replied. "They're short-handed right now. Two of their cowboys got busted up pretty bad a week or so again. They ain't fit to ride."

Zane downed the whiskey in a single swallow. "Thanks. I'll look into it."

"I hear there's been some Indian trouble west of here," Ed remarked. "You hear anything about that?"

"The tribes are angry about the settlers encroaching on their land, putting up fences. There's bound to be a fight sooner or later."

The bartender nodded. "You been to see your people lately?"

"No."

Ed nodded again. Bringing up Zane's ties to the Cheyenne was a touchy subject. Some of the folks in town didn't take kindly to half-breeds.

Lil tugged on Zane's hand, a question in her eyes Grinning, he followed her up the stairs.

Kathleen Taggart sat in the wooden rocker on the front porch, shelling peas. She looked up at the sound of hoof-beats, frowned as an unfamiliar rider mounted on a big buckskin horse trotted down the road toward the house. "Stranger coming," she called to her father, who was inside going over the ranch accounts.

Tobias Taggart stepped out onto the porch, his favorite Winchester rifle held loosely at his side. "That *hombre* looks like trouble."

Kathleen nodded. He certainly did. As he drew closer, she was sure of it. He rode easy in the saddle, yet there was an air of tension about him, as if he never truly relaxed. His holster looked well-worn, as did his boots. His hair—glossy black and straight as a string—fell past his shoulders. His eyes were dark gray and wary beneath of brim of a dusty black hat.

He reined his horse to a halt in front of the porch stairs.

Taggart took a step forward. "Can I help you?"

"I heard you might be hirin'."

"Yeah? Who told you that?"

"The bartender at Sally's."

Tobias grunted softly. "Ed a friend of yours?"

The stranger nodded. "He said you were short-handed just now."

"Yeah. Couple of my men got busted up trying to break a loco bronc." Taggart's eyes narrowed. "You've got some Injun blood in you, or I miss my guess."

A muscle twitched in the stranger's jaw. "You got a problem with that?"

"That depends on you," Taggart said. "You got a name?"

"Zane. And you'd be?"

"Taggart." His gaze darted to the stranger's holster. "What kind of work are you looking for, Mr. Zane?"

"Anything I can get."

"You any good with that hogleg?"

Zane shrugged one shoulder. "I generally hit what I aim at."

"All right. I'm a little shorthanded right now, but I don't need another cowhand. What I need is a man to keep an eye on the place. We've had a couple of steers rustled in the last few weeks."

"Any idea who's behind it?"

Taggart shook his head. "Mark Edling, owner of the Triple E, is bringing a herd of cattle up from Texas. He's eager to buy my south range, but it's not for sale. Not at any price. But Edling wouldn't bother stealing a few head. Anyway, I'm looking for someone to side me who's good with a gun and not afraid to use it. Can you handle that?"

Zane nodded once, curtly.

"All right, you're hired. Pays twenty-five a month and found. You can bed down in the bunkhouse. This here's my daughter, Kathleen. She's off-limits."

Zane grinned wryly. "Right." With a nod in the girl's direction, he reined his horse around and headed for the bunkhouse.

Her father was right, Kathleen thought, as she watched the stranger ride away. He looked like trouble, sure enough. No doubt about it.

Chapter Two

The bunkhouse was empty when Zane opened the door. A wood stove stood in the center of the room. A table and four chairs occupied a space near the door. Cots lined both sides of the room, five on one side, four on the other. Three of the bunks were available, easy to recognize because the blankets were neatly folded at the foot. The three empty bunks were next to each other. He took the last one, which was nearest to the back wall, which left a wide space between himself and the others.

Judging from past experience, he was pretty sure he wouldn't be welcomed by the cowhands. Not only because he was new but because of his Cheyenne blood. The Plains tribes were on the warpath. Three months ago, a war party of Cheyenne had massacred a wagon train about seventy-five miles from Cross Creek. The grisly news had made headlines in the last newspaper he'd seen. Attacks like that tarred all Indians with the same brush.

He dropped his gear on the cot then went outside to unsaddle his horse.

Kathleen had been about to go inside to start dinner when she saw Zane step out of the bunkhouse. She cocked her head to the side as she watched him unsaddle the big buckskin mare. He moved with innate grace as he laid the saddle and blanket over the top rail of the small corral beside the barn and then began to curry the mare with long, easy strokes. Kathleen frowned when she found herself staring at him, admiring the impressive muscles that bunched and flexed in his back and arms as he moved. Annoyed, she looked away. Only to find herself glancing over her shoulder for one more look.

When he finished brushing the mare, Zane stood at the mare's head, his hand idly scratching the buckskin's ears.

Kathleen smiled as the mare lowered her head in what was obviously a sign of pleasure. Whatever else the man might be, she thought, he took good care of his horse.

She felt her cheeks flush when he looked up and caught her staring. Mortified, she turned and hurried inside.

But she was still thinking about him when she went to bed that night.

Taggart laid his fork aside. "You look troubled, daughter. What's on your mind?"

"What? Oh, nothing. More eggs, Dad?"

"Don't change the subject, girl. Something's got your tail in a knot this morning. What is it?"

"Oh, very well. If you must know, it's that new man."

"Zane? What about him?"

"You don't know anything about him, except that he says he's good with a gun."

Taggart shrugged. "At the moment, he's just the kind of fella we need around here."

Kathleen shook her head. She knew her father was worried about the stolen cattle. Maybe Edling was responsible. Maybe Indians. She didn't know which worried her more. "I need to go into town tomorrow."

"Well, I can't take you. I need to go see Tom O'Brian today. He's hurtin' for money and before he went to visit his daughter, he offered to sell me that chestnut mare I've had my eye on."

"Can't you go this this morning?"

"No. He's not home yet. Won't be back until tomorrow at noon. I'm going into town today to withdraw the money from the bank. Tom said if he didn't hear from me by twelve-thirty on Saturday, he'd sell the mare to Tompkins."

Kathleen huffed a sigh. Susannah's party started at twelve. The O'Brian place was a good hour's ride away from the ranch, and in the opposite direction of where she needed to go. By the time her father and O'Brian closed the deal, drank a few rounds to celebrate, and her father returned home, the party would be over.

"Sorry, daughter. I can't spare any of the hands just now. The river's jammed up and it's gonna take them the next two or three days to clear it. And you're not going anywhere alone. Austin saw some Injun sign a few miles south of here. I'll take you to town on Monday."

"But Susannah's party is tomorrow and I promised her I'd be there." Seeing the stubborn look on her father's face, she was about to give up. And then, from out of the blue, she said, "Zane isn't doing anything. He can take me."

"Zane! Are you out of your mind, girl?"

"You said he was just what we needed around here."

"Yeah, for keeping an eye out for Edling and redskins, not escorting you to town."

"I don't care! Susannah's my best friend and I'm going to town, with Zane or without him. It's up to you."

Taggart glared at his daughter. She had her mother's temper, he thought irritably. He had never won a fight with

Helen, and damn few with their daughter. And he knew Kathleen well enough to know she was just pig-headed enough to wait until his back was turned and sneak into town on her own. She might be better off going alone at that, he thought glumly.

But it wasn't a risk he was willing to take. "You'd better let him know your plans today."

"Can't you tell him?"

"No. This is your idea, not mine."

"Fine." Tossing her napkin on the table, she stalked out of the house.

Save for Old Mort who was nursing a cup of coffee, the cookhouse was empty when she got there. "Can I help you, Miss Kathleen?" the old man asked.

"I was looking for Mr. Zane."

"He don't see fit to take breakfast with us."

"Oh? Where is he then?"

Mort shrugged. "He took his plate outside. I don't know where he went."

"Thanks, Mort." Leaving the cookhouse, Kathleen looked around, wondering where Zane had gone and why he didn't eat with the other hands. Had they said something to make him feel unwelcome because he was part Indian?

She found Zane sitting on a stump behind the barn, his empty plate on the ground beside him, a cup of coffee in his hand. He looked up, one brow raised, when he saw her. "You lost?"

"No. I need to go into town tomorrow afternoon. My father would like you to accompany me."

"Is that part of my job?"

"It is now."

Zane nodded. Considering that her father had made it abundantly clear that she was 'off-limits' he found it somewhat surprising that the old man trusted him to see his daughter safely to town and back. But, what the hell. He could think of worse ways to spend the day. "What time?"

"I'd like to leave at eleven-thirty. Please have the buggy ready by then."

"Yes, ma'am."

She glared at him then turned and flounced away.

Zane removed his hat and ran his fingers through his hair. She was a pretty little filly, with her curly red-gold hair and snapping green eyes. It was obvious she didn't like him much, but it was just as well. They had about as much in common as a rattlesnake and a rabbit.

Zane was at the house at eleven-thirty sharp on Saturday morning. He had no sooner hopped down from the buggy than Kathleen came out the front door. Last night, she'd been wearing pants and a baggy plaid shirt, her hair pulled back in a pony-tail. Today, she wore a green-and-gold striped skirt and a shirtwaist that matched her eyes. Her hair fell around her shoulders in thick, red-gold waves. A dainty, white straw bonnet adorned with green and white ribbons perched on her head. She carried a small, gaily-wrapped package in one hand, a reticule dangled from the other.

Taggart had sought him out last night, warning him once again to keep his hands off Kathleen or face the consequences. Looking at her now, he thought risking the old man's wrath might be worth it.

She gave him a cool nod, flinched when he took hold of her arm to help her onto the seat. He walked around the buggy and took his place beside her. He didn't miss the fact that she sat as far away from him as she could, or that she gathered her skirts close so they didn't brush against his trousers.

Grunting softly, he picked up the reins and clucked to the horse.

They drove in silence, with her sitting stiff as a statue beside him. No doubt her father had warned her to keep her distance.

It was pretty country, he mused, glancing from side to side. Mountains rose in the west, their peaks shrouded in dark clouds. Likely a storm coming. White-faced cattle grazed on both sides of the dirt road. A narrow, winding ribbon of blue hinted at a river not far away. Now and then, he caught a glimpse of the T Bar K cowhands off in the distance.

Kathleen slid a sideways glance at Zane, who seemed totally oblivious to her presence. She told herself that was fine with her. He was a drifter and a ruffian, no fit company for gentle folk. Still, she couldn't stop stealing looks at him. He was handsome in a rough sort of way. She wondered what he would look like in a coat and vest and wearing a beaver hat, and then wondered why she cared.

She bumped against him when the buggy bounced over a rough patch in the road, felt a rush of heat when her thigh grazed his. Startled, she quickly pulled away.

"What's the matter?" he asked, his voice gruff. "Too good to touch my kind? Afraid some of my dirt might brush off on you?"

Momentarily taken aback by the vehemence in his words, she stared at him. And then she straightened her spine. "How dare you!"

"Honey, I dare plenty."

"Yes, I can see that."

"A little dirt might do you some good."

With a huff, Kathleen looked straight ahead, her mouth set in a grim line. The sooner they got to town, the better.

He dropped her off at a large house set behind a white picket fence, with instructions to return for her at promptly at 4.30. When he offered her his hand to alight from the buggy, she ignored it, then swept past him as if she were the Queen of England.

With an amused shake of his head, Zane tied the gelding to the hitch rail in front of the house then, hands shoved into his pockets, he strolled down the boardwalk toward Grant's General Store. Cross Creek was a small town by eastern standards, but today was Saturday and the stores were busy. Women from the outlying ranches came into town to shop or simply to mingle with their neighbors. Men gathered at the blacksmith shop, standing around in small groups, talking the weather and politics while they waited for the smith to repair their tools and harness or shoe their horses. Boys ran through the streets, rolling hoops or playing tag, while others played catch in a vacant lot. Girls mostly stayed close to their mothers' sides, helping with their younger siblings, while their mothers did the weekly shopping or shared the latest gossip.

Men and women alike eyed him with thinly-veiled suspicion as he passed by. There had been a time when those looks had bothered him; now, he ignored it. Like it or not, they would never trust him, not while stories of massacres and other equally lurid atrocities made the headlines.

Ducking into the general store, he picked out a pair of black whipcord trousers, two shirts, one a dark gray, the other black, five pairs of socks, and a box of .44 ammunition. It was a good thing he had found work, he thought as he paid for his purchases. Prices were going up. Fifty cents for cartridges. A dollar for a pair of pants, eighty cents for a shirt. It was surprising, the wide variety of goods the store offered—buggy whips, pails in assorted sizes, canned goods, bolts of cloth, jars of candy and sacks of coffee were interspersed with Stetson hats, bonnets, shoes and boots, boxes of cigars, and men's and ladies ready-to-wear.

He paid the clerk, who quickly wrapped his goods in brown paper and tied it with string.

Tucking his package under his arm, Zane sauntered down the street toward Sally's. He had a couple of hours to kill. Might as well try his luck at the card table.

The saloon was empty save for three men playing poker at a table near the door.

"Mind if I sit in?" Zane asked, jerking his chin at the empty chair.

The three men exchanged glances. The man dealing shrugged his approval.

Zane stowed his package under his chair then sat down. He didn't pay much attention to what the men talked about between hands. Most of their conversation was about the price of beef. Buyers in Kansas City were said to be paying over forty dollars a head. That was a pile of money for a good-sized herd. But he had little interest in cattle. Instead, he watched the players.

Abel Jensen, the man to his left, stroked his mustache whenever he thought he had a winning hand. The man to

Zane's right, Paddy Murphy, blinked rapidly. The fella across from him, Dixon by name, didn't have any discernable tells.

Zane won a couple of hands, then began to lose steadily. Eyes narrowed, he watched the man across from him. Dixon was cheating, no doubt about it. He was dealing from the bottom of the deck and he was damn good at it.

When Dixon dealt the next round, Zane caught his wrist as he pulled a card from the bottom.

"What are you doing?" the culprit stammered.

"Stopping a cheat."

The other two men looked at Zane.

"What's that you said?" Paddy Murphy asked sharply.

"You heard me," Zane said, still holding Dixon's wrist. "He's dealing from the bottom."

"That right, Dixon?" Murphy asked.

Dixon glared at him but didn't reply.

Jensen shook his head in disgust. "Well, that explains it. Damn clever of you, to let us win a few hands now and then. I always thought you had the devil's own luck."

Dixon jerked his hand free and pushed away from the table. "He's lying! Who are you going to believe?" He jabbed his finger in his chest. "Me, or that dirty redskin?"

Zane kept his gaze on Dixon. He let his hand slide below the table as the other man's hand slipped inside his coat. "You'd better be reaching for a cigar," Zane warned.

Dixon froze. There was a tense moment when it could have gone either way, then Dixon jerked his hand from inside his coat.

And Zane shot the pistol out of his hand.

From the corner of his eye, Zane saw Ed pull a shotgun out from under the bar. "Jensen, go get the sheriff," the bartender said. "Zane, drop your weapon. There'll be no more gunplay in here today."

Zane hesitated, then laid his .44 on the table.

Five minutes later, the acting Sheriff strode into the saloon.

Kathleen was waiting for him in the buggy when he got there. "You're late."

Zane nodded as he tossed his package under the seat, then vaulted up on the bench. Picking up the reins, he turned the horse toward home.

"What kept you?"

He shrugged. "A little trouble at the saloon. Nothing for you to worry your pretty head about."

"What kind of trouble?"

"I was playing poker with a man who was dealing from the bottom of the deck. When I caught him at it, he drew on me."

Her eyes widened. "What happened?"

"He went to jail."

Kathleen sat back. She had never been in a saloon, of course, but she had heard plenty of titillating stories about what went on inside such places, none of it good.

She shivered as a blast of cold air blew across the road. Looking up, she saw dark clouds gathering overhead. A blinding flash of lightning split the sky, followed by a deafening crash of thunder. She let out a gasp as the heavens opened. In moments, she was soaking wet.

Zane's gaze darted from side to side, seeking a place where they could shelter from the storm. Another flash of lightning revealed what looked like a line shack in a grove of trees. Giving the horse a sharp slap with the end of the reins, he urged the gelding into a gallop.

At the shack, he jumped from the buggy, ran to the other side, lifted Kathleen from the seat and hurried her inside. Shivering, teeth chattering, she ran her hands up and down her arms.

Zane glanced around. There was a small stack of wood piled beside the fireplace, a box of matches on the mantel. Kneeling on the hearth, he said, "Get out of those wet clothes," while he started a fire.

Kathleen stared at him. Was he seriously telling her to disrobe with him in the room?

When the fire sparked to life, he pulled one of the blankets from the cot and thrust it at her. "You can wrap up in that."

"Turn your back," she demanded, though her teeth were chattering so badly she could hardly speak.

Flashing a wry grin, he went to stand in front of the hearth. He could hear her undressing behind him while he removed his hat, shirt, and boots. He kept his pants on, even though they were wet clear though, afraid if he took them off, she might faint, or worse, go into hysterics. He draped his gunbelt over the chair, then held his hands out toward the flames, wishing he'd thought to bring his new clothes in with him. In his haste, he'd left the package under the seat. No doubt they were drenched by now.

"You decent?" he asked.

"Yes."

He turned to find her sitting on the edge of the cot, one of the blankets held tightly around her shoulders, a second one draped across her lap. She'd spread her clothes and stockings over the back of a chair to dry. Her hat was ruined, her shoes a muddy mess. She looked like a drowned rat.

Zane pulled one of the other chairs from the battered table and dragged it closer to the fire. Straddling it, he folded his arms over the back.

She flinched as another drumroll of thunder sounded overhead. Rain hammered on the roof and at the shack's single window. Uncomfortable with the silence and the tension between them, she cast about for something to say. "Do you think the rain will last long?"

He shrugged. "This time of the year, most storms are over pretty quick."

Silence fell between them. Time and again she found herself stealing glances at him. Who was he, really? Where had he come from? Her gaze slid to the gunbelt hanging over the back of the chair. Had he killed many men? Was he married? How long was he going to stay at the ranch? Why did his presence affect her the way it did?

Mortified, she flushed and quickly looked away when he caught her staring.

"Something on your mind?" he asked. "You worried about what people might say if they find out you were holed up in here with a half-breed saddle tramp?"

"Of course not," she said, and then her brows rushed together in a frown. What *would* people say? What would her father say? She pushed the thought from her mind. It was all perfectly innocent. Still, she was sitting here clad in nothing but her undergarments and a ratty blanket. And he was shirtless … Her mouth went dry. His shoulders were wide, his arms well-muscled, his skin the color of old copper.

With a shake of her head, she closed her eyes and prayed that her father had sent someone out to look for her. And then she frowned again. With this storm, he probably thought she had decided to stay in town with Susannah until it blew over.

"Looks like we might be here for a while," Zane remarked, glancing out the window.

With a sigh, Kathleen turned to face him. "Here," she said, offering him the blanket across her lap. "You must be cold."

"Keep it." It was a small room. The fire had warmed it considerably. Better if she kept covered up, he thought ruefully, because even cold and bedraggled, she was a hell of a temptation.

Nodding, she stared out the window. The rain was coming down in sheets. What if the storm lasted all night? She glanced at the narrow cot. Would he expect to share it with her? It was barely large enough for one. But it was too cold for him to sleep on the floor, which was nothing more than rough planks.

As the sun went down, Zane added another log to the fire. His shirt was almost dry and he shrugged it on. He grinned when Kathleen's stomach growled. She had probably never missed a meal in her life.

She looked up at him, a wave of embarrassment pinking her cheeks. "So," she said, "tell me about yourself."

"What do you want to know?"

She shrugged. "Anything you'd like to tell me."

He scrubbed his hands up and down his thighs. His past was unpleasant at best. She was already uncomfortable in his presence. Anything he told her would only make it worse.

Sensing his hesitation, she said, "I'm sorry. I have no right to pry."

"Let's talk about you, instead." His gaze moved over her. You're young and pretty and the right age. How come you're not married with a couple of kids? Are all the men in Cross Creek blind?"

"As a matter of fact, I'm dating a fine young man."

"Is that right?"

"Yes. He works at his father's bank."

He nodded, wondering why the news bothered him.

"Have you ever been married?" she asked.

"No."

Something in his expression made her ask, "Ever been in love?"

"Once," Zane said curtly. "A long time ago."

She waited, hoping he'd say more, but he didn't seem inclined to elaborate.

"You going to marry Mr. Banker?"

"My father expects me to."

"But?"

"I haven't decided." She glanced away. Oliver Plotkin was a handsome young man and they got along splendidly. And yet, she didn't feel any real attraction to him. She enjoyed his company, liked discussing books with him, but when he kissed her, it didn't move her at all. She told herself that was as it should be. Decent young women didn't feel lust. But surely she should feel some measure of desire for a man she was thinking of marrying. She didn't know a lot about such things, but there must be something wrong with her, because when she looked at Zane, it did funny things in the pit of her stomach. When he had taken off his shirt, she'd had a sudden yearning to touch him, to run her hands over arms, to delve her fingers into his hair.

Shame flooded her cheeks. What was wrong with her? Why did he stir feelings inside her she had never felt before. Tears stung her eyes. She was cold and hungry and she wanted to go home.

It was dark now, the only light cast by the flickering flames and an occasional flash of lightning.

"Why don't you get some sleep?" Zane suggested. "I'll wake you if the rain stops and we'll head for home."

Kathleen nodded. What else was there to do? She stretched out on the lumpy cot and closed her eyes.

Rising, Zane paced the floor in front of the fireplace, his gaze constantly drawn to the woman. She had fallen asleep almost as soon as she closed her eyes. Her hair, almost dry now, framed her face. Her lashes lay like dark fans against her cheeks. Her lips, pink and perfect, were slightly parted. Desire rose within him, hot and swift.

Stupid, he thought. Stupid to want something he could never have.

Chapter Three

It rained all through the night. Zane slept fitfully in the chair, his dreams haunted by visions of a past laced with blood and death.

He woke to a quiet dawn. Kathleen lay on her side, the covers drawn up to her chin. She was beautiful, even in sleep.

Rising, he slammed his hat on his head, stomped into his boots, and buckled on his gunbelt before giving her shoulder a light shake.

She woke instantly, her eyes wide. And then she blinked at him. "Oh, it's you."

"You ready to go?"

Nodding, she sat up and ran her fingers through her hair.

He turned his back while she dressed.

Kathleen sighed when she looked at her hat. "Darn. I just bought that bonnet," she muttered as she tossed it into the fireplace. She grimaced when she picked up her shoes. They were still damp and caked with mud. She held them in one hand, her reticule in the other. "Let's go."

"You can't go traipsing out in the mud in your stockings," he remarked, and before she could protest, he swung her effortlessly into his arms, carried her out the door, and kicked it shut behind them.

After settling her on the seat, he hopped up beside her.

Kathleen felt a wave of sympathy for the poor horse, who'd had no shelter from the storm and nothing to eat since yesterday morning. The gelding moved out briskly when Zane lifted the reins, no doubt as eager to get home as was she.

It was obvious her father had been worried and just as obvious that he'd been waiting at the window. He burst out the front door and ran down the porch stairs as soon as they pulled up to the house. "Kathleen!" He lifted her from the buggy and enfolded her in a bear hug. "I've been worried sick! I sent a couple of the boys out this morning to look for you."

"I'm fine, Dad. We got caught in the storm."

Eyes narrowed, Taggart looked up at Zane, still seated in the buggy.

"Nothing happened," Zane said, his voice as cold as the weather. "I'll go look after the horse."

Holding her at arm's length, Taggart looked his daughter up and down. "Are you all right? He didn't ..."

"Of course not! We spent the night in that old line shack."

His gaze bored into hers for a moment and then he nodded. "Come on inside, kitten. I'll have Juanita fix you something to eat while you get cleaned up."

Zane swore under his breath as he unhitched the gelding and rubbed it down, then led the horse into the barn and forked it a generous helping of hay and oats. If Taggart hadn't been Kathleen's father, he would have slugged the man for looking at him the way he had. Dammit!

He'd missed breakfast, but it didn't matter. He was too damn mad to eat. Grabbing his package from under the seat, he stalked into the bunkhouse and tossed his hat on the rack by the door. The rest of the hands were long gone. He shook out the clothes he'd bought yesterday and spread them over a couple of chairs to dry then paced the floor, anger churning deep in his gut. He should have been used to those nasty looks by now. He'd been getting them all his life. But it still stung.

Shit! He dropped down on the cot, hands dangling between his knees. If he didn't need the money so bad, he'd ride on. He grunted softly, knowing it for the lie it was. Knowing he was a damn fool for sticking around when Kathleen Taggart would never be his.

Kathleen thought about Zane as she scrubbed herself clean and washed her hair. Why was he so reticent about his past? How bad could it be? Who were his parents? It was obvious he was a half-breed. Was that why he wouldn't talk about them? What had he done before he came here? He claimed to be good with a gun. Had he been a bounty hunter? A hired killer? Maybe a lawman, but that seemed unlikely.

So many questions, she mused as she dried her hair.

Minutes later, clad in a blue skirt and a white shirtwaist, Kathleen went downstairs. Her father was reaching for his hat when she stepped into the parlor. He was generally pretty easy-going, but she could see that his back was up this morning.

"I want to know what happened last night," he demanded gruffly.

Kathleen's gaze met his, unblinking, unflinching. "I told you, nothing happened," she said, her voice equally sharp. "We took shelter from the storm in the old line shack."

"Why don't I believe you?"

Fisting her hands on her hips, Kathleen glared at her father. "I've never lied to you before and I'm not lying now. Either you trust me, or you don't."

Taggart regarded her for a long moment, then jammed his hat on his head. "I'm going to O'Brian's to pick up the mare. I won't be late.

She blew out a relieved breath, grateful that he wasn't going to pursue the matter any further. "Why didn't you bring her home yesterday?"

"It started to rain shortly after I arrived at Tom's place. I told him I'd pick her up today and lit out for home. I didn't want to take a chance on her getting spooked, what with all that thunder and lightning. Wait until you see her! She's a beaut. Juanita has your breakfast warming." He gave her a quick peck on the cheek before leaving the house.

Kathleen had no sooner taken her place at the dining room table than Juanita bustled into the room and placed a plate of bacon, eggs, fried potatoes and a cup of coffee in front of her. Juanita had come to work for them shortly after Kathleen's mother left the ranch. She had her own little house out back where she lived with three cats and a canary. Her daughter and granddaughter lived in town.

"*Buenos dias, pequeña.*"

Katheen smiled, amused that Juanita still called her 'little one. "*Buenos dias* to you, too."

"Can I get you anything else?"

"Not right now. Oh, wait, could you fix me another plate in a few minutes?"

"Did I not give you enough?"

Kathleen smiled. "It's not for me." It had occurred to her that Zane might have missed breakfast, since the hands ate early. The least she could do was take him something.

With a nod, Juanita returned to the kitchen.

Kathleen had just finished eating when Juanita returned with a covered plate and a steaming cup of coffee. Kathleen didn't know what they'd do without Juanita. She did most of the cooking, helped with the laundry, cleaning the house, and the mending.

"Thanks, Juanita. I'm going to get this down to the new man while it's hot."

Zane glanced over his shoulder, one brow arching in surprise when Kathleen stepped through the bunkhouse door. "To what do I owe this unexpected pleasure?"

She held up the plate. "I thought you might be hungry."

"Thanks."

She placed it on the round table in the corner where the cowhands played poker, then stood there, not knowing whether to stay or go. Wanting to stay, though she wasn't sure why, she said, "I'll wait for the dishes, if you don't mind."

"Fine by me." He pulled out a chair for her, then sat down across from her. "Smells good."

"Juanita's a wonderful cook. She's been with us for years. Practically raised me."

He took a few bites and washed them down with a swig of coffee. "Where's your mother?"

"It's a long story."

"I've got plenty of time on my hands."

"My mother's parents were quite wealthy. We lived with them until I was four or five, when my father got the itch to move to Wyoming. My mother didn't really want to go and, from what I understand, her parents threatened to disown her if she went with him. Feeling it was her duty, my mother agreed to go. She hated the West, hated life on the ranch, but I loved it. I guess I was nine or ten when my grandmother got sick. After a few days, my mother decided to go home and see her before she died. She wanted me to go with her. She tried to persuade me, but my father said I didn't have to go if I didn't want to. My grandmother passed away a few months later, and then my grandfather got sick and passed away. My mother never returned to the ranch. In spite of my grandparents' threat to disown her, they left her their estate. My mother and I exchange letters every couple of months. She's always promising to come for a visit, but she never has."

"You must miss her," he said, his voice gruff.

"Sometimes. But not as much now as I used to."

"What about your father's parents?"

Kathleen shrugged. "He was an orphan." She bit down on her lip, wondering if she dared ask him any of the questions tumbling through her mind. He hadn't been willing to answer them last night. Would he now?

"What is it?" he asked. "I can see you're dying to ask me something."

"I … that is … I was wondering about *your* parents. Are they still alive?"

"No." He finished the last of his meal. Leaning back in his chair, he regarded her over the rim of his coffee cup. "My mother's dead. My father killed her," he said flatly. "And I killed him."

Aghast, Kathleen stared at Zane. What on earth could she say to that? *I'm sorry* seemed woefully inadequate.

"It was a long time ago," Zane said in that same emotionless voice. "He deserved to die and I'm not sorry for what I did. I'd do it again." He cocked his head to the side. "Are you shocked? Disgusted? Horrified?"

"I don't know what to say except why? Why would you do such a thing?"

"My mother was Cheyenne, my father was a renegade white man. I never knew how they got together in the first place, but it wasn't a love match. My old man was a mean drunk, with a violent temper. He liked to hit me and he did it often. One night, he got mad at me. When my mother tried to protect me, he turned on her." He laughed harshly, bitterly. "I was seventeen years old and *she* wanted to protect *me*. When I tried to pull him away, he slugged me. Knocked me out. When I came to, he was still hitting her. And I killed him." A muscle twitched in his jaw. "She died in my arms. Once she was gone ..." He shrugged. "I couldn't stay there, so I left."

Inadequate or not, all she could say was, "I'm so sorry. I didn't mean to pry or bring up bad memories. I'll pick up the dishes later." Pushing away from the table, she stood and hurried out of the bunkhouse as if Satan himself were snapping at her heels.

Zane stared after her, but in his mind's eye, it was his mother he saw, as young and beautiful as she had once been, her hair shiny black, her eyes dark and always filled with love when she looked at him. And then he saw her as she had looked when he regained consciousness, her face swollen, both eyes black, her lip split by his father's fists, her breathing shallow and labored as she gasped for breath.

He had staggered to his feet, grabbed his father's .44 and shot him dead. No one in the tribe had condemned him for what he'd done. He had buried his mother with the help of her family. They had not dignified his father's body with burial. Instead, Zane and his uncles had wrapped his old man's body in a buffalo hide and left it on the prairie, prey to weather and scavengers. No one ever spoke the man's name's again.

Late that night, he had gathered his few belongings and left the village. He'd been seventeen. That had been twelve years ago. He had always intended to go back and visit her grave, see her family, but he never had. Without her there, it didn't seem like home.

He had roamed the West, doing whatever he had to do to survive. He had fallen into bounty hunting by accident. He grinned at the memory. He'd killed a man in a fight. It had been self-defense. There had been numerous witnesses, including the sheriff, and no charges had been filed against him. As it turned out, the man he'd killed had been a well-known outlaw with a hefty price on his head.

Zane had used part of the reward money to buy a black Stetson and a holster, then spent hours on end learning to draw and fire his old man's Colt. It came surprisingly easy to him. In time, he hit what he aimed at ninety-nine times out of a hundred. And suddenly he had a reputation as a fast gun.

Of course, no one liked bounty hunters, but people treated him with a certain degree of respect, not that he gave a damn. Hunting men was easy money. Thus far, he'd never killed an unarmed man or shot one in the back.

He blew out a sigh. He was what he was and no fit company for a decent woman. It had never bothered him before. But it sure as hell bothered him now.

❧   ❧   ❧

Zane had just finished currying his horse when Taggart rode into the yard leading a flashy chestnut mare with a blaze face and one white stocking. He grimaced when he saw Zane.

Zane swore under his breath, wondering if the old man was going to fire him. Damn the old man and his suspicions, though he really couldn't blame him. "Hell of a good lookin' mare," Zane remarked.

Taggart nodded curtly as he dismounted, then turned the chestnut loose in the corral. "I plan to breed her to my stud. She should throw a fine colt."

Zane nodded. The mare had good, clean lines, a beautiful coat, and intelligent eyes.

Whistling softly, Taggart jogged up to the house.

Zane had just put his own mare in the barn when Kathleen came hurrying toward the corral.

She slowed when she saw Zane step out of the barn. "I just came down to see Dad's new horse."

He nodded. Damn, but she was a pretty woman, her cheeks pink, her green eyes sparkling. He followed her to the corral.

"No wonder he wanted her," Kathleen said. "She's beautiful."

He bit back the words, "So are you," certain they wouldn't be welcome coming from him.

Katheen folded her arms on the top rail, acutely aware of Zane beside her. Never, in all her life, had she been so aware of a man's nearness. He was so very male, from his rugged good looks to his masculine scent. Oliver had never affected her like this, never made her insides quiver or her heart beat faster. Never made her so aware of the fact that she was a woman.

She felt a rush of guilt when her father came up beside her, though for the life of her, she didn't know why.

"So, daughter, what do you think of her?"

"She's lovely."

"But not yet saddle broke. I was counting on Slim to break her, but he's not coming back."

"He's not? Why?"

Taggart shrugged. "I guess Edling scared him off."

"I could break her for you," Zane said.

"You got any experience breaking horses?" Taggart asked, gruffly.

"I've worked a few now and then."

Taggart grunted, his dislike for the man obviously warring with his desire to see the mare saddle-broke. "I want her broke gentle," he said. "Do it right and I'll make it worth your while."

Zane nodded. "I'll start in the morning."

Taggart nodded curtly. "Let's go, daughter. Juanita made *flan*."

With a brief glance at Zane, Kathleen followed her father back to the house.

Zane grunted softly. Kathleen Taggart was another filly he'd like to try his hand at. Too bad she was off limits.

Chapter Four

Zane rose at 6 a.m. with the cowhands. Smothering a yarn, he followed them to the cookhouse. He had to admit, the grub was plentiful and Cookie knew his way around a frying pan.

With breakfast over, he saddled the buckskin. Taggart had hired him to keep an eye on things and now seemed as good a time as any to ride out and explore the ranch. He'd work with the chestnut mare later.

Swinging into the saddle, he turned the buckskin west, toward the mountains. He had always loved this time of the day, when the earth was just waking up. A slight breeze tickled the leaves on the trees. In the distance, a couple of young deer nibbled on a patch of buffalo grass.

Zane nudged the mare into a lope, his gaze constantly moving back and forth in what had become second nature. He reined the buckskin to a halt at the top of a verdant hill. For a moment, he sat there, admiring the view. A narrow ribbon of blue cut the valley below in half. A young buck stood at the water's edge, its ears flicking back and forth, head high as it scented the breeze before it lowered its head to drink.

Zane reached for his rifle, then changed his mind, reluctant to shatter the peaceful stillness of the valley. He didn't need the meat and he'd never been one to kill just for the sport of it.

Clucking to the mare, he rode along the top of the ridge until he came to a natural trail leading downward. He had ridden about three miles when he saw the first hoofprints. Reining the buckskin to a halt, he dismounted and followed the tracks on foot. Unshod horses usually meant Indians.

He followed the trail into a heavily wooded area, came to an abrupt halt when he saw a splatter of dried blood amidst a patch of chewed-up ground. Moccasin tracks identified the hunters as Cheyenne. Four warriors. They had made a kill here—likely a deer or an elk—butchered it, and were likely headed home.

Grunting softly, Zane swung into the saddle and followed the faint trail they had left behind to make sure they were headed home and not circling back to the ranch.

Kathleen dressed with care before going down to breakfast. She told herself it was because Oliver had said he might come calling that afternoon when, in reality, it was because she hoped to see Zane. He would be working with the chestnut today. It was the perfect excuse to go down to the barn.

With her stomach in knots, she barely tasted her breakfast.

"You all right, daughter?" Tobias asked.

"Yes, fine."

"What are your plans for the day?"

Kathleen shrugged. "Oh, you know, the usual." It was Monday. Laundry day. With luck, they would get it done early. "I thought I'd go down later and look at the chestnut again. She really is a beauty."

"She cost more than I wanted to spend, but she'll throw some fine colts. O'Brian wants the first one." Taggart wiped his mouth, stood and grabbed his hat. "I'm going into town to see if those new seed catalogs I ordered have come in. Stay close to home while I'm gone."

Kathleen helped Juanita do the breakfast dishes, then spent the next two hours helping her do the wash. As soon as the clothes were drying on the line, Kathleen grabbed an apple and headed out the back door. She forced herself to walk sedately toward the barn.

She blew out a sigh of disappointment when she didn't see Zane outside. He wasn't in the barn, either, and his horse was gone.

Disappointed, she returned to the house to see if Juanita needed help with anything.

Zane followed the tracks for a quarter of a mile. The Cheyenne were headed west, across the river into the wild country.

Brow furrowed, he debated following them to their camp, then decided against it. The four hunters were no threat. They hadn't killed or stolen any of the T Bar K cattle. With a shake of his head, he headed back toward the ranch.

He was about a mile-and-a-half from home when he saw the lake, partially hidden by a stand of timber. The water shimmered in the late morning sun. Deciding a swim sounded like a good idea, he urged the mare into a lope.

After finding a grassy spot along the bank, he unsaddled the buckskin and tied the reins to a low-hanging branch. The mare immediately buried her nose in the lush verge. He'd just stripped off his shirt when he heard a splash. Turning, he glanced upriver, felt a smile play over his lips when he saw Kathleen Taggart swimming toward him with long, even strokes.

She spied him at the same time. Standing in water up to her shoulders, she crossed her arms over her breasts. "What are you doing here?" she exclaimed.

"Same thing you are, I reckon."

"Well, go away."

His smile broadened as he shook his head. "I like the view."

"Go away! I can't get out with you standing there." Kathleen glared at him when he didn't move. Oh, but he was a vile man!

Unfastening his gunbelt, he asked, "How's the water?"

Eyes wide, she stared at him. "You can't come in!"

"Why not?" He set his holster on a rock and reached for his belt.

"You … you're … oh! I don't know what you are."

Laughing softly, Zane removed his belt.

Cheeks burning with embarrassment, Kathleen said, "Please, just go away. My clothes are on a bush a few feet behind you." If only Juanita had needed her help at home, she wouldn't be in this predicament now.

Taking pity on her, Zane turned around. "Come on out, princess. I won't look."

She stared at his broad back and felt a different kind of heat flood her cheeks. His shoulders were broad, his back smooth and beautifully sculpted save for a few faint scars she hadn't noticed that night in the line shack. What had caused them?

With a shake of her head, she sloshed toward the shore, then stood there worrying her lower lip. She had to pass by him to get to her clothes. "Close your eyes."

"What?"

"You heard me. Close your eyes."

Laughing softly, he did as she asked. He listened to her footsteps as she walked past him and then, unable to resist, he took a peek at her. She was tall and slim, her legs long and shapely, her backside nicely rounded. Unable to help himself, he whistled softly.

With a startled gasp, she broke into a run and darted behind a tree.

Laughing, Zane toed off his boots, shucked his trousers, and plunged into the lake. He had expected it to be cold, but it was surprisingly warm. A hot spring, perhaps.

He swam for several minutes, his gaze on the shore.

Ten minutes later, Kathleen reappeared mounted on a pretty palomino mare. Smiling, she called, "I hope you drown," as she reached for the buckskin's reins. "I'll see you back at the ranch." And so saying, she urged her horse into a trot and headed for home, with Zane's mare trailing behind her.

Zane stared after her, not knowing whether to laugh or cuss. Damn. The ranch was close to three miles away. Not a long walk, but hiking over rough ground in a pair of boots while lugging a forty-pound saddle was going to make it seem a hell of a lot long longer.

Kathleen was sitting on the front porch swing when Zane sauntered into the yard. She felt a twinge of guilt when she saw him carrying his saddle. She should have realized he wouldn't leave it behind.

He glared at her as he headed for the bunkhouse.

Well, she couldn't blame him. At the least, she owed him an apology. After all, in spite of her embarrassment that he'd seen her naked, his whistle had pleased her vanity. She should just go apologize and get it over with, she thought. Putting if off wouldn't make it any easier.

With a sigh of resignation, she marched down to the barn. She found him currying the buckskin.

Zane looked up at the sound of footsteps. "What the hell do you want?"

"I came to apologize. Taking your horse like that was a childish thing for me to do."

"It was that."

"I said I was sorry. I didn't stop to think that it could have been dangerous, leaving you on foot out there."

He grunted softly. "I suppose I'm partly to blame," he said with a wry grin. "But the view was worth it."

She stared at him a moment. The view? And then, taking his meaning, she felt herself blush from head to foot. "You, sir, are no gentleman!" Mortified that he would mention what he had done, she stalked back to the house.

Zane chuckled. She was right. A gentleman would have kept his eyes closed, but he'd never claimed to be anything but what he was. And he'd gladly walk another three miles for a second look at her bare backside.

Oliver came calling after dinner attired in his Sunday best. She had always thought him a handsome man, with his wavy blond hair and blue eyes. But she suddenly found herself wishing he had long, black hair and dark-gray eyes.

"I missed you in church yesterday," he said, taking the seat on the sofa beside her.

She shrugged. "I overslept." She saw no reason to tell him about the night she'd spent in the line shack with Zane.

Silence fell between them until her father asked after Oliver's parents.

Kathleen found her mind wandering as their conversation turned to the rising price of beef. Sometimes she found herself wondering if Oliver came to visit her or her dad. Unbidden, came the image of Zane treading water in the lake, the sun gilding his hair, and earlier today, as he introduced the chestnut to saddle and bridle.

"Kathleen?"

It took her a moment to realize Oliver was speaking to her. "Oh, I'm sorry, did you say something?"

"I was wondering if you'd like to accompany me to the dance at the Grange a week from Saturday?"

She hesitated a moment, then murmured, "I suppose so."

Smiling, he stood and plucked his hat from the rack. He shook her father's hand, bid her good night, and walked toward the door.

Because it was expected of her, Kathleen stood and followed him onto the porch.

Murmuring, "Until next week," Oliver kissed her on the cheek.

As Kathleen watched him ride away, she found herself wondering what Zane's kisses would be like.

As if conjured by her thoughts, he strode into view. "I see you had company," he remarked.

"Yes. Mr. Plotkin calls on me frequently."

Zane arched one brow. "Oh?"

"Yes. He's taking me to the Grange dance a week from Saturday night."

He grunted softly. "Are you sweet on him?"

"I don't believe that's any of your business."

"Does he always kiss you like that?"

Appalled, she stared at him. "Were you spying on us?"

He shook his head. "I was just passing by."

"I suppose you think you could do better."

Her words had barely trailed away when he was beside her on the porch, his arms folding around her as he covered her mouth with his. Astonished, she started to pull away but his lips were moving over hers, evoking sensations she had never known before. Her toes curled with pleasure and she leaned into him, relishing the feel of his hard-muscled body against hers. Feeling suddenly weak in the knees, she curled her hands over his shoulders.

She felt bereft when he released her.

"Sweet dreams, Kathleen," he murmured, and left her standing there on the porch, totally bewildered by what had just happened between them.

Zane swore softly. Damn! Hidden in the shadows, he watched Kathleen. She remained on the porch, her fingers pressed to her lips. He hadn't meant to kiss her, nor had he expected her to melt in his arms. In truth, he had expected her to slap him, not that he would blame her.

He stood there, watching her, until she turned and went back into the house.

Hands shoved deep in his pants' pockets, he strolled down to the bunkhouse. He had it bad, he thought ruefully. He was a half-breed. A bounty hunter and occasional hired gun. And she was the boss's daughter.

He would do well to remember that.

Chapter Five

Zane was relaxing in the shade toward the end of the week when four of the T Bar K cowhands came thundering into the yard. One of them was slumped in the saddle. Fresh blood stained his left shirt sleeve.

Taggart came hurrying out the house, with Kathleen and Juanita at his heels.

Taggart barked orders. "Boone, Austin, get Woodard into the house. Juanita, boil some water. Kathleen, get some bandages."

When the injured man had been carried into the house, Taggart looked up at the remaining cowboy. "What the hell happened, Chet?"

"We were rounding up some strays along the north forty when a half-dozen masked men surprised us. They came in shooting and stampeded the cattle. Virgil took a bullet in his shoulder. It knocked him out of the saddle. While me and Austin pulled him out of harm's way, the rustlers took off." Chet shrugged. "We had to decide between Virgil and the cows."

"You made the right choice," Taggart said curtly. "Did you recognize any of them?"

Chet shook his head.

Taggart turned toward Zane. "I want those men, dead or alive. Chet'll show you where to start."

❧ ❧ ❧

Twenty minutes later, Zane followed Chet out of the yard. "How far are we going?"

"It happened in a shallow draw about five miles north of here."

They rode the rest of the way in silence.

Bloodstains and chewed-up ground marked the place where the rustlers had attacked. The trail out of the draw was easy to follow.

"You can go home now," Zane said. "I'll take it from here."

"Six against one." Chet shook his head. "The odds aren't in your favor."

"Let me worry about that."

The cowboy shrugged. "Suit yourself."

"I always do."

Chet hesitated, as if he meant to say something else, then touched his hat brim in farewell and headed back to the ranch.

Zane urged the buckskin into a lope. As the miles went by, he wondered if the rustlers realized they were riding into Lakota territory. His lips twitched in a grin. With luck, the Indians would do his work for him.

As it turned out, luck was something the rustlers didn't have. Zane found their bodies five or six miles later. Or what was left of them. They hadn't died easy, or quickly. Their bodies were pierced with arrows; they had all been scalped.

Zane grunted softly. The Plains tribes were angry and he couldn't blame them. Miners and hunters were invading their hunting grounds, killing the buffalo, polluting the rivers and streams in their endless search for hides and gold. The settlers and the Army had broken one treaty after another. It was only a matter of time before the tribes went to war.

Zane glanced around. The Lakota had run off the cattle and taken the rustlers' horses.

He took a last look at the bodies, then followed the Lakota's trail for a mile or two before he turned the buckskin toward home.

Kathleen stared at the grandfather clock in the hallway. Zane had been gone for almost five hours. She had passed the time helping Juanita around the house, but all the while her thoughts had been on Zane. Where was he? Had he found the rustlers? Or had they found him? Was he lying dead somewhere out there on the prairie?

Virgil was resting in the guest room. She had taken him something to eat earlier and sat with him while he ate. He had fallen asleep as soon as he'd finished.

Later, one of the hands had reported a dead cow and calf and her father had ridden out to look things over. He had returned a short time ago, muttering under his breath.

Juanita was in the kitchen, singing as she made tortillas.

Kathleen's head snapped up at the sound of hoofbeats in the yard. Running to the window, she drew back the curtains, a wave of relief sweeping through her when she saw Zane. She didn't know why she was so relieved. He was nothing to her, and yet ... With a sigh, she admitted she liked him far more than she should. She had known he was a dangerous man the first time she'd seen him, but she hadn't realized the danger would be to her heart.

When her father went outside to speak to him, she tip-toed toward the open door, anxious to hear what Zane had to say. He sat on his horse at the foot of the porch stairs.

"Did you find the rustlers?" her father asked.

Zane nodded curtly. "What was left of them."

"What do you mean?"

"They ran into some Indians who did my job for me. The cows and the Lakota were long gone when I got there."

Biting back an oath, her father said, "We've never had any trouble with the Indians. Hell, I don't even mind when they steal one of our cows now and then."

"That's probably why they haven't bothered you. But the rustlers were on Lakota land and they don't like trespassers."

Taggart nodded. "Mind if I ask what tribe you're from?"

"Does it make a difference?"

"No, I was just curious."

"My mother was Cheyenne."

Taggart nodded again. "Might be handy, having you on our side. Tomorrow's Saturday. Kathleen usually goes into town to do some shopping. I'd like you to take her."

With a nod, Zane reined the buckskin toward the barn.

Kathleen stepped away from the door when her father and Zane parted, unable to stifle the little burst of excitement that bubbled up inside her at the thought of spending the day with her father's hired gun.

Kathleen dressed with care Saturday morning, spent more time than usual in front of the mirror, fussing with her hair. After tucking her shopping list into her reticule, she hurried outside to where Zane waited with the buckboard.

She felt a little thrill as his hands went around her waist to lift her onto the seat before he swung up beside her.

Suddenly tongue-tied, she clutched her reticule in her lap as he slapped the reins against the gelding's rump. The last time they had gone to town, they had ended up spending the night together. She glanced hopefully at the sky, but it was a bright, clear blue. Not a cloud in sight. She told herself she should be relieved.

When Zane slid a look in her direction, she had the distinct feeling he was also remembering their interlude together.

"So, what are you shopping for?" he asked.

"Oh, you know, just a few things Juanita needs. Flour and sugar and ..." She shrugged. "That kind of thing."

"How long will you be?"

"I don't know. An hour or so, I guess. Although I may want to stop and look in on Mrs. Cooper. She just had a baby a week ago and her husband's out of work. I want to make sure she has enough food for her other two children and clothes for the baby."

He grunted softly in reply.

"You don't approve?"

"Makes no never mind to me what you do."

"Well," she replied in a huff, "someone has to look after those who need help. Our ranch is prosperous and I've always tried to help those less fortunate."

"That's mighty neighborly of you."

"That's what neighbors are for."

"I wouldn't know."

Kathleen sat back, brow furrowing at the bitter tone of his voice. "What was it like, growing up with the Indians?"

A muscle twitched in his jaw. For a moment, she thought he wouldn't answer.

"It was better when my old man was away. It's a good way to live. My uncles taught me to hunt the deer and the bear and the buffalo. How to ride. How to fight." His gaze caught hers. "How to take a scalp."

She shuddered in spite of herself.

Zane chuckled. "Sorry. I shouldn't have said that."

"If you're trying to shock me, forget it. I've lived out here since I was seven years old. I know what goes on. Why didn't you stay with the Indians?"

"After I killed the old man, I needed to get away for a while. I'd hated my father as long as I could remember, and yet I wanted to know what his world was like. I always intended to go back home, but …" He shrugged one shoulder. "I never did."

"And now you hire out your gun?

"Sometimes. Mainly I'm a bounty hunter."

"Oh."

"You don't approve?"

"I'm not sure. I suppose someone has to bring in wanted men," she said thoughtfully. "The posters always say 'dead or alive'. "

"Dead is easier."

"You kill them?"

"Only when it's my life or theirs."

Zane dropped Kathleen off at Grant's General Store and then drove down the street to Sally's. He tied the horse to the hitchrack, settled his gun on his hip, and strolled inside. It was quiet this time of day. A couple of the saloon girls were playing blackjack at a back table. He didn't see French

Lil. He figured she was either taking a nap or entertaining in her room. A man in a dapper city suit stood at the far end of the bar, nursing a beer.

The bartender smiled at Zane as he stepped inside. "What'll it be?"

"Whiskey."

"Right." Ed pulled a bottle from beneath the counter where he kept the "good stuff" for his favorite customers. He splashed the whiskey in a glass and slid it across the bar. "I hear you're working for Taggart."

"Yeah."

Ed nodded. "He's a good man. Too bad about his wife."

"You mean about her going back east?"

"Told you about that, did he?"

"Not exactly," Zane remarked. "His daughter mentioned it."

"I always felt sorry for Miz Taggart. Must have hurt her feelings when Kathleen chose to stay with old man Taggart."

Zane shrugged. "If she missed her daughter, she could have come back."

"I reckon so. But she never cottoned to the West. Can's say as I blame her. It's a hard life for a woman, specially one as gently raised as she was."

After leaving the saloon, Zane stood on the boardwalk for a few moments before walking down to the General Store. He didn't see Kathleen through the window, so he went inside and strolled up and down the aisles. The place was well-stocked with everything from gunpowder to bathtubs. The air carried a variety of mingled odors—the rich aroma of plug tobacco, and the leathery smell of boots and saddles, the fragrance of freshly-ground coffee. A barrel filled with crackers stood next to a pot-bellied stove. Counters and shelves were piled high with shirts, pants, and longjohns, as well as bolts of fabric. Kegs and barrels and bins were placed at intervals around the store, filled with sugar and flour, beans and salt, vinegar and coal oil, and dill pickles.

He found Kathleen sitting on a bench in the back of the store, trying on a pair of half-boots. "You about ready to head home?" he asked.

"I guess so." She held one foot out, turning it this way and that, before she removed the boot and placed it back in the box. Rising, she headed for the counter at the front of the store, box in hand.

"I'm ready to go, Mr. Henderson," she said.

The clerk nodded. "I've got your bill right here, Miss Taggart. Shall I add it to your father's account?"

"Yes, please. And I'll take these, too," she said, placing the shoe box on the counter.

Henderson made a notation on inside a small journal. "Tell your father hello for me," he said. "Your supplies are waiting out back."

"Thank you." Tucking the shoe box under her arm, Kathleen moved toward the door.

Zane stepped around to open it for her. "Wait here. I'll go get the buckboard."

Kathleen watched him stride away. She didn't miss the way men quickly stepped out of his path, or the way woman swept their skirts aside. He was about to climb onto the seat when a red-headed woman ran out of Sally's Saloon and hurled herself into his arms. Kathleen couldn't hear what was being said but there was no mistaking the fact that the two were glad to see each other. It was obvious from the easy way he smiled at her. And the way she smiled up at him.

A wave of jealousy ran through Kathleen as she wondered just how well he knew that woman. She tapped her foot impatiently as she waited for him to disentangle himself from the soiled dove.

After what seemed like an hour but was, in reality, only a few minutes, Zane kissed the girl on the cheek and vaulted up onto the buckboard's seat. Taking up the reins, he drove to the general store where Kathleen waited on the boardwalk. He looked at her askance but didn't say anything when she climbed up on the seat beside him before he could get down to help her.

"Pull the buckboard around to the back," she said, her voice cool as she tucked the shoe box under the seat.

With a nod, he drove around to the back of the general store. A young man stood there, ready to help load the supplies. Zane jumped down to help him. He was somewhat surprised by the number of bags and boxes.

When he would have taken the left trail out of town, Kathleen instructed him to turn right. Their destination was a ramshackle house some three miles down the road. Following her directions, he drove around to the back door.

Alighting from the buckboard, she said, "Please bring that large box into the house. And that one, too," she said, her voice still cool." After picking up a small sack, she opened the back door and stepped inside.

Muttering, "Yes, your majesty," under his breath, Zane hopped down, picked up the items she'd indicated and followed her into the kitchen. He set the boxes on the floor and then trailed her into the parlor.

A young woman sat in a broken-down rocker, a baby cradled in her arms. A boy, perhaps four years old, napped at her feet. Another boy, maybe a year younger, slept on a battered sofa.

"Kathleen," the woman said. "I wasn't expecting you. The place is a mess."

"I just wanted to stop by for a minute and see how you were doing. I brought you a few things I thought you could use. And a present for the baby."

"You shouldn't have," the woman said as Kathleen handed her the sack. "I don't know how to thank you."

"There's no need, Annie. Is there anything I can do for you while I'm here?"

Zane glanced around the room, thinking there were a dozen things that needed doing, from filling the wood box to sweeping the floor.

Kathleen noticed the same things. "Zane, would you mind bringing in some wood while I clean up in here a little?"

With a shrug, he went outside.

"Who is that man?" Annie asked.

"He's our new hired hand. You rest now, while I tidy up in here." Kathleen felt her heart melt at the look of gratitude in her friend's eyes.

Finding a broom in the kitchen, Kathleen swept all the floors in the house, changed the sheets on all the beds, and stuffed the dirty laundry into a pillow case to take home. Going into the kitchen, she chopped some of the vegetables she'd brought and dumped them into a pot of water, added a few chunks of meat and some seasoning, and put it on the stove for Annie to cook when she was ready.

When she returned to the living room, she saw that the wood box had been filled. Zane stood beside the front door, arms crossed over his chest. There was no sign of Annie.

"She's in the bedroom," he said. "Are you ready to go?"

"As soon as I tell her goodbye."

Annie stepped out of the bedroom a few minutes later wearing a clean nightgown. She had washed her face and brushed her hair.

"We'd better be on our way," Kathleen said. "I left a pot of stew on the stove."

"Thank you so much for all you've done," Annie said, taking Kathleen's hands in hers. "I don't know how I'll ever repay you."

"No need," Kathleen said. "I'm happy to help. Please let me know if there's anything else you need."

Tears of gratitude glistened in Annie's eyes. "God bless you."

Smiling, Kathleen gave the woman a warm hug. "I'll see you again soon, Annie."

Zane was quiet on the way home. He glanced at Kathleen from time to time, thinking she was the closest thing he'd ever seen to an angel. He had never known anyone with such a generous heart or such a giving nature. It only served to prove how different they were. She doled out happiness and service. He delivered death.

It was after three when they reached the ranch. Zane handed her out of the buckboard his hand holding hers a shade longer than necessary. Without being asked, he carried the boxes and bags into the house. With a nod in her direction, he sauntered out of the house, took up the gelding's reins and led the horse down to the barn.

Kathleen stared after him. He hadn't said a word on the way home. Of course, neither had she. But he looked so distant, sitting there beside her, so withdrawn, she hadn't known what to say. Perhaps it was just as well. She found herself thinking about him far too often these days, wanting to spend time with him when she should be busily engaged in trying to help Annie and some of the others in town who were struggling. Merciful heavens, was he angry because she had asked him to stop at Annie's? Could he be so uncaring?

With a shake of her head, she went into the kitchen to help Juanita put the supplies away. She had to stop spending so much time thinking about Zane, she mused, and more time thinking about what to wear to the Grange dance next Saturday night. She sighed, wishing she was going to the dance with Zane instead of Oliver, but that would never do. The people in town would be shocked if she showed up on the arm of a half-breed.

Chapter Six

Stepping out of the cookhouse in the morning, Zane settled his hat on his head, then saddled his horse. At breakfast, one of the cowhands had mentioned seeing Indian sign out on the south range and he'd decided to ride out and have a look around.

He had just taken up the mare's reins when Austin rode in leading a paint horse. A man rode slumped over the horse's neck. Blood leaked from his side. Boone brought up the rear.

Zane's eyes narrowed when he realized the injured man was Indian. "What's going on?" Moving closer, he lifted the injured man's head.

"Found this redskin …" Austin's words trailed off when he recalled who he was talking to. Clearing his throat, he started again. "He was butchering one of our cattle. We're gonna string him up."

"Like hell. He's just a kid. Can't be more than fifteen or sixteen."

"Some kid. He tried to knife Boone in the back."

"So you shot him?"

"He deserved it."

Muttering an oath, Zane pulled the young warrior off the horse, slung him over his shoulder, and carried him into the barn. Lowering the boy onto the straw outside an empty stall, he untied his hands.

The boy groaned. Then, gathering his strength, he tried to sit up.

"Stop it," Zane said, pushing him back on the hay. "You're bleeding like a stuck pig."

He was looking around for a clean rag when Kathleen and her father hurried into the barn.

"What the hell's going on?" Taggart demanded when he saw the wounded kid. "Austin and Boone came up to the house madder than a wet hen. Said some Injun tried to kill Boone."

"I'll talk to the boy after we get him patched up." Zane looked at Kathleen. "Can you bring me a needle and some thread?"

With a curt nod, she turned and ran back toward the house.

Taggart frowned. "I don't mind the Indians taking a cow now and then, but when they try to kill one of my men, we string 'em up."

"You're not hanging anybody until I hear the boy's side of the story," Zane retorted. Removing his kerchief, he placed it over the wound and applied pressure to it. "He's just a hungry kid."

Zane looked up and met Taggart's eyes. He could see the man was weighing his options. In the end, Taggart grunted his agreement and stalked out of the barn.

Kathleen returned minutes later carrying a large enamel bowl of water, several rags, a sewing kit, and a bottle of whiskey. "What happened to him?"

"I'll know more after I talk to him," Zane said curtly.

"Maybe we should send someone for the doctor."

"It's not that bad."

Looking dubious, she asked, "Have you stitched many wounds before?"

"No."

"I'll do it. You look and see if the bullet's still in there."

Zane lifted the boy and checked his back. "The slug went through the meaty part of his side. I don't think it did a lot of damage."

Nodding, Kathleen threaded a needle. "Pour some of that whiskey over the wounds," she instructed. "Then hold him still as best you can."

The boy let out a hiss when Zane dribbled whiskey over his side, began to struggle when Zane laid hold on him. "Lay still," Zane said, speaking Lakota. "We're trying to help."

The boy stared up at him through liquid black eyes, his mouth a tight line of pain, but he stopped struggling.

Taking a deep breath, Kathleen concentrated on what she was doing. She knew she was causing the young man pain. It was evident in the taut line of his jaw, the way he held himself, but he never made a sound.

After what seemed like hours but was only minutes, she tied off the thread and laid the needle aside. Dipping one of the rags in warm water, she washed away the blood, then gently dried his skin with the other cloth.

Dragging a hand across her brow, she stood and blew out a breath. "I think he'll be all right if it doesn't fester. I'll bring him a blanket and some water."

Zane nodded. "Obliged for your help."

With a cool nod, she gathered her things and left the barn.

The boy made no move to sit up, just stared at Zane, his eyes wary.

Zane asked, "*Teetonka.*"

"You're a long way from home." When the boy didn't answer, Zane stood, one hand resting on the butt of his Colt.

A few minutes later, Kathleen returned with a blanket, a small jug of water, and a covered plate. "I thought he might be hungry."

"I reckon."

She covered the boy, then set the jug and the plate on a nearby bale of hay. She studied the Indian for several seconds. "Is it safe to have him here?"

"I don't think he's in any condition to attack you, if that's what you're worried about."

"Can you blame me? The Indians have been raiding not far from here. I heard what they did to the rustlers."

"I'll keep an eye on him."

With a curt nod and a last wary glance in the boy's direction, Kathleen left the barn.

"You should eat and then rest," Zane told the kid. "If you need me, I'll be outside."

The boy stared at him, but again, said nothing.

Shrugging, Zane left the barn, closing the door behind him.

Outside, he grabbed a dandy brush, and ducked into the corral. The buckskin whickered softly as she trotted up to him. "Hey, girl, how you doing?" He scratched her ears, then ran the brush along her neck and over her back.

He caught a glimpse of Kathleen as she stepped out onto the front porch. She had changed clothes and he realized it was Sunday and she was likely headed to church. A moment later, Taggart stepped outside, all duded up in a boiled shirt and black trousers. The old man handed Kathleen into the buggy that had been brought up to the house by one of the ranch hands, then climbed up beside her, took up the reins, and clucked to the horse.

Damn, she was a pretty woman. He recalled all too clearly how she had felt in his arms, soft and warm. The way she had leaned into him when he kissed her.

He smiled at her when she glanced over her shoulder. She quickly looked away, but not before he saw the blush that stained her cheeks when their gazes met.

He was surprised by the rush of heat he felt, the sudden heaviness in his groin. The old man had warned him that his daughter was off limits, but damn, it might be worth Taggart's wrath to pursue her.

Church had already started by the time Kathleen and her father arrived. They usually sat with Oliver, but this morning they settled quietly into the last pew in the back.

Kathleen usually enjoyed Sunday services, but this morning, she couldn't concentrate on the sermon. All she could think about was the way Zane had looked at her. Reverend Thomas might be talking about repentance, but in her mind she replayed the thrill she'd felt when Zane took her in his arms, the way he had held her, kissed her. What was there about that infernal man that she found so attractive? He was nothing but a half-breed drifter, a hired gun. He would likely stay long enough to earn a few dollars and then be on his way. She told herself she couldn't wait to see the last of him, but it was a lie and she knew it.

After services were over, she begrudged every moment her father spent telling Mr. O'Brian how happy he was with the chestnut. She forced herself to make polite conversation with Oliver, nodded when he reminded her of the upcoming dance. She knew he expected her to invite him to

Sunday dinner, but she wasn't in the mood to spend the evening listening to him ramble on about banking or, heaven forbid, hint at marriage again.

She bid Oliver a quick goodbye, grabbed her father's arm and hustled him toward the buggy before he could start a conversation with another one of their neighbors.

"What's wrong with you?" her father asked as he took up the reins.

"I'm just hungry, that's all. Juanita was making an apple pie when we left the house."

As soon as the midday meal was over, Kathleen changed her clothes and fixed a plate for their patient. Humming softly, she hurried down to the barn, the covered plate in her hands the perfect excuse. With luck, Zane would be there. She found him inside, saddling the chestnut mare.

"You need something?" he asked.

"I brought the boy something to eat."

Zane jerked his chin toward an empty stall. The kid was inside, sleeping soundly. "Probably best to let him rest."

Kathleen nodded. "Juanita always says sleep is the best healer of all."

"I reckon so."

Kathleen offered him the plate she was holding. "You might as well eat this, then."

"Obliged."

Kathleen's eyes widened when his hand brushed hers. Had he felt it, too? That sudden jolt of awareness? She lifted her gaze to his and knew it had affected him, too.

Confused, she thrust the plate into his hands and fled the barn.

Zane stared after her. Damn. He hadn't felt this way about a woman since ... hell, he'd never felt this way.

Back in the house, Kathleen stood at the kitchen window watching Zane work the chestnut. He rode easy in the saddle, as if he was part of the horse, his hands light on the reins as he put the mare through her paces. For a big man, he moved with a kind of fluid grace that was beautiful to watch.

"Kathleen."

She gave a start when her father called her name, felt her cheeks grow hot when his gaze slid past her to the window.

"He did a fine job breaking the mare to saddle," her father remarked. "But then, Injuns seem to have a way with horses."

"Yes."

His eyes narrowed when she turned away from the window. "I trust it's the horse you're admiring," he said, his gaze probing hers.

"Of course. Would you like a piece of apple pie?"

He nodded slowly as he pulled a chair from the table and sat down.

Kathleen busied herself getting two plates and cutting the pie, all too aware of the suspicion lurking in her father's eyes.

Kathleen hung up her apron, ran a hand through her hair, and stepped out onto the front porch. Her father was in his office going over the ranch accounts. Juanita had gone into town to visit her grandchildren.

Kathleen blew out a sigh. It was a lovely night, the sky a midnight-blue sprinkled with millions of glittering stars. All was quiet save for the low whinny of one of the horses and the faint whisper of the wind sighing through the trees.

Her father was going to breed the chestnut to his stallion tomorrow. Kathleen recalled the first time she had seen a stallion cover a mare. She'd been a young girl, maybe nine or ten. She remembered watching, wide-eyed, as the stud reared up on its hind legs. It had been an impressive sight. She also remembered her mother's horrified cry when she caught Kathleen watching, and how her mother had grabbed her by the hand and hustled her back up to the house. A rather embarrassing talk had followed.

The scuff of a boot heel caught her attention. A moment later, Zane emerged from the shadows. Her heart skipped a beat as his gaze met hers.

"Nice night," he remarked.

Throat dry, she nodded, felt her pulse race as he stopped at the foot of the stairs, one foot resting on the bottom step. Try as she might, she couldn't think of a thing to say, couldn't think of anything when he was looking at her. The moonlight silvered his hair and she clenched her hands, wishing she had the right to run her fingers through it, to explore the spread of his shoulders, run her hands down his muscular arms.

He moved up a step. "I was going for a walk," he said, his voice low and intimate. "Wanna come along?"

She shouldn't. Her father wouldn't like it. Oliver wouldn't like it. But when Zane held out his hand, she took it, her whole body tingling with excitement when his fingers curled around hers.

It took only minutes to leave the house behind. His hand was large and calloused, so different from Oliver's. But then, Oliver was a banker, a gentleman. He had never done any hard, physical labor. She much preferred Zane's hand, she thought. It was strong. Strong enough to protect a woman. She remembered how effortlessly he had lifted her from the buggy and carried her into the line shack during the storm.

"Cat got your tongue?" he asked.

"Juanita took the Indian boy something to eat after dinner. He was gone."

"Yeah. He took off while I was in the bunkhouse."

"Just like that?"

Zane shrugged. "He's got no love for the white man, no reason to trust us."

"Why wouldn't he trust you? You're ..."

He lifted one brow, waiting for her to finish the accusation.

She blushed under his knowing gaze.

"The kid was wounded and afraid. He hightailed it for home while I was gone. Damn, I must be getting old. I didn't hear a thing." Zane shook his head. "He's just lucky none of the hands saw him sneaking off and took a shot at him."

"Do you think he'll be all right?"

"Reckon so. I talked to him a little. His name's Teetonka. Seems he was kidnapped by the Crow when he was five or six and then rescued by the Lakota when he was eleven. And even though the Crow and the Lakota are enemies, he spends time in both camps. Damnedest thing I ever heard."

After a moment, Katheen said, "I ... I guess you know that my father's pleased with the progress you've made with the chestnut."

"He mentioned it."

"He's going to breed her tomorrow," she said, and clapped her hand over her mouth, wishing she could recall the words. Talk about breeding was hardly a fit subject to discuss with a man.

Zane grinned. Even in the faint moonlight, he could see the blush in her cheeks. "She'll throw a fine foal."

Kathleen nodded, too embarrassed to speak.

"Are you coming down to the corral to watch?" he asked, enjoying her discomfort.

She had planned on it. Now, she wasn't so sure. She had a quick image of the stallion rising over the mare, the mare nervous and quivering.

She looked up at him when he stopped, her heart hammering in her breast as she waited.

Her eyes were wide with mingled trepidation and anticipation as he drew her into his arms. Moving slowly, he lowered his head and claimed her lips with his. For a moment, he thought she was going to slap him or holler for help. Then her eyelids fluttered down and she melted against him. She trembled like a leaf in the wind as he deepened the kiss, went suddenly still when his tongue plundered her mouth. And then, moaning softly, she welcomed him inside.

"Damn, girl," he muttered when they came up for air.

"Did I do something wrong?"

"Hell, no, darlin'," he growled.

Kathleen stared up at him, waiting, hoping, he would kiss her again, felt her knees go weak as his mouth moved over hers, evoking feelings and sensations she had never dreamed existed. His hands moved restlessly up and down her back, drawing her body closer. Lost in a haze of pleasure, she was oblivious to everything until, abruptly, Zane put her away from him.

And then she heard it. Her father's voice, calling her name.

"You'd better go," Zane said, "before he comes looking for you."

She wanted to ask him to kiss her again, but lacked the nerve to do so. Instead, she turned and ran toward home.

Taggart eyed his daughter with suspicion as she hurried up the porch stairs. When she would have gone into the house, he caught her arm. "Where were you?"

"I … I went for a walk."

"Alone?"

She stared at him like a rabbit caught in a trap.

"Kathleen?"

She had never lied to her father, but it wasn't necessary.

"You were with him, weren't you?"

She nodded, her gaze sliding away from his angry one.

"I need him here, Kathleen. I overheard a couple of the Triple E cowhands in town saying Edling had warned them not to try anything as long as Zane was here. Apparently he has quite a reputation as a fast gun up in Montana. But I'll send him packing if you go sneaking off to meet him again." His gaze bored into hers, then he turned and stalked into house.

Filled with shame, her lips still tingling from Zane's kisses, Kathleen followed her father inside.

From the shadows by the porch, Zane listened to the exchange between Taggart and his daughter. He swore under his breath at Taggart's ultimatum, but he couldn't blame the man. No doubt the old man considered the banker a far better match for his only daughter than a half-breed bounty hunter.

But it stung like hell just the same.

Chapter Seven

Taggart's stallion was a beautiful animal. Coal black with a narrow blaze, it stood sixteen hands high. The stud snorted and tossed his head, nostrils flaring wide when Zane led the mare into the corral. Virgil and Austin sat on the top rail of the corral fence, hats pulled low to shade their faces. Boone and Chet stood on the other side of the corral. Dusty had gone into town to pick up the mail. Old Mort watched from the porch rocker.

Zane glanced up at the house, wondering where Kathleen was. She had been looking forward to this morning, he recalled, as her father led the stud around the mare, who tossed her head and obligingly lifted her tail, signaling she was ready. Had the old man told Kathleen to stay home, or was she too embarrassed by what had happened between them the night before to face him?

The stallion was an impressive sight as he reared up, his forelegs coming down to hold the mare in place. It was over in moments. When the stallion withdrew and backed away, the mare snorted and pranced around the corral.

Taggart led the stud into the barn where a bucket of oats was waiting for him.

With a last glance up at the house, Zane turned the chestnut loose. Taggart had asked him to ride out and check for Indian sign. Whether the old man was really worried about trouble with the tribes or just wanted Zane gone for the day was anybody's guess.

Zane had saddled the buckskin earlier. Swinging into the saddle, he rode out of the yard, heading west.

Kathleen watched Zane leave the ranch yard, a catch in her heart as she wondered if her father had fired him. Still upset with her father about last night, she had watched the breeding from the kitchen window. Breakfast had been strained this morning. Juanita had sensed the tension in the air. She often ate in the dining room with the family, but this morning she had taken her breakfast in the kitchen.

At loose ends, Kathleen went upstairs to her room. She glanced out the window, wondering where Zane had gone, if he was coming back. She looked at the dress laid out on her bed, thinking she needed to mend the hem, and then she shrugged. She wasn't in the mood to sit in her room and sew, or read, or do anything else. She was restless and angry and she didn't know who she was the maddest at, herself for practically throwing herself into Zane's arms, or her father for threatening to send him away.

Five minutes later, clad in pants and a long-sleeved shirt, she ran down to the barn, saddled her favorite horse, stuffed a couple of apples into her saddlebags, and rode out of the yard. She needed some time alone, time to sort out her muddled feelings, and there was no better place to do it than by the river that ran through the meadow to the south.

It was a beautiful day for a ride. She saw a small herd of T Bar K cattle and paused for a few minutes to watch a couple of calves cavort around their mothers. The air was fragrant, the breeze warm. She touched her heels to the mare's flanks and the Palomino broke into a canter. A mile later, the river came in sight, a shallow, twisting ribbon of water that ran summer and winter.

She dismounted at the water's edge and hobbled the mare, then removed the bridle and let the horse graze on the lush grass. Reaching into one of the saddlebags, she pulled out an apple, then plopped down on the grass, her back against a cottonwood tree.

Overhead, a squirrel scolded her, the chatter blending in with the whisper of the water and the quiet song of the wind.

She fed the apple core to the horse, then removed her boots, socks and hat, rolled up her pant legs, and waded into the shallow water. She jumped as a fish brushed against her ankle, let out a startled gasp when a deep voice said, "Don't you know you're not supposed to leave the ranch alone?"

She whirled around to find Zane grinning down at her. "What are you doing here?"

"Your old man asked me scout around for Injun sign."

Kathleen sent a quick glance up and down the river. "Did you find any?"

Swinging out of the saddle, he said, "You should have worried about that before you left the ranch."

"I needed some time alone," she said, hoping he would take the hint. As always, his presence unsettled her.

He didn't leave, of course. Dropping the buckskin's reins, he hunkered down on the ground near the water's edge.

Kathleen stared at him. She tried to hang onto her anger, but found herself admiring the width of his shoulders, the way the sunlight danced in his long, black hair. He really was quite handsome, in a rough-hewn, uncouth sort of way. She had a sudden memory of the kisses they had shared, the warmth and excitement of his touch, the feel of his hard-muscled body against hers … She had liked it way too much.

She flushed when his lips twitched in a knowing grin. She told herself he couldn't possibly know what she was thinking, but that insolent grin said otherwise.

"What will it take to make you go away?" she asked, her hands fisted on her hips.

"A kiss?"

Her cheeks flamed. Merciful heavens! He did know what she'd been thinking!

He cocked his head to the side. "How about it?"

Kathleen shook her head, too flustered by the memory of his kisses to speak, too ashamed of the way she had gone so willingly into his arms. Too afraid her father would find out Zane had been here with her and send him away.

Zane watched her, noting the blush in her cheeks, the uncertainty in her eyes. "Come on," he said, rising. "I'll take you back to the ranch."

She nodded. Wading out of the water, she sat down and dried her feet with an old towel she kept in one of her saddlebags. She pulled on her socks, tugged on her boots, rolled down her pant legs and settled her hat on her head. She looked up when Zane offered her his hand, and the next thing she knew, he was lifting her to her feet, drawing her into his arms.

She was so damn beautiful, he thought, her deep green eyes as wide and scared as that of a doe facing a wolf. He murmured her name as he lowered his head, his lips playing over hers, teasing and tempting. He heard the hitch in her breathing, felt her tremble as he deepened the kiss, his hand sliding sinuously up and down her back, then drawing her body closer, closer.

Kathleen clung to him as the world seemed to spin out of focus and there was just the two of them, alone at the river's edge.

Zane muttered an oath as she writhed against him. Damn, if he didn't let her go now, he never would.

He kissed her again and she kissed him back, every rational thought wiped out by the thrill of being in his arms. His mouth was hot against hers and she strained against him, excited by his touch, by the myriad emotions tumbling through her. She looked up at him, her eyes cloudy with passion, her lips bruised from his kisses.

He blew out a breath, muttered, "Girl, as sure as hell and damnation you're gonna get me in trouble." He reminded himself that she was young and innocent, not some saloon girl to be used and forgotten. Too damn young, he thought, and too damn innocent. But if she kept looking at him like that, she wouldn't be innocent much longer.

Kathleen smiled a smile as old as time as, for the first time in her life, she realized she had the power to entice a man. It was a heady feeling and she reveled in it.

"We're leaving." He removed the mare's hobbles, slipped the bridle over her head. "Right now," he growled. "Before one of us does something she'll live to regret."

Kathleen smiled all the way back to the ranch.

Her smile faded when they reached home. Her father stood on the porch, his expression thunderous when he saw her ride in with Zane. He descended the stairs, hands fisted at his sides.

"Don't bother dismounting, Zane," he said. "You're fired. Kathleen, go to your room."

"Dad …"

"Go to your room, Kathleen Marie Taggart."

Knowing there was no point arguing, she slid from the saddle and ran up the stairs and into the house. This was all her fault. He'd told her he would fire Zane if he saw them together again, but she hadn't really believed him.

"Get your stuff together, Zane, then come up to the house. I'll have your pay waiting."

"Keep it."

"I told you my daughter was off limits."

Zane nodded curtly. "I don't give a damn what you think. I didn't go looking for her and we didn't plan to meet. I found her out on the south range, alone, and I brought her home."

Before Taggart could say anything, Zane spun the horse around and spurred the buckskin into a gallop.

Eyes narrowed, Taggart stared after him. Maybe he'd misjudged the man, he thought as he slowly climbed the stairs. Kathleen was a pretty young woman. He couldn't blame the man for looking. Maybe he owed him a debt for bringing his headstrong daughter back home.

Maybe.

Thinking the old man had done him a favor, Zane rode into town. He would spend a few hours playing poker, get a hot bath at the barber shop, spend the night in the hotel, and move on in the morning. Maybe head up to Elkhorn or Virginia City.

Sally's Saloon was quiet this time of day. Standing at the bar, he ordered a whiskey and was debating whether to order another when French Lil flounced down the stairs. A smile lit up her face when she saw him.

"Zane!" She skipped down the last few steps and threw herself into his arms. "I was just thinking how dull it's been without you and here you are!"

"How's it going, Lil?"

She shook her head. "This town's as dull as dishwater," she said, linking her arm with his. "Why don't the two of us head for San Francisco?"

"Frisco?"

"People are getting rich up there every day. And there's Chinatown, and fancy saloons, and big houses, and ..."

"Whoa, girl," he said, with a laugh. "Slow down. I haven't heard of any bounty hunters or whores making a fortune up there. The only ones getting rich are the railroads and the banks."

"We could go to Nevada. There's a big silver strike."

"Who's gonna mine it, darlin'? You?"

"I was just dreamin', Zane," she said. "It don't hurt to dream."

He thought briefly of Kathleen. "No, I guess not." He glanced toward the back of the room where three men were settling at one of the tables. He jerked his chin toward them. "I'm gonna go see which way my luck is runnin'. How about getting me another whiskey? Maybe you'll bring me some luck."

Things were still tense between Kathleen and her father at breakfast the next morning. Dinner the previous night had been equally uncomfortable. Kathleen had gone to her room immediately after clearing the table and stayed there the rest of the night.

Juanita was unusually silent as she bustled about serving breakfast. As she had last night, she chose to dine in the kitchen. Kathleen couldn't blame her. The tension in the room was so thick, you could have cut it with a rusty knife.

When the meal was over, her father stood and grabbed his hat, then paused in the doorway. "I guess I owe you an apology, and maybe Zane, too," he said, his gaze not quite meeting hers. "He told me the two of you met by accident and he brought you home. I can't fault him for that. As for you, daughter, you're not to go riding alone under any circumstances. As long as there's Injuns prowling around, you're to stay close to home."

Kathleen nodded curtly.

Settling his hat on his head, Taggart muttered, "I'll see you tonight," and stomped out of the house.

What difference did her father's apology make, Kathleen mused with a sigh. Zane was still gone.

CHAPTER EIGHT

Zane glanced up at French Lil. She stood behind his chair in the saloon, one hand resting lightly on his shoulder. He'd been kidding last night when he'd suggested she might bring him luck, but damn if she hadn't. He had won better than two hundred dollars and seemed on the verge of winning another hundred or more today.

His fellow card players were a mixed bag. During the course of last night's game, he'd learned that Jensen owned the hotel. Paddy Murphy and his son owned the stable. Young Sean Murphy worked days and the old man worked nights. Lee, the attorney, rarely took a risk. Zane figured the man didn't have many clients if he could idle the days and nights away playing poker. The fourth man at the table, Glen Abbott, was a drummer just passing through. The five of them had played until midnight and started again this morning after breakfast, minus Sean Murphy, who'd gone to work.

Lil let out a squeal when Zane showed his hand, a full house, aces over deuces, and raked in the pot. He sat back as Paddy Murphy shuffled the cards and dealt a new hand. Zane glanced at his cards and wondered what the hell he was doing still in town. The answer came quickly, even though he didn't want to admit it. Kathleen. He wanted to see her again. Hold her again. Feel her curvy little body pressed against his. *Dammit.* He had to stop thinking about her. It was time to move on. Still, he might as well hang around as long as the cards were running in his favor. When Lady Luck stopped smiling on him, he'd ride on. Alone.

A short time later, one of Lil's steady customers came to claim her. Leaning over, she whispered, "Don't go away, Zane. I won't be long," before she followed the lanky cowboy up the stairs.

He was raking in another pot when Tobias Taggart entered the saloon. The man glanced around until he spotted Zane, then came striding across the room like he owned it. "Can I talk to you for a minute?"

Zane shrugged. "Sure. What do you want?"

"Not here."

Gathering his winnings, Zane followed the rancher to the bar. "What's on your mind?"

Taggart cleared his throat. "I reckon I owe you an apology for jumping to the wrong conclusion the other day, and I'd ..." He huffed a sigh, then blurted, "I'd like you to come back to work."

Zane lifted one brow. "Is that right?"

"Some of the other ranchers have seen Indian sign in the area and I'd feel some better if you were around in case we need to palaver with 'em."

"If they want war, talkin' won't change their mind."

"I'd still like to have you on the payroll. You're good with the horses."

Zane dragged a hand across his jaw. He should say hell, no, and ride on. Taggart might be willing to let him handle his horses, but he'd made it clear his daughter was off limits. It was just as well. White women meant nothing but trouble. Still, he had nowhere to go and no one waiting for him when he got there. Why not stay another month or two and add a few dollars to what he'd earned at the poke table?

Taggart shifted from one foot to the other. "Well, what do you say?"

"You've got yourself a hand."

Sitting on the front porch, Kathleen looked up from the peas she was shelling when she saw two riders coming down the road. She shaded her eyes, felt her heart skip a beat when she realized Zane was one of them. A familiar warmth engulfed her when his gaze met hers. And just like that, the world seemed brighter and filled with possibilities. She couldn't help smiling as the two men reined their horses to a halt in front of the porch.

Zane tipped his hat in her direction, then clucked to the buckskin and headed for the barn.

"I hired him back on," her father said gruffly as he dismounted. "Don't make me regret it."

Kathleen couldn't sleep that night. She tossed and turned for hours, every fiber of her being longing for Zane's touch. What had he done to her, to make her want him so? Certainly Oliver had never fired her imagination or kept her awake nights. His nearness inspired nothing within her, no excitement, no ... passion. She didn't dream of him or spend hours remembering the touch of his hands, the taste of his kisses, the way his very nearness made her come alive. She scarcely thought of Oliver when they were apart. But Zane ... he was in her every waking thought, and lately, in every dream. Was he asleep in the bunkhouse? Or tossing and turning as restlessly as was she?

Unable to settle down, she slid out of bed, pulled on her robe, and tiptoed down the stairs and out of the house. Maybe a little fresh air would relax her.

A full moon hung low in the sky. A warm breeze stirred the leaves on the leaves, lifted the hem of her robe. One of the ranch dogs, sleeping under the porch, whined in its sleep.

She felt her heart leap into her throat when she heard the soft scuff of a bootheel, knew before she looked that Zane had ghosted up to the porch stairs. Even in the dark, she could feel his gaze moving over her.

"You're up late." His voice was low, as intimate as a caress.

"So are you."

He grunted softly. "Got a lot on my mind."

"Oh?" It was hard to breathe, hard to think. "Is something troubling you?"

"Yeah." He climbed one stair. "You are."

"Me?" Her voice emerged as little more than a breathy whisper.

Wood creaked as he climbed the second stair. "You've been driving me crazy since the first time I saw you."

He was close now. Too close. The breeze carried his scent—leather and horse and man. She couldn't see him clearly, but she knew what he looked like, his hair long and black and wild, his eyes as gray as thunderclouds, his nose a blade, his mouth, sometimes curved in an ironic grin … She swallowed hard, remembering his kisses, his tongue dueling with her own, his hands caressing her …

She felt the heat of his gaze like a physical caress and then she was in his arms and he was holding her close, kissing her as if he would never let her go.

"Zane … Zane, no." She tried to push him away, terrified her father would find them together. "We mustn't."

"You want me," he said, his voice whiskey-rough. "Admit it."

"We can't … my father …"

"To hell with him. Come away with me. Now. Tonight."

It was tempting, oh, so tempting. A light flared in her father's bedroom window, followed by the sound of it opening, the snick of a rifle being cocked. "Who's down there?"

"It's me, Dad," she called. "I … I couldn't sleep."

"Are you alone?" She didn't miss the suspicion in his voice. "Yes, of course," she lied. Only it wasn't a lie. As quiet as a shadow, Zane had slipped away.

Zane cussed a blue streak as he made his way down to the bunkhouse. What the hell had he been thinking, asking Kathleen to run away with him? He was a half-breed drifter with nothing to offer her, no home, no future, not even a decent reputation. She would be far better off with that insipid banker. But damn, he wanted her more than his next breath.

Needing to put some space between them, he spent the next two days riding the perimeter of the ranch. By the time he was ready to head for the home place, every tree, fence post and stump carried the Indian mark for friend in both Lakota and Cheyenne.

Riding home Friday evening, he figured he had earned some time off, and there was no better way to spend it than getting drunk with French Lil at Sally's on Saturday night.

Chapter Nine

Kathleen fretted over Zane's absence from the ranch. The last two days, he'd ridden out early in the mornings and hadn't returned until after dark. Her father said he was out looking for Indian sign, but she couldn't help feeling Zane was purposefully avoiding her, though she supposed she couldn't blame him after what had happened the last time they were together. Had he seriously expected her to just pick up and run away with him? In spite of the fierce attraction between them, they hardly knew each other. Maybe she had wounded his masculine pride. Maybe he was angry because she'd refused to admit she wanted him. Whatever the reason, he wouldn't even make eye contact with her now. She told herself she didn't care. He was just a drifter passing through. It would be foolish to let herself care for him.

Oliver came by Friday evening. Sitting with him in the parlor, she couldn't help but notice the differences between him and Zane. Oliver was always well-dressed, his hands and nails scrubbed clean, his hair neatly combed. He was unfailingly polite to her and her father, his manners were impeccable. He owned a lovely home in town, attended church every Sunday. And she felt nothing but friendship for him.

In contrast, Zane's wardrobe was rough pants and well-worn boots, his hands were big and rough and calloused, his hair long and shaggy. He owned little more than his horse and saddle and the .44 Colt riding his hip. She doubted if he had ever been to church. And none of it mattered a whit because he made her feel wanted, desired.

As was his custom, Oliver left at eight o'clock. He bid good evening to her father, kissed her good night on the porch, and reminded her that he would pick her up at seven for the dance tomorrow night.

Kathleen remained on the porch after he'd gone, her gaze constantly straying toward the bunkhouse. Had Zane returned? She told herself she didn't care, that he wasn't worth worrying about, but it didn't help.

She lingered on the porch, hoping that, if he was nearby, he might see her, then chided herself for her foolishness. Hadn't he made it perfectly clear that he didn't want to see her? Well, she didn't want to see him, either.

Blinking back her tears, she went inside and closed the door.

Zane left the ranch early Saturday morning. Taggart had commended him for his long hours checking for Indian sign, but worries about Indians had nothing to do with it, Zane thought as he rode into town. He was purposefully avoiding Kathleen and it was having a lousy effect on his temper. For the first time in his life, he missed a woman's company. In the past, he had loved 'em and left 'em without a second thought. But, somehow, in a remarkably short time, Kathleen Taggart had wormed her way into his heart and it made him as prickly as a porcupine. He'd thought he was hiding it pretty well, but a couple of the cowhands had noticed and asked him what the hell was bothering him.

Cursing himself for being a damn fool, he bought a pair of black wool trousers, a white shirt and a black leather vest, a new pair of boots, and a black Stetson. Whether Taggart liked it or not, he intended to go to the dance tonight and claim one dance with the old man's daughter. Of course, there was always the chance Kathleen would refuse, but it was a risk he was willing to take.

Kathleen sighed as she took a last glance at her reflection. Her dress new and flattered her figure. The green made her eyes look darker, deeper. Juanita had arranged her hair. She wore the pearls her mother had sent her for her sixteenth birthday. If only she was going to the dance with Zane instead of Oliver, everything would be perfect.

She sighed again when she heard her father inform her that Oliver had arrived. Grabbing her wrap, she padded down the stairs.

The Grange hall was already crowded when they arrived. The annual dance was one of the few times the ranchers and townspeople got together to renew friendships and enjoy each other's company. The air was filled with conversation and laughter. The fiddler stood on a raised dais in the corner, tuning up. Long tables covered with white cloths stood against the back wall, groaning under the weight of cakes and pies and tarts, baskets of fruit, and bowls of punch.

"Looks like everyone turned out," Oliver remarked.

Kathleen nodded. Even Annie was there with her husband and children.

"Would you like a glass of punch?" Oliver asked.

"Yes, thank you." She glanced around the room, smiling and waving at old friends, felt her heart skip a beat when she saw Zane saunter through the door. Lordy, he looked handsome tonight. Clad in a new set of clothes, boots, and a hat, she almost hadn't recognized him. She didn't miss the way several of the unmarried girls—and a few of the married women—stared at him.

She was staring herself. She blushed and looked away when he caught her watching him.

A moment later, Oliver returned with her drink. She had no sooner finished it and set the glass aside than the fiddler struck up a tune and Oliver led her onto the floor.

"You're mighty quiet tonight," he remarked. "Is something wrong?"

Wrong? she thought. Everything was wrong.

"Kathleen?"

She forced a smile. "No, nothing."

They danced and visited with some of the other young couples. Kathleen watched Zane surreptitiously. He didn't dance with anyone. Didn't speak with anyone. Just stood against the wall. Every time she glanced his way, she found him looking back at her.

It was late in the evening when he approached her. "Miss Taggart, may I have this dance?"

Oliver bristled like an angry rooster. "See here ..." he began. But Zane silenced him with a glance.

"Miss Taggart?"

Swallowing hard, she took the hand he offered. As they stepped onto the dance floor, she caught her father glaring at her. But she refused to let it ruin the moment. A thrill ran through her as Zane took her in his arms. The dance was a slow waltz. She wondered briefly where he had learned to dance. Surely the Indians didn't waltz. But all that mattered was he was there, holding her too close. She didn't care if it made Oliver angry, didn't care that her father was sure to chastise her. Didn't care that some of the older women looked on with open disapproval. She only wished she could stay in Zane's arms forever.

All too soon, the music ended and a grim-faced Oliver strode toward them.

"Your father asked me to take you home," he said, careful not to meet Zane's eyes.

Cheeks flushed with embarrassment, her head held high, Kathleen followed Oliver out of the hall.

Zane waited a moment, then ducked out a side door.

"What were you thinking, accepting a dance with that dirty half-breed?" Oliver scolded. "The whole town will be gossiping about it at church tomorrow."

"Let them talk!" Kathleen retorted. "I didn't do anything wrong. It would have been rude to refuse him."

"Rude? Rude? The man's a savage. A hired hand. I didn't notice you dancing with Austin or Virgil."

"I don't owe you any explanations," Kathleen retorted, her tone icy. "We are not married. We are not engaged. And after tonight, I never want to see you again."

"Kathleen …" His voice trailed off as a half-dozed Indians suddenly appeared on the road in front of them.

She let out a scream as an arrow whizzed past her cheek and buried itself in Oliver's shoulder. He slumped sideways and tumbled to the ground.

She screamed again as one of the warrior's grabbed her around the waist and hauled her out of the buggy and onto his horse. With a wild cry, her captor raced away into the darkness.

❧   ❧   ❧

Zane slammed his heels into the buckskin's flanks when he heard a woman scream. Kathleen!

He hadn't been very far behind them, but he arrived too late to help. A quick glance at the ground told him half a dozen Indians had attacked the pair. There was no sign of Kathleen. Oliver lay face down on the ground. Zane thought he was dead until a low groan emerged from the man's throat. Dammit! He didn't want to waste time looking after Oliver Plotkin.

Zane sat there a moment while he struggled with his conscience. Every moment he delayed put more distance between himself and Kathleen. He glared at Plotkin, sorely tempted to let the man bleed to death.

Muttering an oath, he dismounted and rolled Plotkin over. Muttering under his breath, he loaded the banker into the buggy, swung up beside him, took up the reins and clucked to the horse. The buckskin trailed behind him.

Zane swore under his breath, quietly cursing the man for not being dead, even as he assured himself that if the Indians intended to kill Kathleen, they wouldn't have carried her away … unless they meant to torture her. But there was no honor in torturing females. Or children.

He hollered for help as soon as he pulled up in front of the house. A few minutes later, Juanita came hurrying out the door. He quickly explained what had happened, carried Plotkin inside, then hurried down to the bunkhouse. He shrugged into a jacket, strapped on his Colt, grabbed his rifle and a box of ammunition, and filled a canteen with fresh water. Returning to the main house, he packed several slices of roast beef, a hunk of cheese, and half a loaf of bread before he lit out after the Indians.

If he was too late, if the Indians hurt Kathleen, Oliver Plotkin was as good as dead.

Kathleen had never been so scared in her life. She tried to pray, but the words wouldn't come. Her mouth was dust-dry, her hands clammy. She felt cold all over even though the night was warm and clear. The arm around her waist was as hard and unyielding as iron. She had risked one glance at her captor's face. His expression behind the war paint was inscrutable, his eyes as black as night. She wondered briefly if Oliver was still alive but her concern for him was swallowed up in fear for her own life. Why had the Indians attacked them? What were they going to do with her? She had no hope of rescue. No one knew where she was. She choked back a sob. If Oliver was dead, no one would ever know what had happened to her.

The Indians rode for hours, stopping occasionally to rest the horses. She huddled on the ground, unable to stop shaking. No one paid any attention to her. Summoning her courage, she edged toward the trees, let out a scream when her captor grabbed her arm and thrust her onto the back of his horse. In minutes, the warriors were all mounted and riding again.

She was exhausted when they finally bedded down for the night. She was too weary to care where they were. When her captor motioned for her to lie down, she was only too happy to oblige. She was asleep as soon as she closed her eyes.

Zane uttered a pithy oath. He had only managed to trail the Crow a short distance before it became impossible to see their tracks in the dark. He considered riding back to the ranch and starting over again in the morning but quickly dismissed the idea. After stripping the rigging from the mare, he spread his bedroll on the ground and put his rifle within easy reach. Lying there, he gazed up at the sky.

"Stay strong, darlin'," he murmured. "I'm coming."

Zane was in the saddle when the sun rose over the distant mountains. The trail was clear now, easy to follow. The Crow were riding due east, hard and fast, not bothering to try to cover their tracks, which meant they didn't know they were being followed. With luck, he would find them before nightfall.

It was near dusk when an instinct honed by years of bounty hunting warned him he was no longer alone. The thought had no sooner occurred to him than he felt a hot, burning pain in his thigh. He grabbed his rifle and spun the buckskin around but he was too late. A second bullet found its mark in his right shoulder. The force of it, the pain, was enough to make him drop the Winchester. And then the Indians were on him, knocking him from the saddle ... and into oblivion.

Chapter Ten

An icy shiver ran down Kathleen's spine as a high, ulu-lating cry sounded from outside the lodge where she was being held. What were they doing out there? What were they going to do to her? How was Oliver? Her father must be frantic, wondering what had happened to her.

She shivered as whoops and hollers filled the air. The Indian who had captured her hadn't mistreated her and though he didn't speak English, he had made it clear she wasn't to leave the tipi. Thus far, she hadn't so much as peeked outside. But she did so now. She had to know what was causing that eerie, blood-curdling sound.

Taking a deep breath, she tiptoed to the entrance and pushed the lodge flap aside enough to see outside ... and let out a cry of her own when she saw two warriors pull Zane from the back of his horse and drag him toward a stout post on the far side of the camp. Strips of cloth had been wrapped around his left thigh and his right arm near his shoulder. Both were stained with blood. Two warriors held him upright while a third yanked his arms behind the post and lashed his hands together. When the warriors released their hold on Zane, he sank to the ground, his head lolling forward. She couldn't tell if he was conscious, but she doubted it. How much blood had he lost?

When she saw the Indian who had captured her striding in her direction, she quickly lowered the lodge flap and scooted toward the buffalo robe in the back of the tipi.

The warrior spoke to her in a harsh, guttural tongue. He handed her a chunk of dried meat and a waterskin, then turned and left the lodge.

Though she had no appetite, she nibbled on the meat. What were they going to do with Zane? He was one of them. Surely they wouldn't kill him … would they? Who knew what savages would do?

Minutes passed. Gathering her courage, she peeked out of the lodge again. Zane hadn't moved. She couldn't tell if he was breathing. Oh, Lord, was he dead?

She gasped when a passing warrior kicked Zane in the side, felt a rush of relief when Zane's head snapped up. Thank heaven, he was alive! But for how long, she wondered, as every man, woman, and child who passed anywhere near Zane hit him, some striking him with their hands, others kicking him. He never made a sound.

She bit down on her lower lip as he struggled to his feet, yearned to go to him when she saw that the wounds in his shoulder and thigh were leaking fresh blood. She knew he must be hurting, yet he glared defiantly at his attackers as they continued to pummel him with their feet and fists. Why did they hate him so? Did they intend to beat him to death?

They tormented him until nightfall. She wished she could go to him, but she dared not leave the lodge. Fear for Zane turned to fear for her own life when her captor entered the lodge that night. He stared at her, his dark eyes curious rather than malevolent. Thus far, he hadn't touched her. Would tonight be different?

He spoke to her in a rough, guttural tongue as he gestured for her to lay down. Every nerve taut, she slid beneath the buffalo robe, her lips clamped together to keep from crying out when he stretched out beside her in the dark.

She flinched when she felt his fingers sift through her hair. He muttered a word she didn't understand, then rolled onto his side. Moments later, his snoring filled the lodge.

Weak with relief, Kathleen closed her eyes but sleep wouldn't come. As quietly as she could, she eased out of the buffalo robe and tiptoed toward the entrance. She stood there a moment, holding her breath, and when the warrior didn't stir, she crept out of the lodge.

Outside, she stood in the darkness, hardly daring to breathe. Clouds covered the moon. Thunder rumbled in the distance. But the camp was quiet.

On silent feet, she made her way around the edge of the camp toward Zane. He was sitting down, long legs stretched out in front of him, his chin resting on his chest.

His head jerked up when she whispered his name. "Kathleen!" he murmured. "Are you all right?"

"Yes. But you …" She bit down on her lower lip. Even in the darkness, she could see the pain in his eyes. "What can I do?"

"Can you bring me some water? And a knife?"

A noise from behind her sent Kathleen scuttling back to the lodge.

Zane tensed as a man materialized out of the darkness, muttered an oath when a shaft of moonlight glinted on the knife in his hand. But the warrior didn't cut him. Instead, he slashed the rope binding his hands together, then pulled Zane to his feet.

"Teetonka." He whispered the warrior's name.

"We go," the young warrior said.

"Not without my woman."

With a grunt, Teetonka put his arm around Zane and half-dragged him behind the nearest lodge, where three horses waited. "You. Here. Stay."

Zane draped his uninjured arm over the buckskin's neck, his every sense alert. Minutes later, Teetonka and Kathleen hurried toward him. Teetonka boosted Zane onto the buckskin's back. When Kathleen started toward Zane, Teetonka grabbed her and thrust her onto the back of a dun-colored horse before swinging onto the back of his own mount.

Riding single-file they rode slowly, quietly, out of the village.

Once they were well away from the camp, Teetonka kicked his horse into a gallop and the other two followed.

Kathleen glanced constantly at Zane. Even in the faint light of the moon, she could see the lines of pain on his face. How he managed to stay on the horse was beyond her.

They rode for hours, constantly changing direction, riding through streams and splashing across rivers, never stopping for more than a few moments to rest the horses.

It was near dawn when Kathleen saw the lodges. Dear Lord, she thought, another Indian camp. Had they escaped one disaster only to find themselves in another?

Their arrival caused a stir as a dozen or more warriors swarmed around them. Kathleen watched in horror as some of the warriors grabbed the Indian who had rescued them.

Zane spoke to one of the Indians and, to Kathleen's surprise, they turned Teetonka loose.

Two warriors stepped forward, lifted Zane from the buckskin's back, and carried him into a lodge. A third warrior gestured for Katheen to follow.

Inside, Zane lay on a pile of buffalo robes. A wizened old Indian woman knelt beside him, chanting softly as she removed his shirt. Kathleen gasped when the woman reached for a knife, but she only cut the seam in the leg of his trousers, exposing the wound.

When that was done, she sprinkled something in the small fire burning in the center of the lodge. Then, using a feather, she fanned the smoke toward Zane until it covered him like a fragrant cloud.

Zane looked up at Kathleen. In a voice raw with pain, he said, "You should go outside."

She shook her head, not willing to leave him.

He didn't argue.

The old woman spoke to Zane in her native tongue, placed a short, fat stick between his teeth, and picked up her knife again.

And Kathleen wished suddenly that she had gone outside. She bit down on her lower lip as the old woman dug the slug out of Zane's thigh, closed her eyes when she turned toward his arm.

When the slugs had been removed, the old woman washed the wounds, spread some kind of thick yellow paste over them, and bound them with cloth. She offered Zane a cup of water, which he drank greedily, then covered him with a trade blanket.

With a faint smile at Kathleen, the old woman shuffled out of the lodge.

When they were alone, Kathleen knelt beside Zane. His eyes were closed, his face drawn and pale. There were tight lines of pain around his mouth. She had questions, so many questions, but he was already asleep.

Overcome with exhaustion, she stretched out beside him and closed her eyes.

It was late afternoon when she woke. Zane was still sleeping. Kathleen groaned softly when she sat up, every muscle protesting the hours she had slept on the hard ground, the exhausting ride to the village. Easing to her feet, she stepped outside. A clump of brush provided some much-needed privacy while she relieved herself.

Returning to the front of the lodge, she glanced at her surroundings. Perhaps two dozen hide lodges stood in a loose circle near a winding river. A herd of horses grazed in the distance. Men, women and children were in evidence, laughing, talking, eating, going about their daily tasks. No one paid her any attention. She wondered where the old woman was. Where Teetonka was. Where the hell she was. All she knew was this was a Lakota camp and the Crow were their enemies.

A few moments later, the old woman hobbled toward her, a bowl cradled in her hands. She smiled at Kathleen as she thrust the bowl into Kathleen's hands, offered her a spoon made of some kind of horn, then pointed at the bowl and made eating motions.

Kathleen nodded and smiled, her expression pensive as she glanced at the bowl's contents. It looked like some kind of stew or soup, but she had no idea what it was made of. Sitting cross-legged in front of the lodge, she said a silent prayer that it was venison or buffalo and not dog or horse, and took a bite. It was bland but surprisingly good.

She had almost finished eating when the old woman returned with another bowl, which she carried into the lodge.

Kathleen remained outside for several minutes, until her curiosity got the best of her and she ducked inside.

Zane was awake, his head resting on a rolled-up hide, while the old woman fed him.

He smiled faintly at Kathleen when he saw her. "You doing all right?"

She nodded. "Better than you."

"Yeah. I feel like I was stomped by a bull. But I was lucky. The slugs didn't hit anything vital. I'll be sore for a while, but …" He shrugged. "Could have been a lot worse."

She nodded again, then remained quiet while the old woman fed him the last of the soup, then held a waterskin to his lips. When that was done, she lifted the bandages to check his wounds, nodded in what appeared to be satisfaction. After replacing the bandages, she gathered the bowl and spoon and hobbled out of the lodge.

"Who is that?" Kathleen asked as she sat beside Zane.

"She's a medicine woman. I don't know her name. Where's Teetonka?"

"I don't know. I haven't seen him since he brought us here."

Zane grunted softly. "We were damn lucky he was at the Crow camp and not here."

She was afraid to ask what would have happened to them if the boy had been here with the Lakota instead of with the Crow. "Is there anything I can do for you?"

"Just keep me company."

Leaning forward, she brushed his hair away from his forehead. His skin was warm but not fever-hot. Surely a good sign. "How can Teetonka live in two places?"

"It's unusual, I'll grant you that. I guess he learned to love the Crow warrior who had kidnapped him. Seems the Crow warrior's wife couldn't get pregnant and her husband decided to do something about it. He kidnapped Teetonka and then, years later, some Lakota warriors raided the Crow camp. One of them recognized Teetonka and took him home."

"That's the strangest story I ever heard."

"I'd have to agree with that."

"Thank you for coming after me, although I'm sorry you got hurt. Are you in much pain?"

He made a vague gesture with his hand. "Some. The old woman gave me some willow bark tea. It's good for relieving pain."

"You should get some sleep."

"Yeah, I think I will. Don't be afraid, Kathleen. No one here will hurt you. The Lakota and the Cheyenne are allies."

"Don't worry about me."

"I can't help it," he murmured. Moments later, he was asleep.

Kathleen stayed by his side, her thoughts wandering homeward. Her father must be worried sick, wondering where she was, if she was still alive. And Oliver … had he survived his wounds? Did everyone think she was dead? How long would it be before Zane could travel? A couple of weeks, at the very least, she thought, before his wounds would have healed enough for a long ride across rough country. How many days would it take them to get back to the ranch? She blinked back her tears, wondering if she would ever see her home and her father again.

Chapter Eleven

Kathleen smiled her thanks the day the old medicine woman provided her with a simple, unadorned dress made of doeskin and a pair of moccasins. She breathed a sigh of relief as she changed out of her soiled clothes and into something clean. Teetonka, equally generous, had offered Zane a buckskin shirt and pants. She couldn't help grinning when she saw her reflection in the river. Even with her hair in braids, she'd never pass for a Lakota.

Kathleen learned a lot in the days and weeks that followed while they waited for Zane's wounds to heal. She discovered that even though people looked and dressed differently, spoke another language, or ate peculiar foods, people were still just people, red or white. Indian men protected their homes and families and hunted for food. Women loved and cared for their husbands and children. They looked after their homes, tended the sick and the aged. Little boys and girls could find fun anywhere—chasing butterflies, swimming in the river, throwing a ball made of rawhide back and forth.

She spent most of her time with Zane, although he was rarely awake much the first few days. Every now and then, when she needed some fresh air or just some time alone, she walked down by the river. It was beautiful there, peaceful, with only the sound of rushing water and the soft sighing of the wind in the cottonwoods.

In spite of her inability to communicate with anyone, the old Indian woman, whose name was Talutah, was adept at getting her message across, whether she was asking if Kathleen was hungry, wished to bathe, or wanted to be alone. The members of the tribe treated her with respect.

Sometimes, when Zane was napping, she sat outside and observed the activity in the village. She watched old men dozing in the sun or telling what she assumed were stories to the children who frequently gathered around them. She saw women skinning game, making jerky, curing hides—a disgusting process if she had ever seen one. Men seemed mostly idle. They strolled through the camp chatting with friends, or sat in the shade making or repairing weapons. She saw children too young to walk being taught to ride, young boys learning how to handle a bow and arrow, girls taking care of their younger siblings.

One evening, when Zane was strong enough to get up and around, they sat outside. On this night, the Indians were having some sort of celebration. There was food and dancing. Oddly, the men and women seldom danced together. She was intrigued by their intricate dance steps, the rhythmic beat of the drum, the way the firelight played over the faces of the dancers.

She glanced sideways at Zane, puzzled by the expression on his face. "What are you thinking about?"

"Nothing."

"I don't believe you."

He shrugged one shoulder. "I was thinking about home, and how long it's been since I've been there."

"How long has it been?"

"Twelve years."

She bit down on her lower lip. Not since he'd killed his father, she thought. Did he ever regret what he'd done? "What did you do when you left? Where did you go?"

"I spent a year or so roaming the Black Hills, living off the land. Eventually, I made my way to some nameless prairie town. My old man had taught me to speak English and on the rare occasions when he wasn't drunk, he told me about his people, their ways and beliefs. It took a while, but I learned to adjust to the white man's way of living, although I never really fit in."

"And you never went back home? Not even once?"

"Why would I?" He stood abruptly and walked away from the fire.

Kathleen waited a moment before she followed him. She found him standing beside the river, staring into the distance. Hesitantly, she placed her hand on his arm. "I'm sorry, Zane."

He grunted softly. "It was a long time ago."

But the hurt and the bitterness were still there. She could see it in his eyes.

She let out a gasp when he suddenly pulled her into his arms and buried his face in her hair. He held her for a long time, his body tense.

Her heart aching for him, Kathleen stroked his back, willing to stand there forever if it would help. He wasn't wearing a shirt and his skin was warm beneath her hands, his muscles taut.

Gradually, he relaxed and there was a subtle shift in the way he held her. She felt a thrill of delight as he rained kisses over her cheeks and along her neck before he claimed her lips. She leaned into him, eagerly returning his kisses. She clutched his shoulders, only to draw back when he let out a hiss of pain.

"Sorry," she murmured. "I forgot you were hurt."

"Yeah." He grinned down at her. "I forgot about it myself for a minute there."

"How soon do you think we can go home?" she asked. "My father must be worried to death, wondering where I am."

He blew out a sigh. "We can leave tomorrow, if you like."

"Are you sure you're up to it?"

"Good enough to travel, if we take it slow. I'll let Talutah know we're leaving."

Once the decision was made, it took less than a day to get ready. Talutah prepared several days' worth of food for their journey, filled a couple of waterskins, and provided them with a pair of bedrolls. She had also washed and mended their clothes as best she could.

They left early the following morning. Teetonka presented Kathleen with a pretty little bay mare for the journey home. Zane packed their gear, saddled his buckskin, and they were ready to go.

Zane said their goodbyes, then helped Kathleen onto the back of her horse before mounting his own. As near as he could figure, they had been gone about seven weeks. No doubt her old man feared she was dead.

"How long will it take us to get home?" Kathleen asked as they rode out of the village, heading west.

"Three or four days, I reckon."

She nodded, wondering again if Oliver had survived. If her father thought she'd been killed. She would find out soon enough, she mused. As long as they didn't run into any more marauding Crow on the way home.

They camped that night in the lee of a mountain. Zane laid a small fire, Kathleen served pemmican and venison for dinner. They turned in early. Kathleen spread their bedrolls on either side of the fire and went to bed fully-clothed except for her shoes.

Zane fell asleep almost instantly, but she lay awake for a long time, thinking about his past. What a rough life he must have had after killing his father. She wondered how he had become a bounty hunter and how many men he'd caught and if he had brought them in dead or alive. Did his conscience ever bother him for killing his father? Or had he felt nothing but satisfaction at dispatching the man who had beat his mother to death? How horrible that must have been. No wonder he often seemed withdrawn. With his past, she was surprised he ever smiled at all.

She bolted upright at the sound of something rustling in the bushes. Indians? A wild animal? Afraid to call his name out loud, she whispered. "Zane."

He woke instantly. "What's wrong?"

"I heard a noise. In the bushes. Over there."

She had no sooner uttered the words than a large brown bear lumbered into sight.

Kathleen let out a cry that emerged from her throat as little more than of a squeak. She had seen bears before, near the ranch, but always from a good distance. She had never realized just how big they were. The horses whinnied nervously as they caught the predator's scent.

"Don't move," Zane warned.

"What are you going to do?"

"Try to scare it off." Reaching for his Colt, he stood up slowly and fired three quick shots into the air.

The bear spun around, faster than Kathleen would have thought possible, and ran away.

"You all right?" Zane asked.

Kathleen pressed a hand to her pounding heart. "Can I come over there and sleep next to you?"

"Sure."

Rising, she gathered her bedroll and quickly spread it beside his. The sooner they got home, the better.

Kathleen woke abruptly, surprised to find herself pressed against Zane's side, her head pillowed on his shoulder, his arm around her waist. And then she remembered the bear. Lifting her head, she took a hasty look around, but there was no sign of it. She wasn't sure which had frightened her more, being captured by the Crow. or the thought of being attacked by that big brown bear.

She should get up, she thought, before Zane woke. But she didn't move. He needed to rest and she didn't want to wake him. That was the excuse she told herself, but the truth was, she liked lying there beside him. Asleep, he didn't look so formidable. She studied his face, his fine, straight nose, his strong jaw, the tempting curve of his mouth, the thick black lashes, his high cheekbones. He really was a handsome man. His long, black hair and copper-hued skin only added to his over-all appeal.

Kathleen bit down on her lower lip when she realized he was awake and watching her through heavy-lidded eyes. She felt her heart skip a beat when his arm tightened around her. His free hand moved to cup her nape, drawing her head closer. Her eyelids fluttered down as his mouth brushed hers. When she sighed, he rolled onto his side and deepened the kiss, his lips moving seductively over hers, his tongue darting inside for a taste. She melted against him, wanting to be closer, then paused.

"What's wrong?"

"I don't want to hurt you."

He frowned, and then he laughed. "You aren't. And even if you were, the pleasure would surely outweigh the pain."

They might have stayed there all day, kissing and caressing, if her stomach hadn't let out a very unladylike growl.

Zane laughed softly as he put her away from him and sat up. Another few minutes, he thought, and her virtue would have been in serious danger.

They saddled up after breakfast. The day passed peacefully enough. They stopped a couple of times to rest the horses. Kathleen had never seen such beautiful country—rolling hills and lush valleys, winding rivers rich with fish. Scattered patches of wildflowers added splashes of bright color to the hillsides, trees provided welcome shade in the heat of the day.

"How did you get to be a bounty hunter?" Kathleen asked when they stopped for something to eat.

Zane shrugged. "I just sort of fell into it. I was in Wichita when I saw a wanted poster. The face looked familiar, the reward was sizeable, and I realized I'd seen him a few days earlier in the town I'd just left. I rode back and found him in one of the saloons. I got the drop on him and turned him in." He chuckled. "They weren't all that easy."

"Seems like a dangerous way to make a living."

"It can be. Hiring out my gun doesn't usually pay as much but in some ways, it's safer."

"Haven't you ever wanted to settle down?"

"No." His gaze moved over her. "Not until I met you."

His words warmed her from head to toe. And repeated themselves in her mind until they drew rein for the night.

When it came time to turn in, she looked at Zane, a question in her eyes. The answer came when he patted the ground beside him. It was wrong, she thought as she spread their bedrolls out side by side, but she didn't care. For these few hours, there was no one to tell her she couldn't love him, that lying close beside him was wrong.

She stretched out on her bedroll, her head again pillowed on his shoulder as she stared up at the stars, all too aware of the man beside her. He smelled of horse and leather and perspiration—scents she had grown up with and rarely noticed. But on Zane, they were … enticing. Or perhaps it was the scent of the man himself. As if sensing her thoughts, he wrapped his arms around her.

Zane held her close. In the faint glow of the dying fire, he could see the yearning in her eyes, hear the faint uptick in her breathing as his hands slid up and down her back, drawing her body tight against his, letting her feel his arousal.

Though no words were spoken, Kathleen heard the question. For a moment, fear of the unknown overshadowed everything else.

And then he kissed her, gently at first, and then with increasing intensity, driving every thought from her mind but the fact that they were alone. He'd told her they would be home tomorrow. She might never have a chance like this again … never be alone and in his arms again.

"Kathleen?"

"Yes," she murmured. "Make love to me."

His gaze searched hers. It was wrong, he thought. Wrong on so many levels. Despite what he had told her, he wasn't the kind of man to settle down in one place and raise a family. He'd been drifting since he was seventeen. He had a price on his head in Sagebrush Flats … But none of that seemed to matter when she slid her hand under his shirt, her nails raking his chest, her hands measuring the width of his shoulders.

One kiss, he thought. Just one more kiss and he would let her go. But when their lips met, it was like touching a match to dynamite. The lingering ache of his wounds disappeared as quickly as their clothes. He kissed her again, their hands and mouths touching, exploring, until they were both breathless with need

"Kathleen," he groaned. "Tell me to stop."

With a shake of her head, she ran her tongue over his lips and along his chest while her hands moved restlessly up and down his back.

And he was lost.

When he rose over her, she pulled him closer, let out a soft cry as he possessed her, his life pouring into her, until they lay spent in each other's arms, sated and content, while the night wind sang them to sleep.

Chapter Twelve

Kathleen woke slowly, reluctant to leave the wonderful dream she'd had. Sighing, she opened her eyes—and found Zane watching her, his expression guarded.

It hadn't been a dream. She had spent the night in his arms—a night she would never forget. Heat flooded her cheeks when she remembered asking him to make love to her, the eager way she had responded to his kisses. The way her hands had boldly explored his hard, muscular body. The warm, sensual pleasure of his hands roaming over her, arousing her, touching places no one had ever touched before.

Zane swore a silent oath as he watched the emotions play over her face—embarrassment, disbelief. But, thankfully, not regret.

Kathleen swallowed hard. "Say something."

He lifted one brow as several replies flashed through his mind, none of which she wanted to hear. "Do you want me to say I'm sorry?"

"Are you?"

"No." He caressed her cheek with his knuckles. "Are you?"

Her gaze slid away from his. "I don't know. I thought … I mean …" Her cheeks grew hotter. "I don't know what I mean."

Like all women the morning after, she wanted to hear that he loved her. And maybe he did. How the hell was he to know?

When she started to roll away from him, he held her fast. "Kathleen, look at me." He swore softly when he saw the tears shining in her eyes. "I've never been in love before. I'm not sure what I feel for you. All I know is that I care for you more than I've ever cared for anyone. Maybe it's love. After last night, I'd like to think so."

They weren't the words she wanted to hear, but at least he was telling her the truth. And try as she might to regret what had happened, she couldn't. She had never been in love before, either, but she was now. Deeply, irrevocably. For better or worse. "We should go."

He nodded. Cupping her face in his hands, he kissed her lightly. He hadn't intended for it to lead to anything else, but one kiss led to another. And then another. He waited for her to pull away, to tell him no, but she clung to him, her body molding to his as she kissed him back. And in that moment, turning away from her was just as impossible as asking the sun not to shine.

He made slow, sweet love to her there, beneath the bright blue sky, and in that moment, he knew he would never willingly let her go.

Kathleen guessed it was close to midnight when they rode into the ranch yard. The house was dark and quiet. After dismounting, Zane lifted her from the back of her horse and into his arms. "You gonna be okay?"

Bone weary, she nodded. "All I want to do is sleep." Her gaze searched his. "Will you still be here tomorrow?"

"I'm not going anywhere." At least not right away. He didn't know if the consequences of the nights they had spent together had occurred to her, but he wasn't leaving until he knew. Giving her a squeeze, he murmured, "Sweet dreams, darlin'."

"Kiss me good night?"

He grinned as he pulled her closer.

Kathleen's eyelids fluttered down as he claimed her lips in a long, searing kiss that left her breathless and wishing they were still out on the prairie, alone.

She sighed as he gave her one last, quick kiss, then took up the reins of their horses and headed toward the barn. As happy as she was to be home, she was going to miss the days and nights they had spent together.

Kathleen opened the front door as quietly as she could and crept up the stairs. She paused in front of her father's bedroom door. She really should let him know she was here. He would have questions, questions she was just too exhausted to answer. There would be plenty of time for that in the morning. She tiptoed into her room, quietly closed the door, and fell into bed, fully-clothed, asleep as soon as her head hit the pillow.

Tobias blinked in astonishment when Kathleen entered the kitchen in the morning. "What ... when ... how ...?" Surging to his feet, he knocked the kitchen chair over as he hurried forward and wrapped his arms around her. "I've been worried as hell about you. All this time, nobody knew if you were dead or alive." He held her away from him and looked her up and down. "Oliver was unconscious and couldn't tell us anything. Juanita said Zane dropped Oliver off, said there'd been an Indian attack and you were missing.

She said he picked up his weapons and lit out again. All these weeks of not knowing if you were dead or alive …" He took a deep breath. "Where the hell have you been all this time?"

Kathleen pressed her fingertips to his lips, stilling any further questions. "All in good time, Dad," she assured him. "But let's eat first. You have no idea how much I've missed Juanita's cooking."

At that moment, Juanita padded into the kitchen with breakfast. "Welcome home, *pequeño*!" she exclaimed. "We have been so worried about you. Sit, sit," she said, motioning to a chair. "I will bring you something to eat."

"*Gracias*, Juanita." Kathleen took her usual place at the table, her stomach growling loudly at the tantalizing scent of bacon and eggs wafting from the kitchen.

"When did you get home, daughter?" Sitting down, Taggart pushed his plate out of the way and leaned forward.

"Late last night."

"Why didn't you wake me?"

"I'm sorry. I know I should have. But I was so tired. Is Oliver all right?"

"Yes, he's fully recovered." His gaze moved over her. "You're well?" He cleared his throat. "The savages didn't …?"

"No! No. They treated me well enough."

"And Zane? Did he survive?"

"He brought me home."

Taggart grunted softly. "After dropping off Oliver, Zane rode out again before Juanita could ask him any questions. All we knew was that he was going after you. But after a week or two, we figured the Indians had killed him, too."

"He was badly wounded by the Crow. You remember that Indian boy we took care of for a short time? Teetonka?

He was at the Crow village, thank the Lord. He helped us escape from the Crow and took us to a Lakota camp."

"What the hell?" Her father slammed his hand on the table. "From one bunch of savages to another?"

Kathleen shook her head. "No. Zane is Cheyenne. The Lakota and the Cheyenne are allies. An Indian medicine woman looked after his wounds. I wouldn't be here if it wasn't for Zane and the boy."

"Where is he now?"

"Down at the bunkhouse, I guess." Sometime during the conversation, a plate of bacon, eggs, and fried potatoes had been placed in front of her. Kathleen picked at it now, her thoughts on Zane instead of her breakfast.

Taggart studied his daughter's face while she ate. She looked different somehow, he thought, but maybe that was to be expected after all she'd been through. "You should go visit Oliver," he suggested, pouring himself a cup of coffee. "He asks about you every time I see him."

"I will. Maybe I'll have Zane take me tomorrow."

"Zane, yes," Taggart muttered, his eyes narrowing as he thought of his daughter and the gunman alone on the Plains. Rising, he grabbed his hat and jammed it on his head. "I'm glad you're safely home, kitten," he said, giving her shoulder a squeeze. "We'll talk more tonight."

Zane looked up from currying the buckskin when he heard footsteps. *Here it comes*, he thought as Taggart strode purposefully toward him.

"My daughter tells me I owe you a debt of thanks," Taggart said, without preamble.

Zane stretched his arm along the buckskin's back. "You don't owe me anything."

"You saved her life. Are you saying her life isn't worth anything?"

"You know damn well that's not what I meant."

"I'd like to give you something to show my appreciation," Taggart said gruffly. "Perhaps a few head of cattle? Or a few acres of land?"

"Forget it."

A muscle worked in Taggart's jaw. "I know the two of you were alone together for a good long time."

Zane shifted his stance as he rested his hand on the butt of his Colt. "I don't think I like your tone or what you're implying."

"She's a lovely girl," Taggart went on doggedly. "Any man would be tempted."

"I took a bullet in my arm and another in my thigh trying to rescue your daughter," Zane said, his voice as cold and flat as his eyes. "I can show you the scars if you don't believe me. I wasn't really in any condition to rape her." At least not in the Indian camp.

Taggart took a step back, repelled by the cold fury in the half-breed's eyes. And then he planted his feet and squared his shoulders. "I'm her father. You can't blame me for being concerned."

"We done here?"

Taggart cleared his throat. "Thank you again for bringing Kathleen home. I owe you a debt I can never repay."

Zane nodded. Despite Taggart's words of appreciation, it wouldn't have surprised him if the old man had fired him on the spot. Taggart hadn't come out and directly accused him of bedding his daughter, but the man obviously suspected something had gone on between them. And he didn't like it one damn bit.

But, with any luck, Zane thought with a wry grin, the old man would never find out.

Kathleen stood at the kitchen window, thinking she would have traded her best dress to know what was being said down by the barn. It was apparent from their stance that harsh words had passed between Zane and her father. They were obviously arguing, but about what? At least it hadn't come to blows, she mused. The two men glared at each other, then her father headed back to the house and Zane went gone back to brushing the mare.

Relieved, she turned away from the window and went to check the pots of water heating on the stove. Before she did anything else, she intended to soak in a hot bath and scrub the trail dust from her hair and skin. And maybe, just maybe, she would find an excuse to go down to the barn and ask Zane what he and her father had talked about.

She had just dragged the tub into the kitchen from the mud room when her father poked his head in the door. "I'm going into town," he said. "Do you need anything?"

"I don't think so."

"All right. Stay close to home while I'm gone."

"I will." She hummed softly as she filled the tub, laid out a towel and a change of clothes, found a fresh bar of soap. With a sigh, she sank into the blissfully warm water and closed her eyes.

Zane watched Taggart ride out of the yard. He hated lying to the man, but he had no doubt the old man would string him up if he found out what had happened out there on the prairie. But Taggart wouldn't hear it from him. That was Kathleen's secret to tell, but he was pretty sure she was in no itching hurry to tell her father about it, either.

Kathleen.

He had wanted her from the moment he first saw her, charmed and amused by her prickly defenses and the way she had tried to deny the attraction that had hummed between them from the very beginning. But damn, once she made up her mind, she didn't hold anything back. And he loved her the more for it.

"Love," he muttered. Was it love? Or just his desire to possess a beautiful woman?

Zane ran the brush over the buckskin one last time and turned her loose in the corral.

He stood there a moment, gazing up at the house. The old man was gone. She was alone.

And they needed to talk. No time like the present, he mused.

Kathleen glanced over her shoulder when she heard the back door open. "Juanita, is that you?"

"*Si, señorita.*" That voice. Far too deep to be Juanita's.

She stared in open-mouthed shock as Zane loomed in the doorway. "You … what are you doing here? Go away."

He leaned his shoulder against the door jamb. "I don't think so."

"I'm taking a bath!" She didn't know why his being there upset her so. They had made love, after all. But, somehow, having him see her in her bath had her blushing from head to foot.

"I can see that. Want me to wash your back?"

She stared at him, cheeks burning, wishing she had the nerve to invite him into the tub with her. "Please, go."

He shook his head. "I like the view."

"You're … you're … oh! I don't know what you are."

"I'm a man who enjoys the sight of a pretty woman. And if that woman is … ah … wearing nothing but water, so much the better."

"My father could come in at any moment!"

"Pretty ladies shouldn't tell lies. I saw him ride out."

"Juanita …"

Ignoring her protest, he pushed away from the door.

Kathleen gasped when he plucked the soap from her hand, then knelt behind her and began to wash her back.

Her shock soon turned to pleasure as his big, rough hands moved over her. How she loved his hands. She closed her eyes, remembering how he had caressed her when they made love, how gentle those hands could be one moment, and arousing the next. She shivered with delight when he kissed her nape, ran his tongue along her shoulder …

Kathleen froze when the front door opened and she heard Juanita's voice calling her name.

Before she could think to respond, Zane was out the back door, leaving her alone and aching for his touch.

Muttering an oath, Zane threw a saddle and bridle on the buckskin and rode hell-for-leather away from the ranch and the undeniable temptation the lovely Kathleen Taggart embodied. For a moment, he lost himself in the sheer exhilaration of the wind in his face, the surging power of the horse beneath him. But it was fleeting. All too soon he was remembering the way Kathleen had looked reclining in the tub, the water barely covering her breasts, her cheeks red with embarrassment as he stared at her. But for Juanita's untimely appearance, he would have carried Kathleen up to her room and made love to her.

He swore softly. He didn't know if it was love or lust. All he knew was that he wanted her, wanted to feel her writhing beneath him again, hear her cry his name as they came together. He loved the way she smiled whenever she saw him. Damn, he had it bad. If he was smart, he'd just keep riding. Even if he wanted to marry Kathleen, old man Taggart would never allow it. And he couldn't blame the man, Zane mused ruefully. Any father worth the name wanted more for his daughter than a half-breed drifter who had nothing to offer her. A man who earned his living with a gun.

A man with a price on his head.

Shit.

CHAPTER THIRTEEN

Zane rode for another hour, refusing to think of anything but the sense of freedom that riding across the prairie gave him. Eventually, he turned his horse toward town and headed for Sally's. He had no sooner walked through the saloon doors than French Lil came running toward him.

"Zane!" she exclaimed, throwing her arms around his neck. "Where have you been? It's been weeks and weeks since I saw you last."

Peeling her arms from around his neck, he said, "I was out of town for a while.'

"Why didn't you take me with you?"

"You wouldn't have liked it where I was," he said, making his way toward the bar. "Believe me."

"Well, you're here now." She batted her eyelashes at him. "Why don't you come upstairs with me and I'll give you a real welcome home."

"Not today, darlin'."

"You never used to say no," she said, with a pout. "Have you found someone else?"

Zane grunted softly. That was the real question, wasn't it?

⚜   ⚜   ⚜

Kathleen spent the rest of the day wandering through the house, unable to concentrate on anything. She made a cake and burned it. She broke a dish, she spilled a pail of milk. She had never been so clumsy, and it was all Zane's fault. Time and again she went to the window, searching for some sign that he'd returned. Where had he gone? Was he coming back?

What was she to think? They had made love but he'd never said he loved her. Had he ridden on looking for new conquests? Tears stung her eyes. Maybe he no longer wanted her.

Needing something to occupy her mind, she went upstairs to write a letter to her mother. Helen loved the East. Her letters were filled with exciting stories of the plays she'd seen, books she'd read, card parties with other matrons, days spent shopping with Kathleen's aunt Deborah.

And always, at the end of every letter, her mother asked when Kathleen was coming for a visit.

Kathleen worried her lower lip between her teeth. Maybe that was the answer. She would go visit her mother …

She looked up at the sound of hoofbeats. Hurrying to the window, she pulled back the drapes, felt a little thrill of relief when she saw Zane ride into the yard. She watched him dismount in front of the porch and all thought of going East fled her mind. Smiling, she ran out to meet him.

"Hey," he murmured, gathering her in his arms. "I was hoping you'd still be in the tub."

She made a face at him. "I'd be all pruney if I was."

"I like prunes."

"You do not."

He laughed. "I've never had one. But I like you." His gaze moved over her. "All wet and slippery with soap suds." He glanced up at the house. "Where's your old man?"

"He hasn't returned from town yet. I can't imagine what's keeping him so long. I thought he'd be home by now."

He took up the buckskin's reins in one hand and captured Kathleen's in the other.

She glanced at their joined hands, his large and rough and scarred, hers smaller, softer, and felt something melt inside her. "I'll be taking a walk tonight after dinner," she remarked.

Zane smiled at her. "I think I will, too. Come on," he said, tugging on her hand. "Keep me company while I unsaddle my horse."

"Where did you go?" Kathleen asked, falling into step beside him.

"I took a long ride, and then went to town."

"Did you see my Dad?"

He shook his head. "No."

Kathleen took a deep breath. And frowned. "Who *did* you see?"

Damn, he thought. No doubt he smelled of Lil's perfume.

"Zane?"

"I stopped by the saloon for a drink."

"Oh?"

Nothing worse than a suspicious woman, he thought. "I bumped into one of the saloon girls."

"I'll bet." There was a world of accusation in her tone.

"Hey, it was nothing like what you're thinking." Hell, after being with Kathleen, he didn't want anyone else. "Nothing happened between us. She asked and I said no."

"Have you been with her before?"

"Do you really want to talk about this?" He stripped the saddle and bridle from the mare and turned her loose in one of the corrals. "Lil doesn't mean anything to me other than ..." He cleared his throat. "Dammit, Kathleen, this is no fit conversation for you to be having."

"Oh? Why is that?"

Zane removed his hat and ran his fingers through his hair. Did she really want a blow-by-blow of his former liaisons with Lil?

The arrival of her father spared him from answering any further questions.

Taggart's gaze darted from Kathleen to Zane and back again. "What's going on?"

"Nothing," Kathleen said. "Zane was just telling me about his trip to town."

"Uh huh."

"Do you know anyone named Lil, Dad?"

Taggart frowned. "What the hell kind of question is that?"

"She works at the saloon," Kathleen said with a shrug. "I just wondered if you knew her."

Taggart dismounted, a splash of dark-red staining his cheeks. "Zane, take care of my horse, " he said curtly, then spun on his heels and headed for the house.

Kathleen stared after him, her mouth agape.

Zane bit back a grin, thinking he and the old man had plowed the same field.

Dinner was quiet and uncomfortable that evening. Every time Kathleen looked at her father, she imagined him in the arms of some over-painted saloon girl. He wouldn't, she thought, couldn't. Could he? She wanted to ask but just couldn't summon the nerve. She told herself he'd flushed because he had been embarrassed by her question, one she'd had no right to ask, not because he knew—and had consorted with—a harlot.

She made a hasty exit when the meal was over and headed straight for the barn.

She found Zane sitting on a bale of hay outside, idly scratching the ears of one of the barn cats.

He shook his head when he saw the look in her eyes. "Don't ask," he said.

"What do you mean?"

"It means I don't know what your old man does when he goes into town, or who he does it with. I don't want to know. And neither do you."

Huffing a sigh, she sat down beside him. Theirs was an odd relationship, she thought. One minute they were in each other's arms and he was making love to her and now he seemed like a stranger. She wanted to touch him, hold him, feel his arms around her, but she didn't have the nerve to make the first move.

Zane swore inwardly as he felt her tension. Making love to her had been a mistake. He had known it was wrong even while it was happening, knew she was too young, too inexperienced, and yet it would have been easier to stop breathing. Thinking she was probably even more confused and uncertain than he was, he took her hand in his. And knew he would never willingly leave her.

Later that night, Zane sat outside the bunkhouse, his attention focused on the main house as he listened to the idle conversation coming from the men inside. Dusty was worried that his girl was seeing someone else. Boone was hoping to win enough money at poker to buy a new saddle. Virgil was thinking about moving on. Chet and Old Mort were playing checkers.

Zane stood when he saw Kathleen descend the porch stairs. She strolled toward the garden on the side of the house. Keeping to the shadows, he followed her there.

When he stepped around the edge of the porch, he found her sitting on the plank bench located beneath a tree. She looked like an angel, he thought, with the moonlight shimmering in her hair. She smiled when she saw him. "Hi."

"Hi." He sat beside her, his thigh brushing hers.

"Would you take me into town tomorrow?"

"Sure, if it's all right with your old man."

"It will be."

"What's the occasion?"

"My father thinks I should visit Oliver."

"In that case, I might be busy."

"Oh?"

"Your father wants you to marry that banker, doesn't he?"

"Yes."

"Is that what you want?"

"You know it isn't," Kathleen exclaimed. "But I feel like I should go see him."

"I don't know why."

"He *is* my friend. And he wouldn't have gotten hurt if it wasn't for me."

Zane grunted softly. He couldn't argue with that.

She looked up at him, beautiful green eyes shining in the moonlight, lips slightly parted. And he did what any red-blooded man would do. He took her in his arms and kissed her until she clung to him, breathless.

"I wish we were alone," she murmured. "I wish …"

He cupped her cheek in his palm. "What do you wish?"

"Don't you know?"

"I reckon I do. But my life wouldn't be worth a plugged nickel if your old man found us together."

Sighing, she rested her head on his shoulder, smiled when she felt his lips move in her hair.

"I do love you," he said quietly. "But we both know your father will never approve."

"We could run away."

"And go where? I don't have a home. I don't know how much longer I'll be working for your father. And when he cuts me loose, I'll go back to bounty hunting. It's the only thing I'm good at. I can't very well drag you around the country with me."

It was all true, she thought bleakly. "Where does that leave us?"

"I guess that's up to you." He gave her hand a squeeze. "You'd better go inside before your father comes looking for you." Rising, he pulled her to her feet and into his arms. "I'll see you tomorrow."

She nodded, her eyelids fluttering down as he lowered his head to hers and kissed her good night. There had to be a way, she thought. Some way for them to be together. Some way to convince her father that Zane was the right man for her.

Sadly, she had no idea how to accomplish it.

They left for town shortly after breakfast. Kathleen wore her second-best dress and took extra care with her hair, hoping her father would think it was because she was going to see Oliver, which couldn't have been farther from the truth. She didn't give a fig for what Oliver Plotkin thought. When she saw him today, she would tell him they could never be more than friends.

She hummed softly as they drove out of the yard. It was a beautiful day and she was with Zane. She thrust all her doubts and worries aside and let herself just be happy.

"You look mighty pretty today," Zane said as they pulled onto the trail leading into town.

"Thank you. So do you."

He snorted softly. "Pretty. Right."

"Handsome, then." She placed her hand on his thigh, something no respectable woman would ever do with a man who wasn't her husband. But it seemed silly to worry about propriety when they had made love, something she hoped they would do again, soon. She blushed at her wayward thoughts. What a hussy she had become. Why, she was almost as bad as Zane's saloon girl. The thought made her laugh out loud.

He slid a sideways glance in her direction. "What's so funny?"

"Nothing."

"People don't laugh for no reason."

"I can't tell you. It's too embarrassing."

When she started to remove her hand from his thigh, he covered it with his own. "I think I can guess."

"You can?" She stared at him, wide-eyed.

"There's no shame in wanting to touch me, or have me touch you. It doesn't make you wicked, darlin'."

"Doesn't it?"

"No. It's normal and natural."

"Maybe when you're married," Kathleen murmured. "I don't know what got into me. " She tried again to pull her hand away, but he refused to let her.

"Leave it," he said. "I like it there."

So did she. She left her hand resting on his thigh until they reached the outskirts of Cross Creek.

Oliver lived in a small white house behind a white picket fence, located on the north end of town.

Zane reined the horse to a halt in front of the place. "How long will you be?"

She shrugged. "Thirty minutes?"

"All right."

"Where will you be?" she asked as he helped her from the rig.

"At Sally's."

"You'd better not be smelling like that saloon girl when you pick me up," she warned.

"I wouldn't dare," he said, stifling a grin.

Taking a deep breath, Kathleen went up the front steps and knocked on the door. The sooner she got this over with, the better.

Oliver's face lit up when he opened the door and saw her. "Kathleen! I just heard you'd made it home. I was coming to see you this evening," he said, ushering her into the parlor. "You're looking well."

"Thank you. So are you."

He gestured at the sofa, inviting her to make herself comfortable. Avoiding the sofa, she sat in the chair beside it instead.

"Tell me how you survived," he said taking a place on the couch.

"Zane came after me."

"I see." There was no mistaking the blatant disapproval in his voice. He paused to take a breath. "The last time we were together, you said you never wanted to see me again," he said quietly. "Can I take it that this visit means you've forgiven me? That there's still a chance for us?"

Oh, darn, this was going to be harder than she thought. "Oliver, this is just a social call between friends. I know you've hinted at marriage several times, but I'm not in love with you. I'm sorry."

He stared at her, his brow furrowed. "It's him, isn't it? That dirty half-breed?"

"This has nothing to do with Zane."

Oliver snorted. "Like hell."

"Believe what you will. I only came by to see how you were doing because I feel partly responsible for your getting hurt and to tell you that I hoped we could remain friends."

"Friends," he sneered. "Right."

Rising, Kathleen murmured, "Goodbye, Oliver." She felt him glaring at her back as she headed for the door.

Outside, she glanced up and down the street. Her visit had taken far less than thirty minutes. She tapped her foot for a moment, then started walking down the boardwalk. She found the buggy parked in front of Sally's Saloon.

Curious, she went up on her tiptoes and peered over the swinging doors.

She spied Zane immediately. He was standing at the bar, alone, a glass of beer in his hand. While she watched, a woman in a bright red dress, her cheeks rouged, her lips painted, sashayed up to him. Kathleen couldn't hear what they were saying, but it was obvious that the woman knew him by the possessive way she took his arm. With a shake of his head, Zane removed her hand from his arm. The woman pouted. And when Zane continued to rebuff her, she planted her hands on her hips and shouted, "You'll be sorry, Zane. You'll see!" And with her threat ringing in the air, she lifted her skirts and ran up the stairs.

Zane downed the last of his drink and turned toward the door. He muttered an oath when he saw Kathleen staring at him. Well, damn. She couldn't have come at a worse time.

Outside, he lifted her into the buggy and swung up beside her. "You ended your visit kind of early, didn't you?"

"It seems that Oliver and I didn't have as much to say to each other as I thought we might."

He grunted softly. He could easily imagine how their conversation went. "You ready to go home?"

"Yes." Feeling as though she were being watched, Kathleen glanced over her shoulder. She was, indeed, being watched. The saloon girl stood on the balcony that overlooked the street. And she was glowering at Kathleen. Pasting a smile on her face, Kathleen put her arm around Zane's waist and kissed him on the cheek. It was petty, she thought, but it sure made her feel good.

"Nice girls don't peek into saloons," Zane remarked as they drove out of town.

"Maybe I'm not a nice girl."

"Maybe I'm a bad influence on you."

She laughed softly. "Maybe I don't care," she retorted. And then frowned. What if someone else saw that kiss and told her father?

She shook the worry aside.

And smiled all the way home.

Chapter Fourteen

French Lil gave the man standing at the bar a sharp look. At first, she'd thought he was a lawman, but she quickly shook that idea aside. He was a bounty hunter, she thought, like Zane. They all had that same wary look, that air of watchfulness.

She sidled up to him. "New in town, aren't you?"

The man looked her up and down. "What's it to you?"

She shrugged. "Just thought I'd make you welcome."

He grunted softly. "You been in town long?"

"Long enough. Who are you looking for?"

His brows shot up. "How do you know I'm looking for anyone?"

"It's a gift."

Reaching into his pocket, he withdrew a wrinkled sheet of paper. After unfolding it, he smoothed it out on the bar top. "Recognize this guy?"

Lil stared at the rough sketch on the poster. She didn't have to read the name below to know who it was. "I might."

"Is he in town?"

Lil shrugged. "How badly do you want to know?"

The man tapped his finger on the amount of the reward. Five thousand dollars.

"How much do I get?" she asked.

"Ten percent."

"Five hundred dollars?" Lil snorted her disdain.

"A thousand?"

"Make it two."

He fixed her with a hard stare, and then he nodded. "Two thousand when I bring him in. Do we have a deal?"

She started to say yes and then frowned. What was she doing? Was she actually going to tell this stranger where to find Zane? And then she remembered how Zane had rejected her in front of Ed and all the regulars not an hour ago. And how that pale-faced ranch woman had kissed him right in front of her.

Lil bit down on her lower lip. Two thousand dollars would give her a stake. She could get out of this town, go to San Francisco or Denver and start over.

"Well?" the bounty hunter asked impatiently. "Do we have a deal or not?"

Lil nodded and quickly gave him the directions to the Taggart ranch before she could change her mind.

CHAPTER FIFTEEN

Kathleen sighed as she sat down to the mid-day meal. She hadn't seen her father since returning from town and she wasn't looking forward to the conversation that was sure to come as soon as Juanita left the dining room.

"So," her father said, "how was your visit with Oliver?"

She shrugged. "I told him that I didn't want him to come courting anymore."

His brows rushed together in a look of disapproval that Kathleen knew all too well. "I don't understand you," he said. "Oliver is a fine, decent man, with a good job and a promising future. He's well-liked and respected by everyone in town. He can give you a good life."

"But I don't love him."

Silence fell between them.

Kathleen bit down on her lower lip, waiting for the words she knew were coming.

"It's Zane, isn't it? You fancy yourself in love with that gunslinger."

She wanted to deny it, but couldn't say the words.

"I forbid you to see that man," her father said gruffly. "He's a drifter, a bounty hunter, and no fit companion for a decent woman."

"You seemed to think he was good enough to drive me to town."

"You needed protection."

"He saved my life. And probably Oliver's, too."

"I'm not saying he doesn't have some good qualities. But you don't breed a mustang to a Thoroughbred."

"Are you comparing me to a mare?" Kathleen exclaimed.

"I'm just saying like should marry like. The good people in town will never accept him."

"I never said I was going to marry him."

Taggart stared at her, his eyes narrowed, and then he sighed. "You're not to be alone with him again. If you want to go to town, you'll go with me or Old Mort. Is that clear?"

"Mort? A lot of protection he'd be!"

"I mean what I said, Kathleen. I'll brook no argument from you. Is that understood?"

"Yes, father."

Taggart muttered an oath. Calling him father was a sure sign that he'd upset her. But it couldn't be helped.

Mouth clamped shut to keep from saying something she'd regret, Kathleen pushed away from the table and went out on the front porch, slamming the door behind her. She stood there fighting tears. She had known this conversation was coming, but hadn't expected it to hurt so much. She didn't want to have to sneak round to see Zane, but her father hadn't given her much choice.

She glanced toward the barn. Was he down there, or in the bunkhouse?

The sound of hoofbeats drew her gaze toward the road. She frowned as a man mounted on a black horse trotted toward the house. He pulled up in front of the porch. "Afternoon, ma'am."

"Can I help you?"

"I'm looking for someone. I heard he works here."

"Oh." She glanced over her shoulder as her father stepped out onto the porch and descended the stairs.

"Can I help you, mister?"

The man reached inside his jacket, withdrew a wrinkled sheet of paper, and handed it to her father.

Taggart looked it over, glanced at Kathleen, and handed the paper back to the stranger. "Come inside. We'll talk."

"What's going on?" she asked.

"This doesn't concern you." Gesturing for the stranger to follow him, Taggart went into the house and into the den. When the stranger stepped into the room, he closed the door.

Kathleen trailed behind them. Inside, she stared at the closed door. What was going on in there? Who was that man? And why didn't her father want her to know? She pressed her ear to the door, but couldn't hear what was being said.

"Is he here?" the bounty hunter asked, his voice sharp.

"Yes," Taggart said. "But I don't want any trouble."

"That's up to him."

"I don't want any gunplay. He's in the bunkhouse. I'll go down there and call him outside. When he clears the door, you can take him."

The bounty hunter nodded. "Obliged for your help. I've got tickets on the morning stage."

"I'm not doing this for you." Taggart thrust aside the guilt niggling at him. Zane had saved Kathleen's life and for that, he was grateful. But he'd seen the way she looked at Zane. The way the half-breed looked at her, and he was sorely afraid that there was something going on between them. Something more than just longing looks. He told himself he was doing the right thing. According to the poster, Zane was a fugitive, wanted for murder in Sagebrush Flats. No matter how he felt about Zane personally, it was his duty as a father to protect his daughter. Just as it was his civic duty as a law-abiding citizen to see that justice was done.

Gesturing for the bounty hunter to follow him, Taggart led the way outside and down to the bunkhouse before he could change his mind.

Zane blew out a sigh when Taggart called his name. Judging from the man's tone, he wasn't bringing good news. Squaring his shoulders, he stepped outside.

And came face-to-face with a shotgun leveled at his chest.

"Drop that gunbelt," the stranger said. "And kick it out of the way."

Zane didn't argue. He had seen first-hand what a shotgun at close range could do.

"Turn around," the stranger said. And when Zane complied, he slapped a pair of handcuffs on him. Glancing at Taggart, the hunter said, "Saddle a horse for him, will ya?"

With a nod, Taggart went into the barn and saddled the buckskin.

"Mount up, half-breed. You," the hunter said, pointing at Taggart, "give him a leg up."

Muttering, "I'm sorry about this," Taggart boosted Zane into the saddle.

The hunter mounted his own horse, slid the shotgun into a scabbard, and took up the buckskin's reins.

Zane fixed Taggart with a hard stare as they rode out of the yard.

From her window, Kathleen watched, wide-eyed, as the man on the black horse rode out of the yard leading Zane's horse. With a cry, she ran down the stairs and out onto the porch, crying Zane's name.

Her father caught her by the arm when she started to run after Zane.

"What's going on?" she demanded. "Who is that man? Where's he taking Zane?"

"He's a bounty hunter. In the morning, he's taking Zane back to Sagebrush Flats to stand trial for murder."

"Murder! I don't believe it!"

"The man showed me a poster with Zane's name and likeness on it. I told you he was no good."

"How could you do this? Why didn't you stop him?"

"I'm a law-abiding citizen, daughter."

She stared at him, tears flooding her eyes. "That had nothing to do with it, and you know it. I'll never forgive you for this," she sobbed. "Never!" And so saying, she ran back into the house and up the stairs to her room, threw herself on the bed, and cried herself to sleep.

She woke to her father's voice calling her name.

"Go away," she said.

"We need to talk, kitten."

"I have nothing to say to you."

There was a long pause. "Dinner will be ready in an hour."

"I'm not hungry."

Another long pause, and then the sound of his footsteps going down the stairs.

Slipping out of bed, Kathleen paced her bedroom floor, her mind in turmoil. If the bounty hunter wasn't leaving until morning, he was most likely spending the night in Cross Creek. And the safest place to keep Zane locked up until then was in the jail. It was still early. If she left now, she could ride into town to see him one last time and hopefully get back before anyone missed her.

She quickly changed into a long-sleeved shirt and pants and pulled on her boots. Using her pillows, she did her best to make it look like she was huddled under the covers taking a nap. If her father took a good look, he wouldn't be fooled. But if he just peeked into her room, it might buy her some time.

Tiptoeing across the floor, she quietly opened her window and shinnied down the tree outside her room. The same tree she had used to sneak out of the house when she was growing up.

Luck was with her and no one saw her as she headed for the barn and quickly saddled her horse. Swinging onto the mare's back, she took the back road that circled behind the house and joined the road that led into town. Once out of sight of the house, she slammed her heels into the palomino's sides and lit out for Cross Creek.

She arrived in town as the sun was going down. After leaving her horse in the livery stable, she hurried toward the sheriff's office. Squaring her shoulders, she marched inside as if she had every right to be there.

Karl Powers looked up, his brow furrowing when he saw her. "Miss Taggart, what are you doing here?"

"I've come to visit one of your prisoners."

"I've only got the one. And it's right sorry I am to see him locked up. But the law's the law and it looks like he broke it."

"I still want to see him."

Powers scratched his head, then shrugged. "I reckon it'll be all right." His gaze ran over her. "You ain't carrying any weapons, are you?"

"Of course not."

"All right. This way."

He opened the narrow wooden door that led into the cell block. Heart pounding, Kathleen followed him. There were three cells. Zane lay on the bunk in the middle one, his arms crossed behind his head, his hat over his eyes.

"Hey, Zane, you've got a visitor."

He sat up slowly, his eyes widening when he saw Kathleen standing behind the sheriff.

"You've got fifteen minutes," Powers said.

He stepped aside, allowing Kathleen to slide past him, then closed the door.

She quickly closed the distance between herself and the cell, her hand reaching through the bars.

"What are you doing here?" Zane asked, taking her hand in his.

"I had to see you."

"Does your old man know where you are?"

"Of course not. I snuck out of the house."

"You rode here alone? Dammit, Katheen, don't you know how dangerous that is."

"I don't care." Tears sparkled in her eyes. "I might never see you again. Did you do what they said? Did you kill a man in Sagebrush Flats?"

"Yeah. But it was self-defense. We got into an argument over a poker game. He accused me of cheating and one thing led to another. He reached for his gun only I was faster. But a jury didn't see it that way. It didn't help that his father practically owned the town and that most of the people in it owed him money. The verdict was unanimous. They were taking me back to jail after the trial. The deputy hadn't shackled my hands behind my back and I made a grab for his gun. Told him to remove the cuffs or I'd kill him. I guess he believed me. I stole a horse and got the hell out of there."

Kathleen bit down on her lower lip. What were the odds he could escape again?

"You should go home," Zane said, stroking her cheek. "This is no place for you."

"It is as long as you're here."

"Kathleen." Leaning closer to the bars, he cupped her face in his palms and kissed her. Of all the rotten luck, he thought, to find Kathleen only to lose her.

Kathleen slipped her arms through the bars and held him tight, tears burning her eyes. The bounty hunter would take him to Sagebrush Flats tomorrow and she would never see him again. "I love you," she murmured, blinking back her tears.

"Hey, don't cry for me," he chided as he wiped away her tears with his thumbs. "I'm not worth one of them."

"There must be something I can do."

"I don't know what it would be." His fingers tunneled into her hair, his gaze moving over her face, memorizing every line.

She flinched when the door opened.

"Time's up, Miss Taggart."

Kathleen clung to Zane, lifting her face for one last kiss.

"Forget about me," he said, his voice thick. "Go home and marry a man who deserves you."

"Tell me you love me."

"I love you, Kathleen. Maybe I loved you all along and didn't know it."

Powers cleared his throat.

"Go," Zane said. "And don't look back."

Sniffling, she turned and walked out the door and out of the jail.

Outside, she sank down on the bench in front of the sheriff's office and let the tears come. She wasn't going home tonight, she thought. She would spent the night here so she could see Zane again first thing in the morning.

Wiping her eyes, she hurried down to the livery stable, crept inside, climbed into the loft and hid behind a bale of hay.

She woke early after a restless night during which she'd come up with a plan. Rising, she shook the straw from her hair, straightened her clothes, and hurried to the general store.

The owner, Franklin Grant, smiled as he unlocked the door. "Why, Miss Taggart, what are you doing in town so early?"

"I need to buy a few things. I'm leaving for Sagebrush Flats this morning."

"Going to Montana, huh?" Watson glanced around. "Where's your father?"

"He's buying our tickets."

"Oh. Well, come on in."

Kathleen ducked inside. It took only minutes to find what she needed: a dress, a change of underwear, a brush and comb, a packet of pins for her hair, a flowered carpet-bag to carry her purchases in. When her stomach growled, she picked up a loaf of bread and asked one of the boys who worked in the store to cut a few slices of cheese.

Returning to the front of the store, she piled her purchases on the counter. "Just charge these things to my father."

With a nod, Mr. Grant pulled out his account book and jotted the items down. When he started to wrap them, she said, ""If you'd be so kind as to put the bread and cheese in a sack, I'll just put everything else in the carpetbag."

"Good idea."

"Thank you so much."

"Have a good trip, Miss Taggart."

"Thank you." With an airy wave, she left the store and hurried down to the stagecoach office.

A bell rang over the door when she stepped inside. The agent looked up. And smiled.

"Morning, Miss Taggart. Can I help you?"

"I need a ticket to Sagebrush Flats, Mr. Cosgrove. Can you please charge it to my father?"

"It's against the rules, but I don't mind breaking them for you," he said with a wink.

"You're too kind."

She heard the rattle and rumble of the stage as he stamped her ticket.

"Have a good trip."

"Thank you."

Clutching her carpetbag in one hand and the ticket and the sack in the other, Kathleen ran outside. The driver took her bag and secured it up top, then handed her inside.

Moments later, the bounty hunter arrived. He wasn't taking any chances, she mused, when she saw that he had shackled Zane's hands and feet. The chains rattled as Zane climbed into the coach. He muttered an oath when he saw Kathleen sitting there.

The bounty hunter climbed in behind him. He rapped on the roof of the coach and a moment later, the stage rocked into motion.

Taggart frowned when Kathleen didn't come down to breakfast. After his first attempt to talk to her last night had failed, he hadn't bothered her again. She was mad as a wet hen, and beyond reason, so he had let her sulk, figuring he'd give her plenty of time to cool off. He knew she was angry with him but hoped that, in the end, she would come to realize that he'd done what he had for her own good, and because it was the right thing to do.

"*Buenos días,*" Juanita said cheerfully as she entered the dining room and set the breakfast tray on the table. "Is *Señorita* Kathleen coming to breakfast?"

"I guess she overslept," he said, pushing away from the table. "I'll just go up and wake her."

Overcome by a sudden sense of unease, he took the stairs two at a time. He didn't bother knocking, just pushed his way inside. One look at the bed and he knew she wasn't in it.

Muttering, "Dammit to hell," he thundered down the stairs and out of the house.

Five minutes later he was riding hellbent for leather toward Cross Creek.

Taggart cursed softly when he found Kathleen's palomino in a stall at the livery. When questioned, the hosteler said he hadn't seen her since yesterday.

His next stop was the jail.

"Yeah, she was here last night," Karl Powers said, wary of the fury blazing in Taggart's eyes. "She came to visit the prisoner."

"Where is she now?"

Powers shrugged. "I haven't seen her this morning. I figured she went back home."

"Is Zane still locked up?"

"No. A bounty hunter came for him about an hour ago, hour and a half. Zane's buckskin is at the livery. I'm not sure what to do with it."

"I'll take it back to the ranch with me," Taggart muttered, then stormed out of the office, a string of curses trailing in his wake. Where the hell was she?

He checked the hotel and the restaurant and then swore again when he passed by the stagecoach office. Inside, Cosgrove confirmed his worse fears. Kathleen had bought a ticket to Sagebrush Flats. The stage had left an hour and a half ago.

Dammit! He'd never catch up with her now.

Kathleen sighed as the stage hit yet another rough spot in the road. She was keenly aware of Zane's disapproval, and equally aware of the salacious looks of the bounty hunter.

They had been traveling for almost two hours when the bounty hunter leaned forward. "It's a long way to Sagebrush Flats," he said. "I figured we might as well get acquainted. I'm Braxton. And you'd be Miss …?"

"Missus," she said, primly. "Missus Zane Taggart."

Braxton stared at her a moment, his expression one of disbelief.

Zane lifted one brow in amusement.

Braxton shook his head. "I never would have believed a fine-looking woman such as yourself would be married to a dirty half-breed," he said with a sneer.

"I'll thank you to watch your mouth," Kathleen said sharply. "That's my husband you're talking about."

Zane winked at her when she glanced his way.

"Mr. Braxton, would you mind changing seats with me?" Kathleen asked. "I'd like to sit next to my husband."

He scowled at her a moment, then muttered, "What the hell?" and took the empty place beside her.

Kathleen quickly took the seat he vacated.

"Nice to see you, wife," Zane murmured.

She smiled as she reached for his hand, the cuffs rattling as his fingers curled around hers.

"Does your father know where you are?" he asked.

"No. But it won't take him long to figure it out."

"He'll probably be on the next stage to Sagebrush Flats."

Kathleen shrugged. "I don't care. I'm where I belong. Where I want to be." Noting the bounty hunter's interest in their conversation, she said, "I'd appreciate it if you'd mind your own business, Mr. Braxton."

With a snort, he pulled his hat down over his eyes, his hand resting lightly on the butt of the Colt holstered at his side.

Kathleen stared at his gun, thinking that, if he fell asleep, she might be able to grab it.

"Forget it," Zane whispered, following her gaze.

"But ..."

"No. I know from experience that bounty hunters only catnap unless their prisoners are locked up. It's not worth the risk." Although it was a risk he'd take if Kathleen wasn't there.

⚜ ⚜ ⚜

It was early afternoon when they pulled into a stage station to change the horses, give the passengers a chance to stretch their legs, and get something to eat.

Braxton cuffed Zane's leg shackles to a table leg, then moved to an adjoining table.

Kathleen sat across from Zane. She had little appetite for the bread and beef stew the station agent's wife served, but forced herself to eat anyway, since she had no idea when they would stop again.

Zane ate without tasting a thing. He was happy to see Kathleen but her being here complicated matters. He was willing to risk his own life if the chance to escape presented itself, but not hers.

It was near dark when the coach stopped for the night. After a fried chicken dinner served by the station keeper's wife, Braxton and Zane stretched out on the floor, along with the driver and the shotgun guard. A cot was provided for Kathleen.

She didn't think she'd get much sleep, but she soon drifted off.

Zane lay on his side, his hands shackled behind his back, his left leg shackled to Braxton's right. They were scheduled to reach Sagebrush Flats the day after tomorrow. He hadn't gotten a fair trial there four years ago.

It was unlikely he would get one now.

Chapter Sixteen

Kathleen sighed as she climbed into the coach. She had gone right to sleep last night, only to be troubled by one nightmare after another—Zane being tried and hanged, being gunned down while trying to escape. Sometimes it was Zane standing on the gallows, and sometimes she was standing there, trembling with fear as the hangman placed a noose around her neck and snugged it tight.

She rested her head on Zane's shoulder, wishing he could put his arm around her, wishing they were alone. She had so much she wanted to say to him, but it was unlikely she would get the chance.

She wished Braxton would stop watching her like a hungry cat at a mousehole. It was disconcerting. Unsettling.

They were about an hour away from the stage station when gun shots rang out. Kathleen bolted upright, her heart pounding. Oh, Lord, were they being attacked by Indians?

Braxton swore as he looked out the window.

Zane leaned forward to see what was going on. Three masked men, riding fast. "Looks like we're about to be held up, darlin'," he said quietly. "Just do what they say. Hopefully, all they want is the strongbox."

A hold-up! Was there no end to trouble? She had been attacked and kidnapped by Indians only weeks ago. And now this. She huddled next to Zane, eyes wide and afraid.

There were more gunshots. Shouts to stop the stage. A harsh cry filled with pain.

Zane swore as the shotgun guard tumbled from the seat. "Braxton, give me a gun."

"Hell, no." Drawing his Colt, he began firing out the window.

"Dammit, man, give me a weapon!"

Braxton turned to glare at him, and pitched forward as a bullet caught him in the throat. Blood sprayed from the killing wound as he slid to the floor of the coach.

Kathleen let out a horrified cry and buried her face against Zane's shoulder. Reaching past her, he leaned forward and scooped Braxton's gun off the floor. "Kathleen, get down!"

Leaning out the window, Zane fired. Three shots. Three dead road agents.

With no hand on the reins, the coach horses gradually came to a stop.

"Is it over?" Kathleen asked.

"Yeah." Reaching for her hand, he pulled her up on the seat beside him, then bent down to search Braxton for the key to his shackles.

Kathleen felt the bile rise in her throat as Zane went through the bounty hunter's pockets.

There was no need to ask if Braxton was dead.

Zane unlocked the cuffs from his hands and feet, removed Braxton's gunbelt and buckled it around his own waist, slid the bounty hunter's gun into the holster, the hunter's cash into his own pocket. He got out of the coach, turned, and reached for Kathleen's hand.

She grimaced when she saw the bodies spread out behind them—the dead stagecoach driver and shotgun guard, the three hold-up men. "What now?" she asked.

"We'll ride for the nearest town. Wait here."

He walked back to where the outlaws' horses stood. Taking up the reins, he led them back to the coach. He removed the saddle and bridle from one of them and tossed the tack inside the coach. After removing the cash from the pockets of the driver and the shotgun guard, he laid the bodies inside the stage, then went through the pockets of the outlaws.

When that was done, he unhitched the team and removed their harness, knowing the horses would find their way back home.

With a last glance around, he said, "All right, let's go."

"Are you just going to leave the other bodies lying out there?"

He shrugged.

"And the stagecoach?"

"When it doesn't show up at the next station, the agent will send someone to look for it. I want to be long gone before they get here."

She bit down on her lower lip.

"What's bothering you?"

"You took their money."

"They don't need it. And we do." He didn't like robbing the dead, but, in this case, it couldn't be helped. He lifted Kathleen onto the back of one of the outlaw's horses, swung into the saddle of the other.

She gestured at the top of the coach. "Could you get my valise?"

He rode closer to the stage and stood up in the stirrups. A saddle and a flowered carpetbag were the only things up there. He snagged her bag and tied it behind his saddle. "You ready?"

With a nod, she took up the reins. Nothing seemed to bother him, she thought with a weary sigh. Not Indian attacks or being shot. Not bounty hunters. Not hold-ups. He really was a most remarkable man.

They by-passed Sagebrush Flats and spent the night in the next town. Kathleen was falling asleep in the saddle when Zane lifted her from the back of her horse, then grabbed her carpetbag. Inside the hotel, he registered them as man and wife under an alias and led the way upstairs.

"I can hardly keep my eyes open," Kathleen murmured as he closed the door to their room. "I'm so tired." With a yawn, she fell back on the bed and closed her eyes, already asleep.

He undressed her down to her underwear and tucked her under the covers, only to stand there, looking down at her while he pondered his next move. They couldn't stay here. He needed to get out of the territory. He'd been a fool to stay as long as he had. He wondered how Braxton had gotten his hands on that old Wanted poster and if there were any more flyers gathering dust in Sheriffs' offices in Montana Territory. Damn. He should probably put Kathleen on a stage and send her home.

Too tired to think, he unbuckled his gunbelt and hung it over the back of a chair, then toed off his boots, peeled off his shirt, and slipped into bed beside Mrs. Jones.

Grinning, he drew her against his side and drifted off to sleep.

Kathleen woke to the sound of rumbling wheels and a door slamming. Frowning, she turned onto her side, and came face-to-face with Zane. A slow smile spread over his face when their gazes met.

"Morning, sunshine," he drawled.

She smiled at him, thinking waking up beside Zane was a wonderful way to start the day.

She laid her hand on his chest—his bare chest—grinned when he exhaled sharply. Feeling daring, she trailed her fingers down his chest to his hard, flat belly.

In an instant, his jeans were on the floor along with her undergarments and he was on top of her, his weight resting on his elbows, his eyes hot.

Her breath caught in her throat as she stared up at him. Heaven help her, she had aroused a tiger. Filled with anticipation, she pulled him closer, surrendering to the sweetness of his kisses, the masterful touch of his hands arousing her. She loved the way they fit together, she thought, as she ran her fingertips over his broad back and shoulders, the unbelievable sensation of his body moving against hers, sweeping her away into a world of their own as two became one …

Later, bodies still joined together, he rolled onto his side, dropping feather-light kisses on her cheeks, her chin, the tip of her nose. Voice ever so quiet, he murmured, "I love you, darlin'. You know that, don't you?"

She smiled at him, feeling like the cat that just ate the canary. "I know. And I love you."

He blew out a sigh, wondering how he could tell her he was leaving her.

She frowned when his gaze slid away from hers. "What's wrong?"

"I've got to get out of the territory. I thought those flyers were out of circulation by now, but …" He shook his head. "If there's one, there's bound to be more. I can't stay here."

His words turned her joy to despair. "You're leaving me?"

"I'll put you on the next stage back to Cross Creek."

"Where will you go?"

"I don't know. The Badlands? Maybe Mexico."

"I'll never see you again, will I?"

Shit. This was even harder than he thought.

Refusing to cry, she pushed him away, scrambled out of bed, grabbed the blanket and wrapped it around her.

Stifling an oath, he went to stand behind her, his arms sliding around her waist. "I don't want to leave you, Kathleen. But I can't drag you from town to town like some camp follower."

She sniffed, but said nothing. She wouldn't beg him to stay.

"If you've got any better ideas," he said, nuzzling her neck, "I'm listening."

Brow furrowed, Kathleen bit down on her lower lip. And then, smiling, she turned to face him. "We can go to New York and stay with my mother until this blows over. No one will think to look for you there."

Zane stared at her. New York! Holy hell.

She looked up at him, head tilted to the side, a challenge in her bright green eyes.

"New York," he muttered. "Are you serious?"

"Why not?"

"If your mother didn't like living in the West, I'm pretty sure she won't be too happy about you bringing home a half-breed bounty hunter with a price on his head."

"Maybe not, but she's too well-bred to say anything, or turn away a guest."

"You might be surprised."

"Will you go to New York with me, Zane?"

How could he refuse when she was looking at him like that? "What the hell," he growled, and claimed her lips with his.

The blanket fell to the floor as Kathleen threw her arms around his neck.

And it was a long time before either one of them got dressed.

The next few days were a whirlwind of travel as they made their way out of the territory. Zane spent an hour or so in one saloon or another along the way, winning more than he lost. That, in addition to what he'd taken from the hold-up men, the driver and guard, had grown into a sizeable bankroll.

They had been traveling from one dirt water town to another for about a week when they finally arrived at a large town. The first thing they did was go on a shopping spree. They each bought two changes of clothes, shoes and hats, as well as personal items, and a large valise to carry everything. Kathleen also bought a nightgown. Zane bought a new rifle and several boxes of ammunition.

Kathleen wasn't looking forward to the journey to New York City. If the weather was good, if the roads were open and they didn't run into any more trouble, the trip to New York City was expected to take seventeen to eighteen days by stage, during which they would change coaches many times. Still, she was excited at the prospect of seeing her mother again, of being with Zane.

They left early the following morning.

The first few days were tiring but exciting. The countryside was ever-changing, the skies clear and blue. Some nights, they stayed in stagecoach stations, some they spent on the ground. By the tenth day on the trail, she was exhausted.

They were out of the territory by then, although Kathleen had no idea where they were.

"You look tuckered out," Zane remarked when they climbed into the coach a few mornings later. "What do you say, the next town we come to, we spend a few nights in a hotel?"

"Sounds like heaven to me." They had been on the road for ten days. Ten days of never being alone with Zane. Ten days of seeing the dirty looks some of the men gave him, hearing whispers of "half-breed," seeing the frightened looks sent his way by some of the women passengers. She wondered if it bothered Zane the way it bothered her.

They stayed at a hotel in a small Iowa town the following night. The furnishings were sparse—a double bed, a three-drawer chest, a single chair by a lone window. But everything looked clean. She spied a porcelain chamber pot under the bed. But it seemed like paradise after ten nights on the trail. The first thing on Kathleen's mind was a long soak in a hot bath. The tub was located in a room of its own on the second floor. The water had gone from hot to luke-warm when Zane knocked on the door.

"You gonna stay in there all night?"

"Maybe, if I can get some more hot water."

"Come on, girl, you're not the only one who wants to get shed of twenty pounds of trail dust."

"Oh, all right," she muttered, reaching for the towel on the chair beside the tub. Dripping water, she unlocked the door.

Zane couldn't decide which was more tempting—the bathtub, or the woman wearing nothing but a towel. The tub won, but only because he didn't like the thought of making love to Kathleen while he was covered in grit and dust.

They went to dinner in the town's only restaurant, then took a walk. There wasn't much to see—a few shops, a small general store, the hotel, a barber shop and blacksmith. And, of course, a saloon. Oddly, there was no Sheriff's Office. And no doctor. Perhaps two dozen houses of varying sizes were scattered within walking distance of the town.

An hour later, they returned to their hotel room. Zane lit the lamp beside the bed, removed his gunbelt and draped it over the back of the chair. Though they had made love several times, Kathleen still felt a wave of embarrassment as she undressed. When she reached for her nightgown, Zane took it from her and tossed it aside.

"I hate for you to cover up that beautiful body," he drawled as he drew her into his arms.

His words, the heated look in his eyes, brought a flush to her cheeks. When he released her to get undressed, she scooted under the covers, her cheeks growing even hotter as she watched him shed his shirt and unbuckle his belt.

He grinned at her as he tossed his belt aside and began to unfasten his trousers. Were all men as beautifully made as he was? He reminded her of a picture of the statue of a Greek god she had once seen in a book—long legs and broad shoulders, every muscle well-defined.

She blew out the light when he climbed in beside her and slid his arm around her shoulders. "Tired?" he asked.

"A little."

He grunted softly.

She spread her hand on his hard, flat belly and whispered, "Not that tired."

With a grin, he pulled her close, his hands roaming over her, making her gasp with pleasure, then giggle when he tickled her. She tried to turn the tables on him, but he didn't seem to be ticklish anywhere. They tusseled for a few minutes and then, in a quick move, he tucked her beneath him and captured her lips with his. The laughter died in her throat as he kissed and caressed her, his tongue like a flame as it dueled with hers, his clever hands working their magic until the world shattered and she floated back to earth to fall asleep in his arms.

They spent two days in town while waiting for the next stage. With each passing day, Kathleen grew more and more nervous about seeing her mother. It had been ten years since Helen left the ranch and her family behind. Would they even recognize each other? Have anything in common other than the blood they shared? Helen had never been happy in the West. An only child born to wealthy parents, she had been spoiled her whole life. Growing up, she'd had only to hint that she wanted something and it had been hers. She had never cooked a meal before her marriage, or made a bed, or swept a floor. She had never adjusted to ranch life. Never really tried. What would they have to talk about?

"Kathleen?"

She looked across the table to find Zane watching her, his eyes narrowed.

"You've hardly touched your breakfast. Is something wrong?"

She shook her head.

"You wouldn't lie to me, would you?"

Kathleen huffed a sigh. "It's my mother."

He lifted one brow.

"We haven't seen each other since I was twelve." She made a vague gesture with her hand. "We've been writing back and forth, you know, but our letters aren't personal. I don't know how she feels about anything important. And my letters are the same. Short, chatty notes about what's going on at the ranch. We've never shared our feelings. I've never told her how hurt I was when she left, or how heart-broken my father was. Maybe just dropping in on her isn't such a good idea."

"You can send her a wire from the next town to let her know you're on your way."

Kathleen pushed the eggs around on her plate and then nodded. "That's probably a good idea."

"It's up to you. But I think you should at least warn her about me."

Chapter Seventeen

Helen Taggart read the wire a second time and then a third. Kathleen was on her way to New York and was bringing a friend. Brow furrowed, she read the message a fourth time. Who was this 'friend' whose name had been omitted? A female friend? Or a young man? Perhaps the one who had been courting her? She frowned. What was his name? Oliver? Yes, Oliver Plimpton? No, Plotkin. A banker. Had he proposed? Perhaps she could persuade them to stay in New York. After all, there was little chance for advancement in a backwater town like Cross Creek. And if Kathleen was no longer seeing Mr. Plotkin, Helen knew several eligible young men from good families.

Kathleen hadn't mentioned an exact date, just that she expected to arrive sometime in the next week or so. Plenty of time to ready her room, Helen thought with a smile.

Ten years since she had seen her daughter. What would Kathleen think of her? Their letters through the years had been brief. They had been careful never to mention why Helen had left the ranch, or anything else that might have caused hard feelings between them. Helen had never told her daughter why she'd left. She wasn't even sure Tobias had fully understood her reasons.

She thrust the past behind her with a shake of her head.

Taking a seat at the delicate Louis XV desk, she withdrew a sheet of monogramed stationery and began writing down the names of her friends who had daughters Kathleen's age, as well as the eligible bachelors she deemed fit for her daughter.

When that was done, she pondered what to serve. It had been months since she'd given a dinner party, and this one had to be special. It was for her only daughter, after all. She could hardly wait to show her off.

Chapter Eighteen

Kathleen breathed a sigh of relief when the next large town they came to had a railroad. Zane bought two tickets and at eight o'clock the next morning, they were on the last leg of their journey east.

Traveling by train was marginally better than by coach. The ride was a little smoother but one had to be on the lookout for stray sparks coming through the windows as they roared along at an amazing twenty-five miles an hour.

Zane elicited the same stares and whispers on the train as he had on the stagecoaches. There was no hiding his Indian heritage—not that he tried. It was there in his high cheekbones, copper-hued skin, and long, black hair. She had assured him that her mother would welcome him but when she saw the way some people, women especially, took pains to avoid him, she began to have doubts.

They reached New York City on a gloomy afternoon six days later.

Kathleen had little memory of the city, which had surely changed somewhat in the last ten years. Zane hailed a hack. Kathleen gave the driver the address, and they arrived at the home she scarcely remembered thirty minutes later.

Zane swore under his breath when he saw the house. House, hell, it was more like a mansion—a huge, sprawling place, two stories high, set in the midst of a large lot surrounded by a wrought-iron fence. A verandah spanned the front of the house. Large trees and flowering shrubs grew on both sides of the property.

"I forgot how big it is," Kathleen murmured as they walked up the flagstone path to the covered porch. Taking a deep breath, she rang the bell.

A long moment later, a tall, angular man with thinning black hair and a pencil-thin moustache opened the door. "May I help you?"

"I'm here to see my mother," Kathleen said, rather curtly. "Is she at home."

The butler's entire attitude changed immediately. Taking a hurried step back, he said, "Please come in, Miss Kathleen. Madame is having afternoon tea in the sun room. You may leave your bags here for now. This way, please."

Feeling totally out of place, Zane followed Kathleen and the butler through a room that was larger than Sally's Saloon. Paintings adorned every wall. Thick carpets covered the floor. The furniture was obviously expensive, as was everything else in sight.

Eventually, they came to a room that featured windows on three sides, offering a view of an immaculate rose garden.

A woman who appeared to be in her late forties sat at a round table covered with a pristine white lace cloth. She wore a modest gown of emerald green. Her eyes widened when she saw Kathleen standing behind the butler.

"Kathleen!" The woman put her cup down so abruptly it sloshed over the rim of the cup and splashed tea on the tablecloth. Rising, she threw her arms around her daughter. "I can't believe you're here!"

The resemblance between Kathleen and her mother was unmistakable. The woman's hair was the same reddish-brown, though a few strands of gray were visible. Her eyes the same shade of green.

The joy in the woman's eyes quickly turned to shock when the butler left the room and she saw the tall stranger standing in the doorway. Her gaze rested momentarily on the gun holstered at his side.

Stepping away from Kathleen, she said, somewhat brusquely, "Who's your guest, daughter?"

"Mama, this is Zane. Zane, my mother, Helen."

Knowing the woman had no desire to shake his hand, Zane nodded at her. "I'm pleased to meet you, Mrs. Taggart." It occurred to him that Kathleen had probably written her mother about Plotkin. No doubt that's who she had been expecting.

Recovering her manners, Helen said, "Please, sit down, both of you." Resuming her seat, she rang a small silver bell. A moment later, a maid clad in a black dress and white apron hurried into the room. "Millicent, bring me a fresh pot of tea and two cups."

"Yes, ma'am."

"Kathleen, I'm so glad to see you. How is your father?"

"He's well." She had sent him a wire the same day she had sent one to her mother, telling him where she was headed and not to worry. "He misses you."

A faint hint of color stained Helen's cheeks.

Clearing his throat, Zane said, "I know you two have a lot of talk about. If you don't mind, I'll just go outside and look around."

Kathleen looked at him, her expression unreadable.

"As you wish," Helen said.

Zane gave Kathleen's shoulder a squeeze, then strode out of the room.

"Who *is* that man?" Helen asked.

"He's one of father's hired hands. And …"

"And?" her mother asked sharply.

"I'm in love with him."

Her mother's cheeks went from pink to pale. "You're in love with that … that *Indian?*"

And at that moment, Kathleen feared coming here had been a horrible mistake.

Zane stalked out of the house and down the flagstone pathway to the street. He stood there, hands clenched at his sides, then turned and walked back the way they'd come. He had known coming here would be a mistake. He had agreed to accompany Kathleen because he loved her, even though he'd been certain her mother would react exactly as she had. Well-bred or not, few whites wanted anything to do with the Indian people. Not that he could blame them. News of the Indian wars had been splashed across the front pages of papers from New York to California, along with vivid descriptions. Stories of atrocities, scalping, farms burned, cattle stolen. Of course, none of the papers told the other side of the story. No mention was ever made of the Indian women, children, and babies shot in cold blood, run down by cavalry horses, impaled on bayonets. Both sides were culpable.

He had been walking for five or ten minutes when he saw a carriage-for-hire coming toward him. He flagged it down and told the driver to take him to the nearest saloon.

"I don't understand you," Helen said. "I thought you were seeing a banker?"

"I was." They had moved from the sunroom to the back parlor. "But I never loved Oliver."

"But a half-breed Indian?"

"You know nothing about Zane," Kathleen said, her temper rising. "He's kind and caring. When Oliver and I were attacked by Indians, Zane rescued me at great cost to himself." There were other things she admired about him, but none that her mother would see as virtues.

"What does your father say?"

"He doesn't know, although I'm sure he suspects." Kathleen bit down on her lower lip and then, before she could stop herself, she blurted, "Why didn't you ever come back to us? I know you hated living on the ranch, but I thought you loved Dad. Loved *me*. Ten years and you never came to see me, not even once."

Helen lowered her gaze. "I'm sorry," she murmured. "Every year I thought, this year I'll go visit Kathleen. But it seemed something always came up. My father fell ill six months after my mother passed away and I couldn't leave him. He lingered for two years before he passed. And then I had to settle the estate. There were a lot of papers to sign and somehow, one year slipped into another and ..." Her voice trailed off.

"Did you ever love my father?"

"Yes, of course. I still do, but ..." A heavy sigh escaped her lips. "I had no idea Tobias was serious when he talked about wanting to move West. I thought it was just idle talk, that he would go to work for my father and we would have the kind of quiet, settled life my parents had. You were seven when we reached Wyoming. I tried to make the best of it, but I wasn't cut out to be a farm wife. I had no idea how to run a home. I was embarrassed because I didn't know how to do the simplest things. And I didn't *want* to do them. It took a whole day just to do the wash, and another day to iron. And another day just to bake a loaf of bread. I had to tend the garden and everything I planted died. I was afraid of the chickens."

She paused to take a breath. "But you, you weren't afraid of anything. I tried to teach you manners and etiquette, the things my mother had taught me. But you had no interest in any of that. You always wanted to be with your father, learning how to ride and rope, hanging out down at the barn, talking to the cowboys. You refused to wear anything but jeans and shirts and when I tried to put you in a dress, you cried. I felt like a failure, not only as a wife but a mother. When my mother took sick and my father called me home, I felt guilty for having a good excuse to go back home where I belonged." She folded her hands tightly in her lap. "Why have you come home now?"

Kathleen looked away. Helen had fled the ranch because she wanted her old life back. Her daughter had run away because it seemed the only way to start a new life with the man she loved.

"Kathleen?"

"Zane is wanted by the law in Montana. I talked him into coming here because I didn't think anyone would look for him in New York." She cringed at the hurt in her mother's eyes even as her own heart ached with the knowledge that her mother hadn't loved her enough to stay.

The saloon felt like home, Zane thought as he stepped through the door, even though it was a lot fancier than anything Cross Creek had to offer. The card tables were covered in green baize. The dealers wore pinstripe shirts and black string ties. Gas lanterns hung from the ceiling. The bartenders wore crisp white shirts and green aprons. The buxom woman in the painting behind the bar wasn't nude although there was no mistaking her generous cleavage.

Zane sauntered over to one of the tables and gestured at the empty chair. The three card players looked him up and down, then shrugged. Zane pulled out the chair and sat down. He picked up his cards one by one as they were dealt. Lady Luck was with him. For the next hour or so, he won more hands than he lost and at the end of two hours, he had turned his stake into two hundred. Not bad for a day's work.

He was about to call it quits when the man on his left said, "You're an Injun."

"Yeah? What about it?"

"Nothing. I just never met one before. What tribe you from?"

"Cheyenne."

"Do you know Crazy Horse?"

"No. He's a Lakota Sioux."

"I hear he's a bad one."

With a shrug, Zane pushed away from the table, gained his feet, and headed for the bar. Standing there, whiskey in hand, he wondered how long Kathleen intended to stay in New York.

Kathleen stood at the window in the bedroom that had once been hers. Nothing had changed since she'd last seen it ten years ago. The same frilly comforter adorned the bed, the same curtains hung at the windows. A small antique desk occupied one corner. The bookshelf that had held her books was empty now. She had taken them with her when they moved West, along with her favorite doll and a little stuffed gray rabbit she had once slept with. The doll and the rabbit sat on a shelf back at the ranch.

Zane's room was two doors down the hall. It was inconceivable that they would share a bed in her mother's house.

Where was he? She had thought to find him outside, but there had been no sign of him in the backyard, or anywhere else. One of the grooms recalled seeing him leave the estate. Where had he gone? Surely not back to Wyoming?

She turned when someone knocked on her open door. "Yes, Millicent, what is it?"

"Madam wanted you to know that dinner is at eight."

"Thank you."

Dropping a curtsey, the maid took her leave.

Kathleen moved to the other side of the room and peered out the window that overlooked the front yard. She breathed a sigh of relief when Zane stepped out of a hired carriage. Tall and strong and handsome, she thought, and felt her heart skip a beat as she watched him stride toward the house.

Helen Taggart was waiting for him when he crossed the threshold into the entry way.

"We dress for dinner," she said. "I wasn't sure if you had a suit of clothes, so I've left a suit that belonged to my father in your room. It's on the second floor, third door on the left."

A muscle ticked in Zane's jaw. After taking a deep, calming breath, he said, "Thank you, Mrs. Taggart." He had a new pair of black pants and a shirt, but he was pretty sure she wouldn't approve of anything he would consider appropriate.

"I don't think I like you," she said. "And I doubt if you approve of me. But I hope we can be civil to one another for Kathleen's sake."

He nodded curtly, then strode past her. Muttering, "We dress for dinner," under his breath, he took the stairs two at a time. It would serve her right if he came downstairs shirtless with his hair in braids.

"Zane? Are you in there?"

The door swung open. "Are you allowed to come in here?" he asked, his face as dark as a thundercloud.

"Oh, my. What did my mother say to you?"

He gestured at the clothes laid out on the bed. "'We dress for dinner,'" he said, mimicking Helen.

Kathleen grinned as she imagined him clad in her grandfather's brown pinstripe suit, vest, and cravat.

"I'm not wearing that," he declared. "Not for her. Not for you."

"Zane ..."

"No. Is there a horse I can borrow?"

"Sure. In the stable, in the back."

"I won't be gone long," he said, with a wink.

And before she could ask where he was going, he kissed her cheek and walked briskly out the door.

Kathleen frowned. Where was he off to now?"

❧ ❧ ❧

Kathleen paced her bedroom floor. Where was Zane? He had been gone for over an hour

She glanced at her reflection in the mirror. Her mother had lent her one of her dresses. The length was a bit short but other than that, it fit well enough. She had never worn such an exquisite gown. She ran her hands over the jade silk, marveling at the softness. At home, she usually wore shirts and pants, since they were more comfortable and easier to work in than skirts and petticoats. The clothes she wore to church were made of cotton, muslin, or wool, depending on the weather.

She had just decided that Zane was gone for the evening when he rapped on the door, then stepped inside. Kathleen stared at him, wide-eyed. He wore a white shirt, black pin-stripe trousers, a black leather coat, and a pair of new black boots. His hair, while still long, had been neatly trimmed. He looked as handsome as the devil and just as dangerous.

"Well?"

"You look fine," she said. "Better than fine."

"So do you." The jade green dress she wore made her eyes look even darker. She'd piled her hair on top of her head in some fancy style and while she looked beautiful, he preferred her hair falling loose around her shoulders.

Kathleen did a slow turn. "Do you like it?"

He nodded as he drew her close. "You're beautiful in whatever you wear, Kathleen," he murmured. And then he grinned at her. "Or when you're wearing nothing at all."

At the sound of a discreet cough, Kathleen moved out of his embrace.

"Dinner is ready, Miss Kathleen."

"Thank you, Millicent." Taking Zane by the arm, she said, "Shall we?"

With a sigh of resignation, he escorted her down the winding staircase and into the dining room.

Kathleen's mother reigned at the head of a long table covered with a damask cloth. Zane couldn't help wondering if the woman had purposefully set out to humiliate him when he saw the number of goblets and glasses and silverware laid out at each place setting. Why did anyone need three forks?

"Just follow my lead," Kathleen whispered as he pulled her chair out for her. And hoped she hadn't forgotten everything her mother had once taught her.

As one course followed another, seemingly with no end in sight, Zane wondered if the meal would ever end. He had never seen so much food, some of it unknown to him. Helen asked him a number of questions he knew were meant to embarrass him in front of Kathleen.

"How do you earn your living, Mr … Oh, dear. I'm afraid I don't know your last name."

"It's Two Shadows," Zane replied.

"How odd."

He shrugged. "In answer to your question, I'm a bounty hunter."

She looked properly shocked but managed to ask, "Where were you born?"

"In a hide lodge in the Dakotas."

"Are your parents still living?"

"No. My father …" Before he could give her the bloody tale of his parents' demise, Kathleen kicked him under the table.

"Really, Mother," she said, forcing a smile. "I'm sure all these questions can wait for another time. These potatoes are wonderful. My compliments to your chef."

"Yes," Helen said with a tight smile. "Andre really is amazing."

Zane made his escape as soon as dinner was over. Kathleen followed him a few minutes later.

"I'm sorry about that," she said. "I'd forgotten what a snob she is."

"Yeah, well," he muttered. "She's not going to sharpen her claws on me. You stay here and visit with her as long as you like. I'll get a room in the hotel."

"Please don't go."

"People have looked down their noses at me my whole life, Kathleen. I'm used to it. But I don't have to put up with it."

"If you go, I'm going with you."

Damn. He couldn't let her do that. She hadn't seen her mother in ten years. Drawing her into his arms, he brushed a kiss across the top of her head. "Forget what I said. I can put up with her for a few days."

She looked up at him, her smile bright. "I love you, Zane Two Shadows. Why didn't you ever tell me your last name?"

He shrugged.

"Does it have any meaning?"

"It was given to me by an old medicine man. He said I carried the blood of two nations and that I would always cast two shadows."

"I think that's kind of profound."

"Profound, huh?" His gaze searched hers. "What time do people go to bed around here?"

"Are you tired?"

"Not exactly. I was just wondering what the chances were of getting you alone anytime tonight."

"I'll come to you an hour after she goes to her room. Do you think you can wait that long?"

I guess I'll have to," he said with mock despair. "But it won't be easy."

Laughing softly, she led him back into the house.

CHAPTER NINETEEN

In the days that followed, life fell into a routine of sorts. Zane ate the first two meals of the day with Kathleen and her mother. Then, in the late afternoon, when the women left to go shopping or make calls, or visit one museum or another, he went into the city and whiled away the hours playing cards in one of the local saloons.

He received a few suspicious looks the first few times, overheard a couple of rude comments about his Indian blood, but he shrugged it off. There were three or four men who came into the saloon at the same time every day—wealthy men who spent their afternoons gambling and drinking while their wives entertained themselves elsewhere. They had no problem with Zane's heritage. Quite the opposite. He had never answered so many questions about Indians or the West in his life.

Today was no different.

"I notice you wear a gun," Jon Alexander remarked as he dealt the cards. He had hands as soft and smooth as a woman's, but then, bankers didn't do a lot of heavy work.

Zane shrugged. "You got a problem with that?"

"No. You just don't see too many men wearing sidearms these days."

"Maybe not in New York City," Zane said. "But out West, every man wears one."

"You any good with it?" Ben Morton asked.

"I generally hit what I aim at."

Noah Abrams grunted softly. "You ever kill anybody?"

Zane nodded curtly.

"Maybe he was a lawman," Kurt Jurgensen suggested.

"Is that it?" Noah Abrams asked. "You were a lawman?"

"I was a bounty hunter."

Surprise flickered in Jurgensen's eyes and the men at the table fell silent.

Zane placed his cards face down in front of him. "You want me to leave the game?"

Alexander shook his head. "Your past doesn't mean anything here. Just the color of your money."

Morton laughed and the tension at the table dissolved like smoke on a windy day.

Kathleen sighed as they went to visit another of her mother's friends. Making calls had been fun at first. She had met a few young women her age, renewed acquaintances with a couple of girls she had gone to school with. She had enjoyed the lunches and seeing the lovely homes, but the novelty soon wore off. Was this how her mother spent her days? Shopping and visiting and wandering through museums, looking at old pictures and ancient statues, going to plays? It had been exciting in the beginning but the novelty soon wore off. After the first few days, her mother had insisted on buying her a new wardrobe. Kathleen had to admit that had been fun.

"After all," Helen had said, "you can't continue to wear my old clothes. Everyone has already seen them."

Kathleen tried to look interested as her mother and Mrs. Jameson discussed a book they had read recently, but her thoughts soon wandered. Life on the ranch had been hard. At times it had been tedious. But she'd always felt useful. She missed cleaning the house and riding her horse and listening to the cowboys swap tall tales.

Most of all, she missed Zane. She rarely saw him alone. She envied him his freedom to come and go as he pleased. She wondered if he was growing as restless and discontented as she was. After all, even playing poker all day had to get boring after a while.

She frowned, remembering the buxom saloon girl back at Sally's. Were there scantily-clad women in the saloons here in town? Was that why he went there day after day? She frowned, remembering that the tarts who worked at Sally's did more than just serve drinks.

Maybe it was time to have a talk with Zane about how he spent his afternoons.

Zane caught Kathleen watching him several times during dinner that night. He didn't know if Helen was aware of the tension radiating from her daughter, but it was coming through loud and clear.

After dinner, they retired to the parlor where Helen took a place at the piano and began to play.

Zane heaved a sigh. He didn't know about Kathleen, but he was more than ready to leave New York. He'd had his fill of city living. Life with the Cheyenne had been hard. There were no modern conveniences, no servants, no formal dinner parties, no need to remember which fork to use. But damn, it had been a hell of a lot better than this.

Helen was in the middle of her third piece when Kathleen stood up.

"Is something wrong?" her mother asked.

"I've got a headache. I think I'll go up to bed. Zane, may I have a word with you?"

Helen cleared her throat. "Not in your room, dear. Use the den."

A flicker of irritation flashed in Kathleen's eyes. "Yes, of course." Pivoting on her heels, she swept out of the room.

Zane stared after her. She was mad, he thought, mad at him. But he had no idea why.

With a nod in Helen's direction, he followed Kathleen down the hall.

She turned on him the minute he closed the door behind him. "What do you do in the saloon all day?"

He lifted one brow, surprised by the question. "I play poker with a few of the men in town. What do you think I'm doing?"

"Are there …"

"Are there what?"

"Girls there? Girls like French Lil?"

"Is that what this is all about?" With a shake of his head, he drew her into his arms. "I don't want anyone but you. Don't you know that?"

With a sigh, she laid her head against his chest. "Forgive me?"

"There's nothing to forgive." He stroked her hair. "I know you're having a good time with your mother and her friends, but …"

She looked up at him. "But I'm not."

"No?"

She shook her head. "If it wasn't for that wanted poster, I'd say let's go home."

"To hell with the poster. I'm ready to go when you are."

"But it isn't safe."

"There are other towns."

She stared up at him. He was talking about settling somewhere else, which was the only smart thing to do. She knew that, but, somehow, hearing him say it made it real.

"I know, it's a lot to ask," he said quietly.

"Where were you thinking of going?"

"I hadn't thought about it until now. There's no hurry." He tilted her head up and kissed her lightly. "Come on, we'd better get out of here before your mother gets the wrong idea."

In bed later that night, Kathleen smiled inwardly. Zane was right, she thought. They had plenty of time to decide where to go and until then, they could stay here. Was he asleep? Or feeling as restless as she was? Sitting up, she stared at the door. It was well after midnight. The house was quiet …

Slipping out of bed, she eased open her bedroom door and tiptoed down the hallway toward Zane's room. She hesitated a moment, then slowly opened the door … and found him standing on the other side.

"What are you doing here?" he whispered.

"What do you think?"

"I had the same idea." Taking her by the hand, he drew her into the room and closed the door, shutting out the rest of the world.

The telegram arrived first thing in the morning. The message was brief.

Kathleen come home.
Your father is ill.
Diagnosis uncertain.
Juanita

Zane hitched the team to Helen's fancy carriage and drove Kathleen and her mother to the train station to make reservations. The next train headed West left at 8:30 the next morning. They would take the train as far as possible, then catch a stage to Wyoming. On the way home, Kathleen wondered why she and Zane hadn't taken the train sooner than they had. But that didn't matter now. What mattered was getting back to the ranch as soon as possible.

CHAPTER TWENTY

Helen Taggart wasn't one to waste time. As soon as they returned home from the station, she summoned the butler and the housekeeper. She informed them she would be leaving the city in a few hours and explained what they were to do—and not do—in her absence.

Kathleen went up to her room to pack,

A few minutes later, Zane followed her.

He stood in the doorway while she tossed clothes and underwear and shoes on the bed. She was certainly taking more than she came with. Her hands were shaking as she folded one thing after another, only to stop abruptly and sink down on the floor.

With a sigh, Zane went to her. Lifting her to her feet, he sat on the edge of the bed and cradled her in his arms. "It's all right, love," he murmured, stroking her hair. "Go ahead and cry."

It was like a dam breaking. Tears flooded her eyes and ran down her cheeks. Every tear was like a knife in his heart. If not for him, she would be home where she belonged.

Her next words twisted the knife. "I … I never … never should have left him," she sobbed. "I was all he had."

Not knowing what to say, he simply held her close, wondering if her feelings for him had changed. If she would resent him now, for taking her away from the ranch.

Gradually, her sobs subsided and she sat quiescent in his arms, her eyes closed.

Zane glanced up when he heard footsteps. A moment later, Helen stood in the doorway, her mouth pursed, her expression one of disapproval.

He looked at her over Kathleen's head, daring her to say something.

With a humph, Helen continued on down the hallway.

They gathered for the afternoon meal a few hours later. Kathleen's eyes were still red and swollen when she came downstairs and he knew she'd been crying again. He hoped like hell the old man didn't die before they got back to the ranch. He'd never forgive himself if that happened.

And maybe she wouldn't, either.

There was little conversation at the table.

When the meal was over, Zane excused himself and left the house, glad for a respite from the weight of Kathleen's grief, and Helen's obvious disapproval. He took one of the saddle horses and rode into town.

Helen cleared her throat. "Kathleen, how are things at the ranch?"

Kathleen blinked at her mother. In all the time she'd been here, her mother had never mentioned the ranch, or Tobias, even once. "We were prospering. Dad bought a new mare and bred her to his stud. The herd was growing." She shrugged. "We lost a few head to some Indians, but that's normal."

"Is it just the two of you?"

"Of course not. We have four or five cowhands. And Juanita. Dad hired her after … hired her ten years ago. She does most of the cooking and helps me with the cleaning and the laundry." Kathleen grinned. "Actually, I help her."

"I see."

Kathleen stared at her mother. Was she mistaken, or was her mother jealous? Of Juanita?

Helen took a deep breath, her cheeks pinking. "Is your father seeing anyone?"

"Of course not!" Kathleen exclaimed, shocked to think that her father would see another woman when he was still married. And then she frowned. "Are *you* seeing someone?" she asked. Why was she even asking such a question when her father was ill, maybe dying? Folding her napkin, she pushed away from the table. "I need to finish packing."

Helen stared after her daughter, her brow furrowed. She wouldn't have been surprised if Tobias was visiting one of the soiled doves at Sally's. After all, a man had needs. And he was, after all, a virile, handsome man. Or he had been the last time she'd seen him. Ten years was a long time. No doubt he'd changed. But then, so had she.

They arrived at the station at 7:45 the next morning. "Better to be early than late," Helen said.

A porter stowed their luggage and showed them to their seats. Three other people were already onboard.

Kathleen and her mother sat together. Zane sat on the wooden seat facing them. It was, he thought, going to be a long ride, what with Helen glaring at him like he was the son of Satan.

More people boarded the train—couples with kids, single men, a pair of nuns, a drummer, and a woman dressed in mourning.

At 8:25, the engine chugged to life. Five minutes later, the whistle blew, and the train lurched forward.

Kathleen stared out the window. How bad was her father? How would she live with herself if he passed away before she could apologize for the harsh words she had hurled at him in anger? He couldn't die, not before she told him she loved him.

She slid a glance at her mother, still surprised that Helen had decided to go home with them. How long would she stay before she ran back to New York?

And what about Zane? How dangerous was it for him to return to Wyoming? What were the chances another hunter from Montana would track him down to Cross Creek? And how had Braxton discovered Zane was in Wyoming? Once Zane had seen them safely home, would he stay? And if he didn't, what then? He had talked of settling elsewhere ...

Feeling suddenly queasy, she leaned back and closed her eyes.

By the time they reached the end of the line, Kathleen vowed never to ride the train again. She hadn't been nauseous on the stage going east, but for some reason, traveling by rail didn't agree with her at all.

Her mother suggested it might have been something she ate that upset her stomach.

Zane said nothing. He noticed that Helen grew increasingly nervous as Cross Creek drew closer. For the first time, her veneer of self-control was slipping. He wondered at the sudden change in her, from the take-charge woman who had an opinion on everything to the one who rarely spoke, her thoughts obviously turned inward. It was blatantly apparent that she wasn't looking forward to returning to the ranch. Was she afraid, and if so, of what? Or was it merely anxiety at the thought of seeing her husband again after so many years? Either way, it was none of his business. He had worries of his own.

After what seemed like months but was only weeks, they reached Cross Creek. Zane left Helen and Kathleen at the stage depot to collect their baggage while he went to the livery to rent a buggy for the women and a mount for himself. He wondered briefly what had happened to the buckskin. Had the owner of the livery sold the mare to pay for her upkeep? He was sure gonna miss her.

Returning to the depot, he loaded their valises into the buggy, helped the women get settled, and handed Kathleen the reins.

When they were on their way, he swung onto the back of the rented horse and fell in behind them.

He had a feeling their homecoming wasn't going to be pleasant and, for one quick moment, he thought of turning around and riding hell for leather for the Black Hills.

The ranch was strangely quiet when they arrived.

Kathleen reined the team to a halt in front of the porch, climbed down from the seat, and ran into the house, leaving her mother to fend for herself.

"Dad?" She turned at the sound of footsteps, but it was only Juanita, who ran forward and threw her arms around her.

"Where's my father?" Kathleen asked. "Is he …?"

"He is upstairs, resting. He will be so happy to see you."

After removing her bonnet, Kathleen ran up the stairs and into her father's room. All the drapes were drawn. Her father lay propped on a couple of pillows, his eyes closed. A sheet covered him. He'd lost a little weight, she thought, but other than that he looked well.

"Dad?"

His eyelids fluttered, then opened. "Kathleen?"

"Yes, it's me." Blinking back tears, she went to his side and took one of his hands in hers. "I'm so sorry for what I said. I didn't mean it. You're the best father any girl ever had, and I love you."

"There's nothing to forgive," he said, his hand squeezing hers. "I'm just glad you're home." Seeing the concern in her eyes, he said, "No need to fret, kitten. I feel fine. The doctor says I'm good as new. But Juanita insists I rest every afternoon. It's nonsense but if I don't do what she says, I don't get any dessert."

Kathleen smiled, relieved that in spite of his weight loss, he seemed like his old self.

"Tobias?"

His eyes widened at the sound of Helen's voice. And then he looked at Kathleen. "Is that …?"

"Mama came home with me." Kathleen stepped away from the bed. "I'll just leave you two alone." She turned when she reached the door, felt a catch in her heart when her mother perched on the chair by the bed and took his hand in hers.

Smiling, Kathleen closed the door.

Zane was waiting for her downstairs. "How is he?"

"He looks fine. He said Juanita makes him rest during the day. His eyes sure lit up when he saw my mother."

He grunted softly as his gaze ran over her. "How do you feel?"

She shrugged. "Glad to be home."

He nodded as he took her in his arms. They hadn't had much time alone in New York. Helen had made sure of that. It felt good to hold her in his arms without her mother looking on in disapproval.

Kathleen tugged on his hand, leading him toward the sofa. He took the place beside her, their hands still entwined. "What are we going to do now?" she asked.

"What do you mean?"

"Are you going to stay here?"

"If you want me to."

"Is it safe?"

He shrugged one shoulder. "I've given it some thought. I think it was just an unlucky coincidence that Braxton saw that poster. It looked pretty old and faded. Probably not too many still floating around."

Kathleen nodded, relieved. She had been so afraid he would ride on and she would never see him again. "How do you think that bounty hunter tracked you to the ranch?"

"Beats the hell out of me." Zane stood at the sound of footsteps coming down the stairs. "I'll get your luggage and bring it in and then I'm going down to look after the horses. I'll need to take the buggy and the saddlehorse back to town tomorrow, or ask one of the hands to do it."

"Will you come to dinner?"

"I don't think so."

"Will I see you later?"

"I reckon so." He kissed her lightly, quickly, then strode out of the house.

Chapter Twenty-One

Kathleen was glad when dinner was over. She didn't miss the veiled looks that passed between her mother and father, though she couldn't quite decipher them. Pleading that she needed to unpack, she made her escape upstairs. She smiled as she opened her wardrobe, thinking she would be the best dressed woman in town as she began hanging up all the clothes her mother had bought her in New York. Her wardrobe, usually almost bare, soon overflowed with all the colorful dresses, shoes, and hats that she would have little use for here on the ranch.

From Juanita, Kathleen had learned that her father had come down with the grippe, a contagious disease that was often fatal, and only Juanita's constant care and many visits by the doctor had pulled him through. Thankfully, he had recovered.

Her mother moved into the guest room. After seeing the way her parents looked at each other, Kathleen couldn't help wondering how long they would sleep apart.

With a faint smile, she wondered how soon she would be able to make love to Zane again. She missed being in his arms, the desire in his eyes when he held her close, the way her whole body came alive when he caressed her, the thrill of touching him in return, the sound of his voice when he whispered he loved her.

She wondered if he would ever ask her to marry him.

They had arranged to meet in the barn after everyone else had gone to bed. Kathleen found Zane inside, stroking the neck of his buckskin mare.

He looked at her over his shoulder and smiled. "I can't believe your old man didn't leave my horse in town."

"See, my father's not all bad," she said with a grin.

"Well," Zane drawled, "he'd have to have some good in him to have raised you." His gaze searched hers. "He brought your palomino home, too. Everything all right between you and your old man now?"

"Yes, thank goodness."

He grunted softly. "Did you tell him I came home with you?"

"Not yet. I asked my mother not to say anything, either."

"He's not going to like it when he finds out I'm here."

"I know." Looking up at him, she curled her hand around his nape. "Kiss me, Zane."

Drawing her closer, he covered her mouth with his. Her lips were warm and soft and yielding. And sweet, so sweet. Falling back on the straw, he drew her down beside him, so they were face to face. His hands skimmed her breasts, her thighs, rested lightly on her belly for stretched seconds. Little sounds of pleasure rose in her throat, igniting his desire for her. They had made love before, yet he was strangely reluctant to take her now.

She pressed her body to his, yearning to be closer, her hands eager as they caressed him in return.

She paused when he stilled. "What's wrong?"

"Are you still sick in the morning?"

"What?"

"You heard me."

She stared at him a moment, not comprehending, and then her eyes grew wide. "You don't think I'm …"

His silence was answer enough.

"But how …"

He lifted one amused brow. "The usual way, I reckon."

She rested her hands on her belly. A baby? "But … we've only made love a few times."

"I hear it only takes once."

"You seem so sure."

He heard the mild accusation in her voice. "I recognize the signs."

"Oh?" Accusation turned to hurt.

Zane shook his head. "Stop thinking what you're thinking. Indian women get pregnant, too, you know. I wasn't my mother's only child." He'd had two younger brothers. Neither had survived childhood.

Kathleen sat up. "Pregnant." Why had the possibility never occurred to her? "Oh, my."

"Yeah," he muttered ruefully. "Your old man's gonna kill me."

"What are we going to do?"

Zane shrugged. "Either we get married, or we don't. I guess that's up to you." Or, more likely, Taggart. Would her old man prefer to have a half-breed for a son-in-law, or face the scandal of his daughter having a baby out of wedlock? "Do you want me to tell your father?"

Kathleen's eyes grew wide. What would her father say? What would he do? She didn't think her father would really kill Zane. Then again … She shook her head. "I should tell him. After all," she said, dryly, "he won't shoot me. I'll tell him tomorrow. You keep out of sight until then."

Zane didn't know about Kathleen, but he didn't get any sleep that night. He had never considered marriage, or fatherhood, or settling down. He'd been free to come and go as he pleased for most of his adult life. He had never missed having a home or a family. Never wanted either one. But the thought of settling down with Kathleen didn't sound so bad. She was warm and caring and beautiful. And he loved her.

He hadn't been kidding when he suggested her father might take a shot at him. It was, in fact, a very real possibility. Stealing a woman's virginity was right up there with horse stealing and cattle rustling, both hanging offenses in the West. It was unlikely that any jury in Cross Creek would convict Taggart for seeking retribution against the man who had defiled his only daughter.

Shit! He'd known pregnancy was a possibility. His only excuse was that the saloon girls always took precautions to prevent that happening and, like most men, he rarely thought about it. But he was sure as hell thinking about it now.

Taggart frowned when he heard a knock at his bedroom door. It was after eleven, he thought as he threw back the covers. Good news never came late at night.

"Helen?" He couldn't have been more surprised if he'd found a pot of gold on the other side of the door. "Is something wrong?"

"Can we talk?"

He lifted one brow. Except for the few brief moments they'd had together when she visited him this morning, it had been ten years since she stepped foot in the bedroom they had once shared. He took a step back, his nostrils filling with the familiar scent of her perfume when she walked past him.

"Everything's the same," Helen murmured as she settled into the easy chair in the corner.

He closed the door, then leaned back against it. "Not everything. My bed is lonely at night."

"Tobias …"

"Why did you leave us?"

Clenching her hands in her lap, she said, "I told you why."

He snorted. "Because ranch life was too hard? Because you felt like a failure? So you proved it by running away."

"That's not fair!"

"You could have stayed. But you were too proud to ask any of the women in town for help, too concerned with your own petty problems to give a damn about Kathleen. Dammit, Helen, a girl needs her mother. Even a mother who's so self-centered, she'd rather turn tail and run away than make an honest effort to do the right thing." He dragged his hand over his jaw. "Why are you here now?"

"Juanita's wire … it said you were sick. I thought you were … that … that if I didn't come now I … I might never get the chance to tell you how … how sorry I am for leaving you and Kathleen, and …" She looked away as tears flooded her eyes. She had been too proud to come back and admit she'd made a mistake, that her social standing in the community didn't fill the emptiness in her heart. That no matter how many dances she attended, or how many charity events she organized, her bed and her heart were still empty at the end of the day. Too stubborn to admit she missed her husband and her daughter. She hadn't realized just how much she had missed until Kathleen arrived in New York, a woman fully-grown who was practically a stranger. How could she have been so foolish? She only hoped the people she loved would forgive her.

"Helen?"

"I was too proud to admit I'd made a mistake. Too afraid of being rejected to ask you to take me back. And afraid … afraid that after so long, you wouldn't want me anymore."

Taggart groaned low in his throat as he crossed the room and knelt in front of her. "It's not all your fault," he said, his voice thick. "I was too hurt and too proud to write and ask you to come home."

She looked at him, her eyes red and swollen, her cheeks damp. "How could we have been so foolish?"

"I don't know." His gaze searched hers. "I've missed you so damn much. All these years wasted. Are you … is there any chance you're here to stay?"

"If you want me to."

With a wordless cry, he pulled her down into his lap, his arms wrapping around her, hugging her tight. "I never stopped loving you."

"And I never stopped loving you."

Taggart shook his head. "We're just a couple of old fools, aren't we?"

Helen nodded. And then she frowned. "Tobias? I have a confession to make."

Thinking the worst, he growled, "What is it?"

Sniffling, she said, "I still can't cook."

Kathleen woke bleary-eyed and feeling as though she hadn't slept a wink. She had tossed and turned all night. Try as she might, she hadn't been able to come up with a simple way to tell her father she was pregnant. It might be easier to tell her mother, she thought, maybe easier for another woman to understand.

And maybe not.

She threw the covers aside and went to stand in front of the dresser. Looking in the mirror, she turned this way and that. Were her breasts fuller? Her stomach rounder? With a shake of her head, she turned away. She couldn't be more than eight or nine weeks along. Surely it was too soon for anyone to notice.

Feeling a familiar queasiness, she pulled the chamber pot out from under the bed.

Helen paused outside her daughter's bedroom door. Was Kathleen sick? She knocked once and when there was no answer, she opened the door and peered inside.

"Kathleen!" Hurrying to her daughter's side, she put a steadying arm around her shoulders. "Are you all right?"

Kathleen bit down on her lower lip.

Frowning, Helen went to the pitcher on top of the dresser. She poured a small amount in the bowl and wet a washcloth, then filled a glass with water. She carried both back to Kathleen.

"Here," she said, handing Kathleen the glass and the cloth. "Rinse your mouth."

Sniffling, Kathleen rinsed the foul taste from her mouth, then wiped her face. Taking a deep breath, she stood, her gaze on the floor.

Brow furrowed, Helen asked, "Are you ill?"

"Not exactly," Katheen whispered, still not meeting her mother's eyes.

"What, exactly?" Helen asked, afraid she already knew the answer.

Kathleen lowered her head and burst into tears, her cheeks burning with shame.

With a sigh, Helen drew her daughter into her arms. "It's his, isn't it?"

Kathleen nodded.

"Your father will kill him," Helen muttered, thinking if Tobias didn't, she surely would.

Kathleen wept until she had no tears left.

Tugging on her hand, Helen led her daughter to bed, sat and pulled Kathleen down beside her. "Did he take you by force?"

"What? No! No, never."

"How could you let him touch you?"

Shame turned to anger and strengthened her spine. "I'm in love with Zane," Kathleen declared. "I'm proud to be carrying his child!"

"You're nothing but a child yourself."

"I'm not a child! I'm twenty-two years old."

Lips pursed, Helen stood. "Get dressed. We need to tell your father."

As soon as her mother left the room, Kathleen shinnied down the tree outside her window, and ran barefooted down to the bunkhouse. Too late, she realized she should have taken time to dress, but it was too late to turn back now. Fortunately, her gown was made of flannel and covered her from head to foot. A look around told her all the cowhands had already ridden out for the day. She found Zane in the barn.

He looked up at the sound of her footsteps, relieved when he saw her. It wasn't easy, keeping out of sight of the hands. He wondered how much longer he'd have to hide from her old man.

One look at Kathleen's face and he took her in his arms. "What's happened? What are you doing out here in your nightgown?"

"My mother … she heard me being sick this morning …"

"Damn," he muttered. "So, she knows."

"She's waiting for me to get dressed so we can tell my father. What are we going to do?"

"What do you want to do?"

"I don't know." She looked up at him, tears swimming in her eyes. "Maybe we should just run away."

"Is that what you want?"

"I don't know. He's going to be so disappointed in me."

Zane snorted. "He's not going to blame you. And he's not going to stop loving you."

She sniffed back her tears. "What will he do to you?"

He shrugged. "Horse whip me, maybe. Hell, it's what I deserve."

"I'm to blame, too. I could have said no."

Holding her at arm's length, his gaze searched hers. "Are you sorry we made love?"

"No."

"Sorry about the baby?"

She spread her hand over her abdomen, then shook her head.

"Do you love me?"

"You know I do."

"If your father doesn't shoot me on sight or throw me off the ranch, he might insist we get married to spare you the shame of having a child out of wedlock. How would you feel about that?"

"Are you proposing, Mr. Two Shadows?"

"I guess I am."

"Then my answer is yes."

Pulling her back into his arms, he kissed her. "I love you, darlin'. Let's go face the music together."

Tobias stared at Helen. "What do you mean, she's pregnant?"

"I mean, she's going to have his baby."

"I'll kill him for this. I took him in, gave him a job, and this is how he repays me?" Muttering an oath, his face red with rage, he grabbed the Winchester from the rack over the mantel.

"Tobias! What are you going to do?"

"Same thing I'd do to any marauder!"

"Wait!" Helen grabbed his arm. "I know how you feel. I don't like it, either. But even a husband like Zane is better than no husband at all. At least get them married before you do anything rash."

"Married! You want me to let that half-breed bounty hunter marry my daughter? What will people think?"

"What will they think when she has a baby out of wedlock?"

Taggart paused. Did he want Kathleen to be subjected to the scorn of the town? To be the topic of ugly whispers and conjecture? To be snubbed by her friends? Did he want his grandchild to be known as a bastard? He put the rifle back on the rack, then sat down heavily and cradled his head in his hands. How could he let his little girl marry a man like Zane? Dammit! What else could he do?

Standing on the front porch, Kathleen took a deep breath, smiled weakly when Zane squeezed her hand.

"Come on, darlin'," he said. "We might as well get it over with."

She nodded. "I love you, no matter what."

"I hope you still feel that way when this is over," he said ruefully. "Dammit, Kathleen, I never meant to hurt you."

"Stop it. It's as much my fault as yours. Maybe more. Unmarried women are supposed to say no."

He laughed, then pulled her into his arms and kissed her, long and hard. "*Hoka hey!*" he murmured. "It's a good day to die."

Chapter Twenty-Two

Kathleen took a deep breath, let it out in a long, slow sigh, opened the front door and stepped into the living room.

And came face-to-face with her parents.

Her father's eyebrows shot up when he saw her in her nightgown. Before he could say anything, Kathleen said, "It's not what you're thinking. I climbed out the window this morning to warn Zane that you knew about … that you knew."

Tobias grunted, his eyes dark with anger as he glared at Zane. "I should peel the hide from your body an inch at a time, you dirty half-breed. I took you in, gave you a job, and this is how you repay me? By stealing my daughter's virtue? If I shot you where you stand, no one would blame me."

Kathleen slid a glance at Zane. He stood there, his head high as he met her father's angry gaze, but she could feel the tension in him.

Helen laid a hand on her husband's arm. "Tobias …"

"Keep out of this, woman." His gaze shifted to Kathleen. "What do you have to say for yourself, daughter?"

"I love him, and if you harm a hair on his head, I'll never speak to you again. I know you're hurt and angry and I don't blame you. But Zane is the father of my child. He's going to be my husband. And if you don't like it, then we'll leave." She smiled inwardly as Zane gave her hand a reassuring squeeze.

"So, that's it?" Taggart growled. "Either I approve or you're leaving?"

Kathleen swallowed hard, and then nodded.

Shoulders slumped in defeat, her father said, "I hope you don't regret it," then he tuned and stomped out of the room.

Kathleen looked at her mother. "He's never going to forgive me, is he?"

"I'm sure he will, in time," Helen said quietly. "He's forgiven me for leaving."

Zane went out on the front porch while Kathleen went upstairs to dress. Helen joined him there a few moments later.

"What are your plans now?" she asked, her voice cool.

"I intend to marry Kathleen as soon as possible. Beyond that ..." He shrugged.

"Do you mean to leave the ranch?"

"I guess that's up to your husband, Mrs. Taggart."

"I know we got off to a bad start," Helen said, her gaze sliding away from his. "And I won't say I'm happy with the thought of you marrying my daughter, but I hope you'll stay on at the ranch. Kathleen loves it here."

"What about you, Mrs. Taggart? Are you staying?"

"Does your decision to stay or leave rest on mine?"

"No. Whatever I do is up to Kathleen." He cocked his head to the side. "You didn't answer my question."

"I'm staying. I've got a lot of catching up to do."

A faint grin twitched his lips. "Good day to you, Mrs. Taggart."

With a nod, Helen went back into the house. She stood in the entryway a moment, then went upstairs to her daughter's room. "Kathleen, may I come in?"

"Of course."

Helen stepped into the room and closed the door behind her. "Zane intends to marry you," she said, without preamble. "Is that what you want?"

"Yes."

Helen nodded. "I don't want people counting the months on their fingers when your baby comes, so this is what we're going to do."

Zane looked up when Kathleen joined him on the porch. "What took you so long?"

"I had a long talk with my mother."

He grunted softly. "That can't be good."

She sat on the top step and patted the place beside her.

After a moment's hesitation, he dropped down beside her.

"My mother has decided that we're going to tell people we got married in New York."

"What? Why?"

"She doesn't want people counting the months until the baby comes."

"That's too damn bad. We're getting married right away whether she likes it or not."

"Let me finish. We're going to have a quiet wedding in the church, and the reason will be that my father wasn't in New York for the first wedding, so we're getting married a second time so he can give me away."

Zane shook his head, amazed at her mother's solution. "Is this okay with you?"

Kathleen shrugged. "Is it okay with you?"

"I don't care how we get hitched," he said, slipping his arm around her waist, "as long as we do."

"I love you, Zane." She cupped his cheek in her palm and kissed him. "I'll be the best wife I can."

"And I'll try to be the kind of husband you deserve. How soon is this wedding taking place?"

"Ten o'clock tomorrow morning, at the church."

"I guess I'd better go into town and buy some new duds. How about you?"

"My mother left her wedding dress here when she ran away. She wants me to wear it. She's airing it out now. It's a little musty."

"You'll be a beautiful bride no matter what you wear," he murmured, and pulled her into his arms.

A loud cough behind them drove them apart.

"Breakfast is ready, *Señorita*."

"*Gracias*, Juanita."

Rising, Zane took Kathleen's hands in his and lifted her to her feet. She smiled at him. Maybe everything would work out after all. "We might as well eat."

"You go ahead. I'm not ready to sit down with the family just yet."

She started to argue, then kissed his cheek instead. "Will I see you later?"

"Count on it." He kissed her lightly, then descended the stairs.

Kathleen watched him stride down to the barn. Then, with a sigh, she went into breakfast.

Zane saddled the buckskin and rode into town. When he reached Sally's, he tossed the mare's reins over the hitchrack and headed straight for the bar. Is wasn't quite eleven o'clock.

"Kinda early for you, isn't it?" Ed, the bartender, remarked.

"It's been a rough morning," Zane muttered. "Just give me a double whiskey and don't ask any questions."

Grunting softly, the bartender poured two fingers and slid the shot glass across the bar.

Zane tossed it back and asked for another. How had his life changed so drastically so damn fast? He was getting married tomorrow morning. He was going to be father. His future in-laws hated him. And he was going to have to live under their roof until he earned enough money to buy or build a house for Kathleen and the baby.

Shit.

Turning away from the bar, he glanced around the room. Although it was early, there were three men playing poker at a table in the corner.

He was heading in their direction when French Lil came flouncing down the stairs. She came to an abrupt halt at the bottom of the staircase when she saw him.

Eyes wide, her face suddenly pale, she stammered, "You … you're … you're alive."

Brow furrowed, Zane stared at her. Why had she assumed otherwise? When he took a step toward her, she turned on her heel, intending to run back up the stairs. She let out a gasp when Zane darted forward, grabbed her by the arm, and spun her around.

"What did you do?" he growled.

"Me?" she squeaked. "No … nothing."

His eyes narrowed as a horrible thought crossed his mind. And yet, even as he tried to dismiss it, he knew it was true. "You wouldn't happen to know a bounty hunter name of Braxton, would you?"

She shook her head vigorously.

"Don't lie to me, damn you. You told him where to find me, didn't you?"

"No! No. I would never do that!"

"What did he offer you?"

"Nothing!"

"Dammit, don't lie to me! What did he give you?"

"I …"

"You were angry because I refused you, is that it? So you sold me out to get even."

She started to deny it, but something she saw in his eyes changed her mind. "He offered me half the reward. I was going to use it to make a new start."

"You damn whore. I want you to leave town now. I don't ever want to see your lying face again." He slapped her once, then pushed her away. "You're lucky I don't kill you."

She stumbled backward, then turned and bolted up the stairs. A moment later, he heard a door slam.

Cursing under his breath, he headed for the poker table.

He'd been playing about an hour when Lil came down the stairs again. Dressed for traveling, she carried a flowered valise in one hand and her reticule in another. Avoiding his gaze, she pushed her way through the swinging doors. Damn treacherous female, he thought, his anger rising again. Kathleen might have been killed because of her.

Huffing a sigh, he tossed a dollar in the pot. One more hand, he thought, and he'd head back to the ranch.

CHAPTER TWENTY-THREE

It was dusk when he returned to the T Bar K. Kathleen was sitting on the porch, a pensive expression on her face. She stood when he dismounted. "I wasn't sure you were coming back."

"Sorry." He took the stairs two at a time. "I guess the time got away from me."

"You don't have to marry me if you don't want to, Zane."

"Hey! Don't talk like that." Slipping his arm around her waist, he drew her up against him.

"You've been with that saloon girl, haven't you?" Kathleen said, her voice icy.

"Yeah. But not for the reason you think. She was right surprised to see me. Made me wonder why." A muscle clenched in his jaw. "Turns out Braxton offered her half the reward to tell him where I was."

"Oh, no!" Kathleen shook her head. "Why would she do that? I thought she was sweet on you."

"She liked my money," he said ruefully. "I told her to get out of town."

"Do you think she'll go?"

"She will if she knows what's good for her."

"Dinner will be ready in a few minutes."

"Yeah."

"You can't avoid my parents forever. You'll be part of the family tomorrow."

He nodded. She was right.

"Come on in and wash up."

Heaving a sigh, he followed his future bride into the house, thinking he would rather face a firing squad than sit down to a meal with Kathleen's disapproving parents.

"Since you're about to become our son-in-law," Taggart said as he passed a bowl of potatoes to Helen, "perhaps you could tell us a little about your past."

Zane groaned inwardly. "What would you like to know?"

"I know you were a bounty hunter, but not much beyond that."

"There isn't much."

"Where were you born?" Helen asked.

"In a Cheyenne lodge."

A look of distaste flickered in her eyes.

"How do you intend to support my daughter?" Taggart asked. "You don't intend to live in a Cheyenne lodge, do you?"

"I was hoping to stay on here for a while. If that doesn't sit well with you and Mrs. Taggart, we'll move on."

"And do what?" Helen asked.

"Whatever the hell is necessary," Zane snapped, pushing away from the table. "I'm through answering questions."

Kathleen glared at her parents as Zane left the room. The slamming of the door told her he'd left the house, as well. "I hope you're happy," she said. "Zane isn't to blame for what happened between us. At least not entirely. And if you can't treat him with the respect he deserves, then we'll leave tomorrow morning."

"Kathleen …"

"I have nothing more to say." Rising, she left the house.

She found Zane down by the corral, scratching the buckskin's ears. "I'm sorry about that."

"I'd rather face a war party of Crow than sit through another meal with your parents."

"I guess I can't blame you. I wouldn't blame you if you left and never came back."

"It'll take more than your parents to drive me away," he murmured, taking her in his arms. "But I'm not living under your old man's roof." He would never feel comfortable making love to Kathleen, knowing her father was only a few doors away. "I'll sleep in the barn."

"Our last foreman was married. He built a house not far from here. We can stay there, if you want to."

"I can't ask you to do that."

"You didn't ask." She looked up at him, her expression one of amusement. "Would you rather sleep in the barn, alone?"

"What do you think?"

"I think I want you to kiss me."

"Pretty forward, aren't you?"

"Kiss me, Zane."

Crushing her close, he covered her mouth with his, his tongue seeking hers while his hands caressed her. She was his in every way that mattered, he thought. The ceremony tomorrow was only window dressing. As far as he was concerned, the real marriage between them had taken place the first time they made love.

Kathleen was as nervous as any other young bride as she slipped into her mother's wedding dress. It was a beautiful gown, with a high neck, long sleeves, and a floor-length skirt that swished when she walked. It had yellowed a little over the years but her mother had aired it out and it didn't look bad at all.

"Something old," her mother said as she fastened the long row of buttons in the back

"Something new," Kathleen murmured, stepping into her shoes.

"Something borrowed," her mother said, as she set her veil in place. As light and airy as a spider web, it trailed on the floor behind her.

"And something blue," Kathleen added as she picked up her bouquet of forget-me-nots.

"You look lovely, daughter," Helen said, eyes shining with unshed tears. "Are you sure this is what you want? It's not too late to change your mind."

"Months too late," Kathleen said, resting her hand on her belly. "Please be happy for me as I am."

Blinking back her tears, Helen hugged her daughter. "I wish you all the happiness your heart can hold."

Zane couldn't think of a time when he'd felt more ill-at-ease than he did standing next to the minister in front of the altar, waiting for his bride.

Juanita and her husband sat in the second pew.

They were there as guests, but also as witnesses.

Taggart walked Helen to the first pew, then returned to the vestibule. A moment later, he came down the aisle with Kathleen at his side.

Zane sucked in a breath when he saw her. Never, in all his life, had he seen anything more beautiful than Kathleen in her mother's wedding gown, her cheeks flushed, her eyes shining with happiness. He felt a tightness in his chest when she winked at him, and he knew he could put up with Taggart's dislike and Helen's disdain as long as he could share his life with the woman he loved.

"Who giveth this woman to be married to this man?" the minister asked.

"Her mother and I do," Taggart said, sounding as though the words were being ripped from his throat. A muscle worked in his jaw as he placed Kathleen's hand in Zane's.

Zane paid little heed to the words of the ceremony, his whole attention on Kathleen, until the time came to say, "I do."

Moments later, came the welcome words, "I now pronounce you man and wife. You may kiss the bride."

He drew her into his arms gently, murmured, "I will love you as long as I live," and claimed his first kiss as her husband.

He surrendered his bride to her parents, stood aside as they hugged her, politely accepted Taggart's curt, "Congratulations."

Outside, Taggart took Zane aside. "Helen and I are taking a short trip to Cheyenne so she can do a little shopping. She thought you and Kathleen might like some time alone, although it seems unnecessary to me. Can I count on you to look after things at the ranch while we're gone?"

"Yessir."

"If you need anything from town, just charge it to the ranch account."

Zane nodded. He stood aside as Kathleen's parents hugged her again.

Kathleen and her folks had come to town in the buggy. Zane had left later and ridden the buckskin.

After Kathleen's final goodbye to her parents, he tied his horse to the back of the buggy, then lifted his bride onto the seat and swung up beside her.

"Let's go home, Mr. Two Shadows," she said, her smile stretching from ear to ear.

"Whatever you wish, Mrs. Two Shadows," he said as he took up the reins. "I can't believe your parents went off and left us home alone."

"I think they're going on a second honeymoon," Kathleen said. "I've been hearing some interesting … uh … sounds from their room late at night."

Zane looked at her, one brow raised, and then he laughed as he imagined crusty old Tobias Taggart making love to his prim and proper wife.

But when he looked at Kathleen, a vision in white satin and lace, he had no trouble at all imagining her in his bed, in his arms. Suddenly anxious to ease his longing and turn his thoughts into reality, he urged the horse into a canter.

Kathleen felt suddenly shy as she removed her veil and placed it over the chair in her bedroom. She didn't understand her nervousness. It wasn't as if they hadn't made love before. Zane had seen her naked. She was carrying his child. And yet … she blushed when he drew her into his arms.

Zane frowned, puzzled by her shyness. "Do you want me to leave while you change?"

She looked up at him, speechless.

"Kathleen? Are you having second thoughts?"

"No! No. I …" She shook her head. "I'm just being silly." Going up on her tiptoes, she clasped her hands behind his neck and kissed him. "I guess I'm having bridal jitters. I don't know why. It's not like we haven't made love before, but …"

"But never as man and wife. And never under your father's roof."

She nodded, relieved that he understood.

"I can turn out the lights if it will make you feel better."

"Don't you dare. I …" Her gaze slid away from his as her cheeks grew hotter. "I like looking at you."

"And I like looking at you."

"Then look," she said, and turned her back so he could unfasten her gown. She shivered with pleasure as he kissed every inch of bared flesh until she stood there in nothing but her undergarments, her skin tingling under his smoky gaze.

Murmuring, "My turn," she peeled away his coat and tossed it on top of her gown. His shirt quickly followed. He obligingly heeled off his boots, unfastened his belt, and removed his trousers, until they were both in their underwear.

With a low growl, Zane backed her toward the bed, lifted her onto the mattress, and stretched out beside her. In between long, slow kisses and caresses, the last of their clothing disappeared.

Zane rested his hand on the gentle swell of her belly, his fingers moving lightly back and forth. "I don't want to hurt you."

"You won't," she said, her voice husky with desire as she pulled him down on top of her. "You won't."

Whispering her name, he tangled his fingers in the wealth of her hair as his body merged with hers, two halves made whole in a dance as old as time.

Chapter Twenty-Four

Helen's gaze rested on the sight of her slim, pale fingers entwined with her husband's much larger, darker ones. Her cheeks warmed as she felt his gaze on hers. "It was generous of you to let Kathleen and Zane have the ranch to themselves for a while."

"I didn't do it for them," he said.

They were lying side-by-side on the bed in their hotel room in Cross Creek.

"It seems strange for us to be together," Helen murmured. "And yet, it seems as if we've never been apart." Her gaze met his. "Have I changed much?"

"You look even more beautiful now than you did the last time I saw you," he said, his voice gruff with emotion.

"Flatterer."

"It's the truth."

Desire swept through her as his calloused hand caressed her. And with it, a sudden rush of jealousy. She hadn't found the nerve to ask the question that was eating her alive. But she had to know. "Did you ever … while we've been apart …? I wouldn't blame you if you had, but did you …?" Her voice trailed off as her courage disappeared.

Tobias frowned at her. "Did I what?" he asked. And then he knew. "Not with anyone that mattered," he said. "And not very often." He took a deep breath. "And you?"

She turned onto her side so she could see his face. "You're the only man I've ever loved. The only man I've ever wanted," she said quietly. "And I still want you."

"Helen!"

He wrapped her in his arms, holding her so close she could scarcely breathe, but she didn't care. This was where she wanted to be, where she belonged.

Why had it taken her so long to admit the truth?

Chapter Twenty-Five

Kathleen woke in Zane's arms. A slow smile spread over her face as she remembered yesterday … and last night … and how wonderful it had been when they made love. Both times. She trailed her fingertips down his cheek, thinking that as much as she had enjoyed his lovemaking before, being married had made it even better and more meaningful.

"What are you smiling at, wife?" Zane asked.

"You'll laugh."

"Why?" Propping himself on one elbow, he kissed the tip of her nose. "Tell me."

"I was thinking that sharing your bed as your wife was even better than before."

"Ah." Of course she would feel that way, he mused, being a good, God-fearing woman.

"Well," he said, "now that it's legal, I see no reason not to do it again."

Juanita was waiting for them in the kitchen when they went downstairs. She poured them each a cup of coffee, scrambled a dozen eggs and served them up with bacon and fried potatoes.

"It smells wonderful," Kathleen said.

"*Gracias.*" Reaching into her pocket, she withdrew a sheet of paper. "*Señor* Taggart left this for you," she said, handing it to Zane.

He grunted softly as he looked it over.

"What is it?" Kathleen asked.

"Your father left me a list of chores and things to do while he's gone." And it was a heck of a list. Check the fences in the south pasture, as well as the waterholes. Repair the broken harness in the barn. Exercise the stallion. Patch the hole in the barn roof. Exercise the horses. The list went on and on.

Leaving Kathleen and Juanita to clean up after breakfast, Zane went down to the bunkhouse. The hands were waiting for him.

"I guess congratulations are in order," Dusty, the foreman, said.

"Thanks."

The other four cowboys nodded and added their good wishes.

"Let's get to work," Zane said, and issued the orders for the day, sending Chet and Austin to ride fence and Virgil and Boone to check the waterholes. He grinned as he watched the hands mount up. He'd kept the best job for himself, he mused, as he saddled the stallion. The black was a beauty, with perfect conformation and built for speed. After tightening the cinch, he swung into the saddle and touched his heels to the stallion's sides. Once out of the yard, he gave the horse its head. It was like riding the wind, he thought as he bent low over the animal's neck and headed for the hills.

Kathleen felt a rush of envy as she watched Zane ride out of the yard. It wasn't fair, she thought. He got the fun job of exercising her father's prize stallion and she was stuck in the house washing dishes.

Following Kathleen's gaze, Juanita made a shooing motion. "Go, *Señora,*" she said. "I will finish up here."

"Are you sure?"

"*Sí.* Hurry now."

Hurry, she did. She didn't bother to curry or saddle the mare but climbed onto the palomino's bare back and lit out after Zane.

Zane had just reined the stud to a halt when he heard hoofbeats coming up fast behind him. His hand curled around the butt of his Colt as he glanced over his shoulder. And grinned when he saw Kathleen riding toward him, her hair flying loose in the wind, her cheeks pink with excitement.

"Are you crazy, woman?" he exclaimed when she drew up beside him. "Riding like that when you're in the family way?"

She frowned at him. "I'm fine!"

"Yeah? What if that mare stepped in a prairie dog hole? Or you fell off?"

She glared at him. "I've never fallen off a horse in my life!"

"There's a first time for everything." Dismounting, he lifted her from the back of the mare and into his arms. "You need to be careful," he said, combing his fingers through her hair. "You're riding for two now."

She smiled up at him, thinking she had never been so happy in her life. Her parents were back together. She was having Zane's baby. And, she thought, as her eyelids fluttered down, he was going to kiss her.

Damn, but she was sweet, Zane mused as his mouth ravaged hers. She clung to him like a cocklebur, making little sounds of pleasure as he deepened the kiss, his hands stroking her back, cupping her breast.

He lowered her carefully to the ground, one arm drawing her body against his.

"Make love to me," she whispered.

As if he needed urging.

The grass was soft and cool beneath them as they undressed, the stream that flowed nearby the perfect serenade as he rose over her, his mouth hungry for the taste of her. He kissed her again and yet again as he sheathed himself deep within her velvet warmth, silently thanking *Ma'heo'o*, the Great Spirit, for bringing them together.

Lost in a hazy afterglow, it was a moment before Zane realized they were no longer alone. Holding Kathleen close to shield her nakedness, he looked over her shoulder, his whole being tensing as he gazed into the leering eyes of a half-dozen mounted warriors, their faces painted for war. Covering Kathleen's mouth with his hand, he whispered, "Don't move."

"What's wrong?"

"Maybe nothing."

"You're scaring me."

"Just do as I say." Lifting his hand in the age-old gesture for peace, he focused his gaze on the warrior he thought was their leader and said, "*Hau, kola.*"

The warrior grunted, his hand tightening around the lance in his hand.

Zane muttered an oath, certain they were about to be killed, when another warrior urged his horse between Zane and the leader. The second warrior gestured at Zane and said, "*Le mita kola.*"

There followed a rapid conversation during which Zane realized the second warrior was Teetonka.

After several tense moments, the war leader lowered his lance and backed away.

"Get dressed," Teetonka said, speaking Lakota. "We talk."

"Kathleen, it's all right. Get dressed."

"With all these Indians watching?"

"This is no time for modesty." Rising, Zane pulled Kathleen to her feet, stood behind her while she turned away and dressed as quickly as she could. Zane kept his gaze on the warriors as he tugged on his pants and shrugged into his shirt, careful to keep his hands away from his Colt. "Teetonka, what's this all about?" he asked, as a third warrior dismounted and bound his hands behind his back.

"The Crow attacked our village. Many warriors were killed. Hunting was bad this season. No buffalo. My people are hungry." He grinned impudently. "We came to steal cattle."

"You don't have to steal them, my brother. Come to the ranch with me. You may take as many as you need."

Teetonka's eyes narrowed with distrust.

"I give you my word," Zane said. "No harm will come to any of you."

With a curt nod, Teetonka spoke to the others, assuring them that they could trust the *wasichu* as he untied Zane's hands.

Five minutes later, Zane and Kathleen were leading the way back to the ranch.

✤ ✤ ✤

Virgil and Boone looked up as Zane and Kathleen rode into the yard, trailed by half a dozen Indians. The cowhands exchanged alarmed glances, then both reached for their guns.

"Keep 'em leathered!" Zane shouted.

"What the hell!" Boone exclaimed.

"You heard me. Kathleen, get into the house and lock the doors."

To her credit, she didn't argue or ask questions, but did as he asked.

"Relax, boys," Zane said. "They're only after a few cattle. Go cut five of the best from the herd out in the back pasture."

"Why the hell are we givin' these redskins our cattle?" Virgil asked belligerently. "Hell, they're painted for war."

"Right. And they're hungry. Now, do you want a fight on your hands, or do you want to keep your hair?"

Boone and Virgil exchanged glances, then mounted up and headed for the back pasture where Taggart kept twenty head or so.

"Anything else you need, *kola*?" Zane asked.

Teetonka shook his head. "You good friend." Pulling the knife from the sheath at his side, the warrior cut a shallow furrow in his palm. Riding closer to Zane, Teetonka handed him the blade. With a nod, Zane made a similar gash in his own palm and the two men clasped hands.

"Now blood brothers," Teetonka said.

"Blood brothers," Zane agreed. "If things get bad in the village, you are welcome to set up your lodges back there, in the trees by the river."

"Pilamaya, kola."

The sound of lowing cattle preceded the five head cut from the herd. Still mounted, Zane watched the warriors drive the cattle out of the yard. When the dust settled, he dismounted and led the buckskin to the barn, wondering what Taggart would think when he learned what had happened here today. Not that he really gave a damn one way or the other, Zane thought. It was easier, and a damn sight safer, to feed hungry Indians rather than fight them.

And then he grinned, remembering how Kathleen had felt in his arms, the look on her face when she realized they were no longer alone.

If he was lucky, maybe he could talk her into making love outside again tonight if he promised that only the moon and the stars would see them.

Chapter Twenty-Six

Helen smiled at her husband. They had spent the last two days in Cheyenne, talking over old times, taking long walks, dining out. Making love.

Now, sitting on the swing on the hotel porch, she cleared her throat. Opened her mouth, and closed it again.

"What is it?" Tobias asked.

"I …"

"Spit it out, woman."

"What would you say to going back East? There are some things I need to take care of if I'm going to be gone long. Or …" She pursed her lips a moment, then said in a rush, "I thought maybe we could spend part of the year in the East and part of the year on the ranch, now that Zane is there to look after things." She bit down on her lower lip, certain he would reject the idea.

"Is that what you want?"

She nodded.

He drummed his fingertips on the arm of the swing. "Sort of a compromise," he remarked.

Helen nodded again. "We can spend most of the year on the ranch, if you like. But I would like a little time in New York."

"I think it's a prime idea," he said after a moment's thought. "I'm not as young as I used to be. Might be nice to take a few months off every year and just relax." A slow smile spread over his face. "I always liked making love in that big brass bed."

Chapter Twenty-Seven

Kathleen stared at the note in her hand. She had read it three times and she still couldn't believe it. Her mother and father were on their way to New York City, where they intended to stay for the next five months, and would return to Cross Creek in time for their first grandchild to be born.

Zane grinned when she showed it to him.

"I should have known you'd be happy," she said. "You never did get along with my father. Or my mother."

"I'll try harder when they get back." Swinging her up into his arms, he twirled her around the room. "Just think, a whole five months all by ourselves. What do you want to do first?"

"I know what you want to do," Kathleen said with a laugh. "Zane, you fool, put me down. I'm getting dizzy."

The next few weeks passed peacefully. For the first time in her life, Kathleen truly felt like a grown-up. She was in charge of the house. Lady of the manor. She had always wanted to rearrange the furniture in the parlor and yet she had been reluctant to do so, wanting everything to stay the way it had been when her mother left, worried that any changes might upset her father. Now, with Juanita's help, she aired the carpets, shook out the drapes, rearranged the two easy chair so they were across from the sofa, and placed a low table between them.

And when that was done, she decided to redecorate her bedroom. She was a married woman now, not a little girl. She replaced the ruffled curtains with white lace ones, replaced the pink bedspread with a dark blue one, and made room in the dresser and the wardrobe for Zane's clothing.

And one bright summer day, she asked Zane to take her into town.

"What's the occasion?" he asked.

"I need to buy some material and some yarn," she replied. "I thought I'd make some baby clothes and booties. Annie said she'd teach me to knit."

The baby, he thought, glancing at her softly-rounded belly. Her pregnancy was obvious now. Still, he sometimes went a whole day without thinking about it, and about the changes it would make in their lives.

"Do you want me to go inside with you?" Zane asked as he pulled up in front of Grant's General Store.

"That would be nice," Kathleen replied as he helped her alight from the buckboard. Then, seeing the expression on his face, she said, "But you'd rather not?"

He shrugged.

"You'd rather go to Sally's wouldn't you?"

"I would like a drink," he admitted. "One drink. No more."

She mulled it over, then sighed. What harm could it do? That hussy, Lil, had left town. "One drink," she said. "Promise?"

"I promise." He kissed her cheek, tethered the horse to the hitch rail, and sauntered down the boardwalk toward the saloon.

With a rueful shake of her head, Kathleen stepped into Grant's.

Zane took a deep breath as he strode toward the bar. There was nothing in the world like the smell of a saloon, he thought. Sawdust, whiskey, cigar smoke, the scent of pickled, hard-boiled eggs.

"Well, well," Ed, the bartender, drawled as he poured Zane a shot of whiskey. "I thought we'd seen the last of you."

"Yeah, I thought so, too. It was a close call."

"I heard tell Mrs. Taggart was back at the ranch. Any truth to that?"

Zane nodded. "Yep, although she's gone off on a trip with the old man."

"No shit?"

Zane shrugged. "Looked to me like things were heating up between them."

"I won't believe til I see it. You want another?"

"More than my next breath. But I promised Kathleen I'd only have one."

Ed smiled a knowing smile. "I heard ya got hogtied."

"'Fraid so, but I'm not complainin'."

"Come back again when you can stay longer," the bartender called as Zane headed toward the door.

Zane lifted a hand in response, then pushed his way through the batwing doors. He stood on the boardwalk a moment, his eyes narrowed as he glanced up and down the street, an old habit from his bounty hunting days. All seemed quiet until a man rushed out of the bank and vaulted onto the back of a horse. Moments later, Oliver Plotkin ran out the door.

"Stop that man!" he hollered. "We've been robbed."

Without thinking, Zane drew his Colt and fired. The bullet caught the thief in his left shoulder and he toppled from his horse. The bandit rolled to his side and pulled his gun as Karl Powers ran out of the blacksmith shop, rifle in hand.

Time seemed to stand still as Powers and the robber fired within a second of each other. The blacksmith's shot went wide. The robber's bullet caught Powers in the chest.

The thief was scrambling for his horse when Zane fired a second time. The man fell forward and lay still.

In seconds, a dozen men emerged from the stores up and down Main Street. One man called for Doctor Joe to look after Powers. Another man went after the undertaker.

Oliver Plotkin pushed his way through the crowd, grabbed the canvas sack stuffed with the bank's money, then hurried back into the building and slammed the door.

Zane had just holstered his Colt when Kathleen came running down the street toward him. "Are you hurt?"

"Not a scratch."

"You could have been killed!"

"Hey, I'm fine. Are you ready to go home?"

The next couple of weeks were busy ones. Time seemed to be flying by, Kathleen mused as she folded a load of laundry. Zane had hired two new cowboys—Rollie Simpkins and Daryl Barker—who were down on their luck. Under his direction, the cowhands spent their days moving the herd from the south pasture to the north, clearing debris from the river, checking the depth of the waterholes, and keeping a lookout for rustlers and Indians.

Zane spent his days looking after the horses. He replaced one of the corral gates, gave the barn a thorough cleaning, tossed out some old harness and rope he found in the tack room. He spent part of the day exercising the stallion and working with the chestnut mare, who was due to deliver a foal in March or April.

Kathleen often found herself standing at the kitchen window watching Zane. He moved with a kind of lithe grace, every movement sure, with no wasted motion. She especially liked to watch him work with the horses. He seemed to have a bond with each one. He had even won the trust of the black stallion. Watching Zane put the horse through its paces was like watching a ballet, she thought. Man and beast, moving in perfect rhythm. Of course, she was busy, too, and as the days went by, she was more and more grateful for Juanita's help. Washing the clothes and hanging them to dry went faster when there was someone to talk to while you worked.

In the evening, Kathleen usually sewed gowns for the baby while Zane familiarized himself with the ranch accounts. She was able to answer most of his questions, and while he couldn't sign checks on the ranch account, she could. But it was the baby who occupied her mind. What would their child look like? she wondered. Would it have Zane's black hair and coppery skin? Or take after her? Maybe a combination of the two?

Now, waiting for Zane to come in for dinner, she rested her hand on her belly. She knew Zane hoped for a son, but boy or girl, she didn't care, as long as it was born healthy. Doctor Joe had assured her that everything was fine. Still, childbirth was a scary thing. Whenever the women at church got together for quilting parties or sewing bees, the conversation inevitably led to babies. Some of the women had had difficult pregnancies. Darcy Evans had been home alone when her baby came. Years ago, her friend, Annie, had delivered a stillborn child.

Kathleen shook her morbid thoughts away when she heard the front door open.

"There's my girl," Zane said, striding into the living room. Reaching for her hand, he pulled her to her feet and into his arms. "How are you feeling?"

"I'm fine. I hope you're hungry. Juanita made fried chicken and rice for dinner."

"I'd rather taste you." Lowering his head, he kissed her, slow and easy, loving the way she always melted into his embrace, the way she pressed herself against him, the little sounds of pleasure she made deep in her throat as she kissed him back.

Lying in Zane's arms later that night, Kathleen was almost asleep when she felt the baby kick for the first time. Startled, she let out a gasp of surprise.

"What's wrong?" Zane asked. "Are you in pain?"

In a voice filled with wonder, she said, "I just felt the baby move."

"Does it hurt?"

"No." Grabbing his hand, she placed it on her belly.

"I don't feel anything." He started to lift his hand when he went suddenly still.

"Did you feel it?"

"Yeah," he murmured, his voice filled with the same wonder as hers. Propping himself on his elbow, he gazed down at her. And then he kissed her ever so tenderly. "I love you, Kathleen."

"I know."

"Taking me for granted, huh?"

"No, never. I love you, too."

Lying down again, Zane slipped his arm around her and drew her closer, wishing he could find the words to tell her how much she meant to him, but he couldn't get them past the lump in his throat.

Chapter Twenty-Eight

In the morning, Kathleen woke with a smile as she remembered how tenderly Zane had kissed her the night before, the sweet sound of his voice telling her he loved her. She pressed her hand to her belly, hoping to feel the baby move again, but to no avail. Maybe he slept days and kicked at night.

Still smiling, she slid out of bed, pulled on her robe, and went downstairs. She found Zane in the dining room, having a cup of coffee with Juanita.

"*Buenos diaz, pequeña,*" Juanita said, beaming at her. "*Senor* Zane was telling me you felt the baby move. Is exciting, no?"

"Very," Kathleen said, taking a seat at the table.

"I think a big breakfast is in order," Juanita decided. "After all, the baby is moving now. We must feed him more." She glanced from Kathleen to Zane. "What would you like?"

"Ham and eggs and fried potatoes," Zane said.

"*Pequeña?*"

"That sounds fine. *Gracias,* Juanita."

With a nod and a smile, Juanita hurried into the kitchen.

"Why didn't you wake me up?" Kathleen asked.

Zane shrugged. "I thought you needed the rest."

"You're a very thoughtful husband."

He grunted softly. He had no idea how a husband should behave, especially when his wife was pregnant. "What are you going to do today?"

"I'm not sure. What are you going to do?"

He shrugged. "I know what I'd like to do."

Kathleen smiled a knowing smile. "Oh?"

His gaze moved over her. "Can't you guess?"

"I'm pretty sure I can. I'll tell Juanita we'll finish up the new curtains for the parlor tomorrow."

After breakfast, Zane saddled his buckskin and Kathleen's palomino. Juanita had packed them a lunch and he stowed it in one of his saddlebags, then tied a blanket behind the cantle, and hung a canteen over the pommel.

When Kathleen was mounted, he checked the stirrups and the cinch before swinging onto the buckskin's back. He didn't know a lot about pregnant women. Hell, he wasn't even sure she should be riding.

Kathleen frowned when he just sat in the saddle, looking at her. "Did you change your mind?"

"I was just wondering, I mean, is it safe for you to ride in your condition?"

"I'm sure it's safe for another month or two."

"All right. We'll take it slow and easy."

But Kathleen had other ideas. She touched her heels to the palomino's sides and the mare broke into a gallop.

Muttering an oath, Zane lit out after her.

Kathleen let out a wordless cry of exhilaration as the palomino flew across the prairie. It was a beautiful day, the air cool with the hint of fall, the sky a brilliant shade of blue. She grinned as she glanced behind her. Lord, was there anything more beautiful than Zane on a horse, his long black hair tossed by the wind. How she loved him.

Knowing he was worried about her, she slowed to a trot and then a walk.

"Dammit, woman, what are you doing? You scared the crap out of me."

"I'm sorry. Truly. But I've been cooped up in the house for so long. Forgive me?"

"I should put you over my knee and paddle your behind."

Eyes flashing, she said, "I'd like to see you try it."

"Don't tempt me. Let's rest the horses here."

It was a lovely spot, a grassy meadow surrounded by cottonwood trees. A river gurgled a few yards away.

Zane dismounted then lifted Kathleen from the saddle and into his arms. He held her close for several moments, then swatted her behind.

And laughed when she stuck her tongue out at him.

He loosened the saddle cinches on the horses and turned them loose to graze. Grabbing the blanket, he spread it on the riverbank. "Feel like a swim?"

For answer, she removed her boots and began to undress.

He watched her, thinking she had never looked more beautiful than she did now, carrying his child.

"Mr. Two Shadows, I don't intend to swim alone."

"Sorry, I was admiring the view."

She blushed under his heated gaze, felt her body tremble with desire as he undressed. Lord have mercy, how she wanted him.

"Kathleen," he said, taking her into his arms, "is it all right for us to make love? It won't hurt the baby?"

"No. Juanita said it's okay until the last month or so, although I can't imagine you'll want me when I'm big and fat."

"I will always want you," he said as he lowered her onto the blanket. "Old and fat, gray and toothless, you will always be beautiful to me."

She laughed softly, until he covered her mouth with his, his hands boldly caressing her, until she was mindless with wanting him. She was more than ready when his body covered hers, filling her, making her complete.

They went for a swim after making love. Then, still naked, they ate the lunch Juanita had prepared.

"We should always have our meals like this," Zane said, grinning.

Kathleen stared at him as if he'd lost his mind. "I'm sure my mother would object."

"I doubt if your old man would be too happy, either."

"Or Juanita."

"What about you, Kathleen? Are you happy?"

"To be naked?"

"To be my wife."

She frowned at him. What was he thinking? They had just made love. She was carrying his child. "Of course I am. What's wrong?"

He took a deep breath and let it out in a long sigh. "Are you ever sorry you didn't marry Plotkin?"

She stared at him in disbelief. Sorry she hadn't married Oliver? Comparing the two men was like comparing a stallion to a gelding. "What brought that up?"

He shrugged one shoulder. "Forget it."

"Zane, I never loved him. I wouldn't have married him if he was the only available man in town. I love you. You must know that."

"I do," he said, looking a little sheepish. "I just want you to be happy"

"Well, I am, so stop worrying. I don't want anyone but you."

Feeling like a fool for letting an old insecurity rear its ugly head, he pulled her into his arms and buried his face in her hair. For a man who had never been in love before he had sure as hell fallen hard.

"Coming here was a good idea," Taggart said. "I'd forgotten there were some good things in the East."

"I'm glad. I was afraid you were sorry we came, but I didn't want to say anything."

"It's good for a man to spend a little time in civilization," he said with a grin. "Good not to worry about the weather. Good to smell something besides horses and cattle. But don't get me wrong," he added hastily, "I still love the West."

Helen grinned at him. "I think what you really enjoy is good whiskey and a steak at Delmonico's"

"I can't argue with that. But it's also nice to see my woman in silk and lace instead of cotton and denim."

"So many years wasted," Helen murmured. "I wish I could turn back the clock."

Taggart shook his head. "No use lamenting the past," he said, taking her in his arms. "I'm just grateful to be here, with you."

"I don't feel old enough to be a grandmother," she said.

"You don't look like one."

"I don't feel like one, either."

"Let's pretend we're newlyweds," he said, waggling his eyebrows, "and this is our honeymoon."

"You've changed," Helen said as he swung her into his arms. "You weren't this romantic when I married you."

"Being with you again makes me feel like a young stud."

"Well, be gentle," she said, wrapping her arms around his neck. "I'm not a young filly anymore."

Chapter Twenty-Nine

It was Saturday night and payday. With a whoop and a holler, the cowhands had all cleaned up and ridden into town, even Old Mort.

Juanita had gone home after dinner.

Humming softly, Kathleen sat in the living room hemming a blanket for the baby.

Zane stood in front of the fireplace, staring at the flames. After a moment, he turned away and began to pace the floor.

Frowning, Katheen set the blanket aside. "Is something wrong?"

He shook his head. "Just feeling restless, I guess. There's a storm coming."

"Oh?"

"Can't you smell it?"

With a shake of her head, she glanced out the front window. "The sky looks clear to me." The words had scarcely left her mouth when dark clouds scudded across the moon. A sharp crack of lightning made her jump. Seconds later, the heavens unleashed a deluge. "I guess you were right."

He'd gone to stand at the window. Rising, she went to his side, smiling faintly as his arm automatically went around her waist.

"I always loved a good storm," he remarked. "The wildness of it, the violence."

She shuddered as a shaft of lightning struck one of the trees in the yard. There was a burst of flame that was quickly extinguished by the downpour.

"I'm going down to the barn and check on the horses," Zane said.

"Do you think that's a good idea?"

"I won't be gone long." He gave her a quick hug, grabbed his hat and a jacket from the coat rack and ducked out the door.

Kathleen pulled the blanket from the back of the sofa, wrapped it around her, and went to stand on the porch. Eyes straining, she tried to see Zane, but he was lost in the darkness. A few moments later, she saw a flash of light in the barn as he lit a lantern.

She loved the rain, but she had always been a little afraid of the lightning. She bit down on her lower lip as it crackled across the heavens. She was about to go back inside when a rider appeared out of the darkness. "Dusty?" she called. "Is that you?"

He wheeled his horse toward her. "Trouble in town," he hollered. "Austin's dead."

With a tip of his head, he raced down to the barn.

Kathleen paced back and forth, troubled by his news, and worried that, storm or no storm, Zane would insist on going to Cross Creek. She took a deep breath when he came riding toward her.

"I've got to go into town," he said, shouting over the rain. "Dusty will stay here with you."

"What are you going to do?"

"Find out what the hell's going on. I'll be back as soon as I can."

Before she could protest, he was gone.

A short time later, Dusty knocked on the door.

"What happened?" she asked as she invited him in.

"I'd best stay out here. I'm soaking wet."

"Don't be silly. It's freezing out there. At least come inside out of the wind."

Removing his hat, he stepped into the entryway. "Me and Old Mort were having drinks at the bar," he said. "Virgil and Chet were playing poker with some of the Flying W cowhands. Austin and Boone were flirting with one of the dance hall girls when Big Jim Hobie came in. He rides for the Triple E. I don't know what Hobie said, but it was obvious he didn't like it when Austin put his arm around the girl. Next thing I knew, Austin and Hobie were staring each other down. Before I could say or do anything, they'd pulled leather. Austin drew first and Big Jim went down. Austin was holstering his weapon when another Triple E cowhand shot him in the back."

"That's murder!" Kathleen exclaimed.

"Damn right. All hell broke loose. Chet and Boone carried Austin down to the undertaker's and I lit out for home."

Oh, Lord, Kathleen thought. What was Zane walking into?

The rain had let up a little by the time Zane reached town. Most of the shops were closed. The sheriff's office was dark and likely to stay that way until the town fathers got together and hired a new sheriff, since no one had stepped forward to replace Karl Powers, who had died of the injury sustained in the bank robbery. Raucous laughter backed by a piano that was badly out of tune emanated from Sally's. While he watched, a chair exploded through one of the windows.

Dismounting, he tethered the buckskin, settled his holster on his hip, and pushed his way into the saloon. A hell of a fight was in progress. He watched a moment, then pulled his Colt and fired three shots into the air.

It had the desired effect.

The piano went silent.

The fighting stopped and all eyes swung in his direction. "I want everybody out of here except for the Triple E cowhands and the men who work for me. "

There was some grumbling from the men, but they filed out of the saloon.

Boone, Virgil, Chet, Simpkins, Barker and Old Mort moved to one side of the room. Six Triple E cowhands gathered at the end of the bar farthest from Zane. Ed stood at the other end, idly polishing a glass. His shotgun rested on the bar top.

Zane's gaze swept the room. "Somebody want to tell me what the hell's been going on here?"

"I'll tell you," the bartender said. "Two of your boys were flirting with my new girl. One of the Triple E hands took exception and the two men involved drew on each other. Your man, Austin, was a shade faster on the draw. That would have been the end of it if Glancy, there, hadn't shot Austin in the back. His only defense is that he's pretty liquored up."

"Hey, you in the black vest," Zane called. "Keep your hand away from your holster unless you want to lose it."

Startled, the cowboy raised both hands over his head.

"Boone, you and Chet haul Glancy down to the jail. Mort, you and the others go on home. Tell Kathleen I'm fine but I won't be home tonight."

There was some mumbling and empty threats from the remaining Triple E hands as Boone and Chet half-dragged the shooter out the door, but nobody made any sudden moves.

"I'll be staying at the jail tonight," Zane said. "If I see anybody poking around, I'll shoot first and ask questions later." His gaze moved over each of the Triple E cowboys before he backed toward the door and stepped outside. He stood there a moment, listening, but he didn't hear anybody coming after him.

Chet and Boone had Glancy locked up when he reached the jail. "You guys go on home. Tell Dusty to stay with Kathleen until morning."

"Don't you want one of us to stay here and side ya?" Chet asked.

"Thanks, but I need you fellas to go back to the ranch and look after things. You might want to stick close to home in case some of Edling's boys come sniffing around looking to get even."

"What'll we tell the missus?" Boone asked.

"Tell her I'll be home as soon as I can."

Nodding, the two men filed out of the room. Zane locked the door behind them, then looked in on his prisoner, who was sleeping it off.

Muttering an oath, he sank into the chair behind the desk. What the hell was he doing here? And why hadn't the town elected a new sheriff? Wishing he was home in bed in Kathleen's arms, he propped his feet on the desk, pulled his hat down low, and closed his eyes.

It was, he thought glumly, going to be a long night.

Kathleen thanked Boone for letting her know that Zane was spending the night in town, closed the door, and sank down on the sofa, her arms folded over her belly. He could have been killed, walking into a situation like that. One careless shot …

She drew in a deep, shuddering breath. He had once earned his living as a bounty hunter. He knew how to take care of himself. She told herself that over and over again as she curled up on the sofa. But the knowledge offered no comfort and no assurance.

She wept until the patter of the rain lulled her to sleep.

The sound of someone pounding on the jailhouse door roused Zane. He groaned as he sat up and stretched his back and shoulders. If he had to spend another night in the jail, he was sleeping on a cot in one of the empty cells.

He called, "Hold on, I'm coming," as he gained his feet and opened the door. He found half-a-dozen of the town's businessmen waiting on the boardwalk. "What do you want?"

Franklin Grant, owner of the general store said, "It's obvious our town needs a sheriff. The town council got together early this morning and decided you're the best man for the job."

Zane snorted. "Are you serious?"

Six heads nodded in unison.

"You're the only one with any experience," Ed, the bartender said, stepping forward.

"Yeah, as a bounty hunter."

"Well, that's only one step away from a lawman," Paddy Murphy said.

"And nobody else wants the job," Jensen, the hotel owner added.

"What makes you think I want it?" Zane asked dryly.

Ed clapped him on the shoulder. "Think of it as doing your civic duty."

Zane shook his head. "You do know I'm wanted for murder in Sagebrush Flats, don't you?"

"We know," Oliver Plotkin said. "But we aren't forgetting how you stopped a bank robbery and saved the town's money."

Zane stared at Plotkin, unable to believe the man was speaking in his behalf.

"It's unanimous," the attorney, J.J. Lee said. "Every businessman in town is behind you, so what do you say?"

"I'll have to talk it over with Kathleen."

"And if she approves?" Ed asked.

Zane huffed a sigh. "I guess you've got yourself a sheriff."

The sound of Juanita singing in the kitchen woke Kathleen. Feeling as though she hadn't slept a wink, she sat up on the sofa, where she'd spent the night. What time was it? When was Zane coming home? All she knew was what Dusty and Boone had told her—There had been trouble at the saloon, Austin had been killed, and Zane was spending the night at the jail and would be home as soon as he could. A glance at the grandfather clock in the corner told her it was nine o'clock.

She sprang to her feet at the sound of footsteps on the porch and ran to open the door.

"Zane! I've been so worried about you!" Her gaze ran over him from head to foot. "Are you all right?"

"Yeah." Lifting his head, he sniffed the air. "Smells like bacon. Let's eat. I'm starved."

"What happened last night?" she asked, following him into the dining room. She smiled her thanks as Juanita put their breakfast on the table. "Please, join us," Kathleen said.

Juanita went into the kitchen and returned with her own plate.

"So?" Kathleen urged.

Zane shrugged. "There was some trouble in the saloon over a girl. Both men were a little drunk and they drew on each other. Austin was one of them. He drew first. When he turned away, one of the Triple E cowhands shot him in the back. And I put his killer in jail."

"You don't have the authority to do that, do you?" Kathleen exclaimed.

He shrugged one shoulder. "Nobody objected."

"Well, thank God you weren't hurt."

"I'll go into town later and see about a casket for Austin." Kathleen nodded.

"I'll have to hire someone to take his place, and see about a burial. Maybe you should write your old man and let him know what happened."

"I will."

"Oh. There's one more thing," Zane said. "I've been sworn in as the new sheriff."

Chapter Thirty

Kathleen wasn't sure how she felt about Zane being a lawman. For one thing, it meant he would be gone most of the day and probably some nights, too, at least until he found a deputy. Fortunately, Dusty was a reliable foreman. He had been with the ranch for years and knew almost as much about running the place as did her father. Zane told Dusty to see about hiring another cowhand or two. And … she blinked back the tears stinging her eyes. She had been so emotional lately. Annie had come to visit her a few days earlier and assured her it was the pregnancy and it would pass. This morning, Juanita had also assured her it was perfectly normal.

She forced a smile as Zane entered the kitchen a few minutes later. It was his first day as sheriff. He looked mighty fine, she thought, as she ran her fingers over the badge pinned to his black leather vest.

"Are you sure you're okay with this?" he asked, drawing her into his arms.

"Not really, but the town needs you," she replied. "Just remember, I need you, too."

"I'll look for a deputy," he promised. "Maybe two. And I'll ask around and see if I can find us a couple of cowhands. In the meantime, you take it easy, you hear?"

She nodded. "I'll miss you."

"I'll miss you, too. If you need anything, send Old Mort after me. I'll try to get home tonight, even if it's just for an hour or two."

Kathleen frowned at him. "Who's watching the prisoner now?"

"Paddy Murphy. I asked him to stay so I could come home and kiss my wife."

"You will be careful, won't you? Promise me."

"I'm always careful." He kissed her then, a long, slow kiss that made her toes curl. "I love you, darlin'."

"Love you, too."

Muttering, "Damn," he gave her one more kiss, then strode out of the house before his desire to carry her back to bed overcame his sense of duty.

"It's damn glad to see you, I am," Paddy Murphy said when Zane entered the jail later that morning. "I'm not cut out for this."

"Thanks for filling in for me. Can you think of anybody in town who might want the job of deputy?"

Murphy shook his head. "No, but I'll ask around. Ed might know somebody."

"Thanks. Any chance I could count on you to stay here tonight?"

"I don't know …"

"How about for a few hours?"

"I reckon," Murphy said, looking put upon. "What time do you need me?"

"Six?"

"I'll see you then. Glancy had breakfast an hour ago."

"Thanks."

Murphy turned to leave, then paused. "Say, Harry Cosgrove has a grown son who just mustered out of the cavalry. Sure and he might be lookin' for work."

"Obliged."

With a nod and a wave, Murphy sauntered out the door.

Zane removed his hat and hung it on the rack. His prisoner was asleep. Zane stood there a moment, just looking around. The jail was a square brick building with windows on either side of the door. A wood stove stood in one corner. A number of flyers were tacked to a cork board on the wall across from the battered desk.

With nothing else to do, he perused them—most of the wanteds were for robbery and murder, with rewards ranging from two hundred dollars to a thousand.

He was going through the desk drawers when the door opened and a tall man with short brown hair and a faint scar down one cheek strode into the room. The Colt on his left hip looked at home there.

"Can I help you?" Zane asked.

"Mr. Murphy told me you were looking for a deputy. He said I should stop by."

"And you'd be?"

"Frank Cosgrove."

Zane nodded. "Murphy said you were in the cavalry."

"Five years. That was enough for me and I didn't re-enlist."

"Can you use that hogleg?"

Cosgrove nodded.

"All right. I'll give you a try," Zane decided. "I'll need you here nights when there's a prisoner. Starting tonight.

Otherwise, just as back-up if trouble starts. Think you can handle it?"

"I think so."

Zane opened one of the desk drawers and pulled out a deputy's badge. "I'm pretty sure there's an oath of some kind but I have no idea what it is." He chuckled softly. "And no idea what the pay is, for you or for me." Handing Cosgrove the badge, he said, "Consider yourself sworn in. Why don't you look around while I go talk to the town council?"

"Yessir."

Zane grinned. Not too many men had ever called him 'sir.' "I won't be gone long."

Frank Cosgrove turned out to be a good choice. He was quiet, efficient, and he turned out to be a hell of a shot. He didn't mind spending nights in the jail.

The circuit judge rode into town two days later. The trial started at ten the following morning.

Zane swore under his breath when he saw Mark Edling sitting in the front row backed by a half-dozen of the Triple E cowhands. There was going to be trouble, sure as hell, he thought, as one witness after another testified that they had seen Glancy kill Austin in cold blood.

The jury deliberated for twenty minutes.

The verdict was guilty. The sentence was death by hanging to be carried out the next morning.

Zane and Cosgrove escorted Glancy back to the jail. Zane had deputized two other men to stay at the jail with Cosgrove.

"I won't be gone long," Zane told Cosgrove, "but I need to go home, get cleaned up, and see my wife. I'll be back no later than four or five."

Frank Cosgrove patted the Colt at his side, checked the ammo in the rifle he held loosely at his side. "You go along," he said. "We'll be all right."

"I don't expect any trouble until after dark," Zane said. "You and the others stay inside until I get back. Be sure to lock up after me. And don't open the door for anybody but me."

Kathleen came running out to meet him as soon as he dismounted. Pulling her into his arms, he held her tight, breathing in the scent of her hair, reveling in the press of her body against his. "How's the baby?"

"He's fine. We miss you."

"I miss you, too." He put his arm around her waist and they went into the house. "I hired a couple of deputies."

"Does that mean you'll be home more now?"

"Yeah. The trial was today. They're hanging Glancy tomorrow morning. Once that's done, things should quiet down."

Kathleen grimaced. She knew a lot of people who loved to watch a hanging. She had never been one of them. "Will you be home nights after … after tomorrow?"

"I should be. I might have to stay late on Saturday nights, though. And I have to go back to town in a few hours."

"You're expecting trouble, aren't you?"

"I'm afraid so. Edling and some of his men are in town. They weren't happy with the verdict."

"You don't think they'll try to break Glancy out of jail, do you?"

"I'm sure they will. Either that, or they'll try to stop the hanging tomorrow." He brushed a kiss across her lips.

"Let's not worry about that now. I need a bath and something to eat. Want to wash my back?"

"You know I do." She forced a grin, but deep inside, she trembled with fear, sorely afraid that there would be gunplay and he would be hurt. Or worse.

Washing Zane's back led to kissing, which led to touching, which led to a lot of water on the floor when he stepped out of the tub, lifted her into his arms and carried her to bed.

"I love making love to you," he murmured, his voice thick with desire as he caressed her out of her clothes, his hands sliding seductively over her body, arousing her, pleasing her, until she cried his name, begging him to take her.

Only later, wrapped in his arms, did she remember, with a blush, that Juanita was downstairs.

Kathleen sat propped up in bed, the sheet drawn over her, while she watched Zane dress. "I wish you didn't have to go back tonight."

"Me, too." He buckled on his gunbelt, settled it on his hip with practiced ease. "Listen," he said, sitting on the edge of the mattress, "don't worry, all right? I've got three men backing me up. I'll be fine. I used to hunt men for a living, remember?"

"I know." She forced a smile she was far from feeling. "Be careful."

"Always." He kissed her again, tenderly, whispered that he loved her, and left the room.

She waited until she was sure he was out of the house before she let the tears fall.

Riding into Cross Creek, Zane sensed the tension that gripped the town. From talking with Ed, he'd learned that there had never been a hanging within the town limits. In days past, the ranchers had dealt with rustlers. Stealing a man's horse or his cattle was a hanging offense and ranchers had taken the law into their own hands. Justice had been swift and final. But times had changed, he thought with a rueful grin. Law and order had come to Cross Creek.

He reined the buckskin to a halt in front of the jail, pulled his rifle from the scabbard, and knocked on the door.

"Who is it?"

"It's me, Cosgrove. Open up."

The door opened slowly until Cosgrove saw Zane and then he stepped back.

"Any trouble?" Zane asked.

"No. Just Glancy mouthing off, saying we'd be dead before he was."

Zane snorted. "Anybody comes busting through that door, Glancy will be the first one to go down. I'll see to that." He tossed his hat on the rack, nodded at the two men he'd hired as temporary deputies. He had seen them around town, but didn't really know them. The younger one, Charlie Richards, was short and thick-set, with a wide face and a shock of wheat-colored hair. The other man, Bob Wade, was older. Of medium-height, he was built solid. He looked like a hard man, one who wouldn't hesitate to shoot first and ask questions later. The kind of man you wanted at your back.

"I'm going out to walk around the town. Wade, why don't you come with me?"

They strolled in silence for a time, pausing now and then to peer into the shadows.

Zane pushed his hat back on his head. "Mind if I ask you something?"

Wade shrugged.

"You wanted by the law?"

Without hesitation, Wade said, "Not in Wyoming."

"What are you wanted for?"

"I robbed a bank in Colorado a few years back," Wade admitted with a shrug. "I was flat broke and my wife was dying. Lots of medical bills I couldn't pay. You gonna fire me?"

"Hell, no."

"Mind if I ask you something?" Wade asked with a wry grin.

"As long as you don't mind if I don't answer."

"What gave me away?"

"Just a feeling," Zane said, with a grin. "I've been a wanted man myself. Let's go check the saloon."

The usual crowd was inside. Paddy Murphy, J.J. Lee, and Abel Jensen were playing poker along with a man Zane didn't recognize. A dozen or so cowboys were gathered at the bar. The upcoming hanging was the main topic of conversation. Four Triple E riders were huddled around a table in the back, a bottle of whiskey between them.

Wade jerked his chin in their direction. "Priming themselves for trouble, or I miss my guess."

"Yeah. Let's go."

They made a slow circuit of the rest of the town before returning to the jail.

It was, Zane thought, going to be a tense night. Sleep was out of the question. Cosgrove and the two deputies sacked out in the empty cells. Zane catnapped in the chair behind the desk, coming awake at the slightest sound—footsteps on the boardwalk outside, the howl of a cat, the screech of an owl. A bad omen, he thought. Some of his people believed that the cry of an owl presaged death.

He shook the thought away. For the first time in his life, he had something worth living for.

Dawn came slowly. Zane stirred at the sound of the town coming awake—the crowing of a rooster, the rattle of an early stagecoach arriving, the sound of someone hammering on the jailhouse door.

Rising, he lifted the bar, opened the door, and peered cautiously outside. At first, he didn't see anything, and then he saw the paper nailed to the door. The message was short: *Give us Glancy or we'll take him.*

Well, shit, he thought, as he ripped the paper from the door and crumpled it in his hand. If they wanted a fight, they'd get one.

At 9:50, Zane shackled Glancy's hands behind his back and they headed for the make-shift gallows that had been quickly erected behind the courthouse. Zane had a shotgun in his hands, aimed at Glancy's back. Cosgrove, Wade, and Richards flanked him. To his surprise, the bartender, armed with the Greener he kept behind the bar, fell into step with them. And as they made their way down the street, other men joined the group. Zane grinned when Oliver Plotkin, looking a little pale but carrying a .44 Colt, came out of the bank and fell in behind them.

A dozen Triple E cowboys were waiting at the foot of the gallows. They exchanged worried looks when they saw the number of armed men flanking Zane and his prisoner.

Zane halted near the steps and his men fanned out beside him. "If there's any gunplay, Glancy will be the first one I kill," he said, his voice like ice over steel. "And then I'll come after the rest of you."

There were some shouted threats, some nasty references to his mother, some name-calling, but none of the Triple E cowhands made a move toward their holsters.

Zane marched Glancy up the stairs, his shotgun leveled at the prisoner's back every step of the way. He shook his head when he saw a number of women and kids gathered around. He had never understood the fascination some people had for hangings. It was a bad way to go. The Indians believed a man's soul was forever trapped inside his body when he was hanged.

The prisoner's face went fish-belly white when he saw the noose.

"Any last words?" Zane asked.

Glancy shook his head. His legs began to shake when the hangman put the hood over his head. He let out a harsh sob as the noose was snugged tight.

The Triple E cowboys fell silent.

The crowd held its breath.

Zane muttered an oath as the hangman sprang the trap. Thankfully, the fall broke Glancy's neck. Some condemned men weren't so lucky and they slowly strangled to death. He'd seen one instance where a couple of onlookers had grabbed hold of the prisoner's legs and given a hard jerk to break his neck and end his helpless struggles.

"It's over," Zane said, his gaze raking the crowd. "Go home."

Kathleen was waiting for him when he returned to the ranch. One look at her tear-stained face, and he took her in his arms. "Hey, there wasn't any trouble," he said, giving her a hug. "You wasted all those tears."

"Don't tease me, Zane. I've been worried to death."

"I know. I'm sorry, darlin'."

"So, what happened?"

"The Triple E hands made some threats, and things might not have turned out so well if a number of the men in town hadn't backed me up. Even Plotkin sided us."

Kathleen blinked at him. "Oliver?" She couldn't imagine her friend doing any such thing.

"Yeah. He's got a lot of nerve for a banker. I might have misjudged him."

Kathleen nodded. "Maybe I did, too."

"Well, if you've changed your mind, it's too late. You're mine now."

"I haven't changed my mind, silly. It's you I love, now and always."

Taking her hand, he headed for the kitchen. "I need a cup of coffee and something to eat," he said. "And then I need to feel my woman's arms around."

"Well, you've come to the right place, sheriff," she said with a saucy grin. "I think I can satisfy all of your desires."

"Honey," he drawled. "I know you can."

In the days that followed, Zane discovered that he rather liked being a lawman. Other than arresting a drunk or two on Saturday night, there wasn't a lot of crime in Cross Creek.

If there were no prisoners in the jail, he rode into town for a few hours every day after breakfast, stayed until four or five and headed home, leaving Frank Cosgrove in charge.

It was an arrangement that suited Zane perfectly, giving him time to do a little work around the ranch, check on the cowboys, and spend time with Kathleen.

He generally stayed in town late on Saturday night, just in case there was trouble.

And to please Kathleen, he took her to church on Sunday.

He was, he thought with a rueful grin, turning into a solid citizen.

As time went on, Kathleen's worry about Zane being the sheriff lessened though it never went away. She didn't worry much during the week, but all her fears resurfaced on Saturday nights when the cowboys got paid and went into town to kick up their heels.

But today was Sunday and they were getting ready for church. She smiled as Zane slipped on his jacket. Was there ever a more handsome man? She never failed to notice the way female heads turned whenever they went into town.

"You ready, Mrs. Two Shadows?" he asked as he settled his hat on his head.

"Yes, indeed, Mr. Two Shadows."

"Are you sure we need to go to church today?" he asked. "You look as pretty as a Christmas present waiting to be opened."

She smiled at the compliment even as she shook her head. "I'm afraid you'll have to wait a little while to open it."

With an exaggerated sigh of resignation, he opened the door.

He hated waiting.

The church was full when they arrived. Kathleen nodded at Annie and Susannah and some of the other ladies she knew as she and Zane slipped into one of the back pews.

Zane took her hand as the choir began to sing. There was little similarity between the Cheyenne belief in Heaven and that of the white man. The Cheyenne believed *Ma'heo'o* created all life, both physical and spiritual, and that included all plant and animal life. They believed the world consisted of seven levels. Like their allies the Lakota, the Cheyenne participated in the Sun Dance, which was the most sacred event of the year.

He didn't find much comfort in the preacher's sermon, which was on the Ten Commandments, especially the sixth one, Thou shalt not kill. Heaven knew he had violated that one numerous times, though mostly in self-defense.

After church, Zane lingered on the edge of the crowd while Kathleen visited with her friends. A few of the men nodded in his direction, a couple of the townspeople came up to congratulate him for keeping the peace during the hanging.

Kathleen was smiling when she sought him out. "Are you ready to go home?"

"Yes, ma'am," he assured her with a wink. "And I'm looking forward to opening that present."

Chapter Thirty-One

Helen leaned over her husband's shoulder as he read Kathleen's letter. "Sheriff!" she exclaimed. "Zane is the new sheriff?"

Taggart swore under his breath. "What the hell was the town thinking, electing a wanted man?"

Helen shrugged. "It says right there that no one else wanted the job."

"It also says we've lost another cowboy." Taggart swore again. "Pack your bags. I think we'd better go home." Seeing the look on her face, he said, "What?"

"Can't we wait a few more days?"

"Why?"

"We have tickets to the opera at the Bowery Theater next Saturday night, and the McAlister's are having a grand party afterward. I bought a new dress …"

Muttering under his breath, he said, "Fine, we'll go to the theater, but the day after that, by damn, we're going home."

Chapter Thirty-Two

Kathleen groaned as she levered out of the easy chair in the living room. She felt as big as the chestnut mare and wondered briefly if horses experienced depression during their pregnancy and if they ever had cravings in the middle of the night.

She didn't know what she would do without Juanita, who had pretty much taken over all the household chores, so that all Kathleen had to do was tidy her room and make the bed. Zane had bought a bassinet from the cabinetmaker in town and she had sewn a blanket for it. She often sat in the rocker in their room and imagined their child sleeping inside. Somehow, it made the baby seem even more real. Being a mother seemed a daunting task. As an only child, she had never spent much time around babies, never looked after one. What if she dropped it? Or had no milk? What about colic? And croup?

She thrust her worries aside when she heard the front door open. Zane was home.

Smiling, she lumbered down the stairs and into his arms.

"I missed you, too," he said, holding her close.

"Have you had dinner?" she asked.

"Yeah. I could use a cup of coffee, though. Oh," he said, reaching into his pocket, "you got letter from your parents."

She opened it on the way into the kitchen. "They're coming home," she said.

"Yeah? When?"

Kathleen glanced at the date on the letter. "This was written a couple of weeks ago."

Zane grunted softly. They could be back any day now. "Is that all it says?"

"My father felt they should come home, now that you've got a job in town." Laying the letter aside, she struck a match to light the stove and filled the coffee pot with water.

Muttering under his breath, Zane sank into one of the kitchen chairs. He wasn't looking forward to her father's return. "I've been thinking," he said, choosing his words with care. "There's a furnished house for rent in town. It's a nice place. What would you think about moving there after your parents get back?"

Kathleen stared at him. "You want to move to town?"

Catching her hand, he drew her down on his lap. "You know your father and I don't get along. Likely we never will. Besides, a married couple should have a place of their own." He stroked his fingertips down her cheek. "If we lived in town, I could come home for lunch and I wouldn't have to travel back and forth."

She nodded, but she didn't look convinced.

"It's up to you," he said. "Just promise me you'll think about it."

She thought of little else in the next few days. He was right, it would be nice if he could come home for lunch. And she would be able to spend more time with him if he didn't have to travel back and forth from the ranch to town.

But leave the ranch? She bit down on her lower lip. She loved it here. Of course, it would be nice to be closer to Annie and Susannah. And closer to the doctor when the baby came. What would her parents think? Would they be glad to get Zane out of the house? She frowned. Maybe they'd like to be alone. And maybe it would be good for her. As long as she lived at home, she would always feel like their little girl …

Three days later, she still hadn't made up her mind.

Needing some fresh air to clear her head, she walked down to the barn to gather the eggs.

Her Appy whinnied as she approached. Kathleen grinned as she reached into her apron pocket. "Here you go, girl," she said, offering an apple to the mare. "I have one for you, too," she told the chestnut. Producing two more apples, she fed them to the chestnut mare and the stallion.

It was such a lovely day, she hated to see them locked up. Finding a lead rope, she led her Appy into the large corral and turned her loose, then went back for the chestnut mare.

She bit down on her lower lip as she regarded the black. The stallion was big and a little wild. She stood there for several minutes, undecided, until the stud whinnied piteously.

With a huff of resignation, she reached for the bridle outside the horse's stall, slipped it over his head, and attached the lead tope. She was about to open the stall door when Zane yelled, "Don't!"

Startled, she dropped the lead rope and stumbled backward, only to trip over a bale of hay and land on her rump. "What's the matter with you?" she exclaimed as he slid from the back of the buckskin and rushed toward her.

"Damn, girl," he said, reaching for her hands and pulling her to her feet. "What were you thinking?"

"I was just going to put him in one of the corrals. He hasn't had any real exercise for a few days."

"That damn stud is only half-broke. If he took it into his head to take off, you'd never be able to stop him."

Looking properly chastised, she murmured, "I didn't think of that. What are you doing home, anyway?"

He shrugged. "I'm not sure. I was making the rounds when something told me to head for home. Must have been my mother's spirit warning me you were in danger."

Kathleen lifted a skeptical brow.

"She was a medicine woman, you know. Able to talk to the spirits." Leading Kathleen out of harm's way, he unlatched the stable door and led the stallion into the small corral. Once freed, the horse began to run and buck.

Kathleen stared at the stallion, his coat blue-black in the sunlight. He was a magnificent animal, well-muscled, powerful. She looked at Zane, who was also well-muscled and powerful, and felt a sudden ache to be in his arms. "Are you home for the day?" she asked, a twinkle in her eyes.

"Yeah." When he caught her staring at him, a slow smile spread over his face. "Was there something you wanted me to do?"

She answered him with a smile of her own as she took his hand in hers. There was no need for further questions as they walked back to the house.

Upstairs, they undressed each other and climbed into bed.

"I don't want to hurt you," Zane said as his hands drifted over her breasts and belly. "Are you sure this is all right?"

"Yes."

Lying face-to-face, they traded kisses and caresses until just touching wasn't enough. Still afraid of hurting her,

Zane slid underneath her, his arms holding her tight as she moved against him, the tension building, growing, until pleasure exploded between them and she sagged against him, spent and satisfied, and more in love than ever.

Her parents arrived home in the middle of a thunderstorm, laden with luggage and boxes. Helen hugged Kathleen, then insisted she sit down and open the presents they had brought.

Her mother had never been one to skimp and Kathleen was overwhelmed by the dozens of clothes, gowns, and blankets her mother had bought for the baby.

"The crib should be here in a week or so," Helen said. "Here, this one is for you."

Kathleen lifted the lid on a large box and found half-a-dozen dresses with expanded waistbands and three voluminous nightgowns.

Zane stood beside the fireplace, arms folded over his chest.

Taggart sat in his favorite easy chair, a faint smile twitching his lips as he watched his wife and daughter *ooh* and *ahh* over tiny baby things. Clearing his throat, Taggart's gaze moved to Zane. "I heard you lost another man."

Zane nodded. "And hired two to take his place."

Taggart grunted. "Any trouble with the Triple E?"

"No."

"So, I hear you're the new lawman."

"That's right."

Taggart shook his head. "Kind of like hiring a wolf to protect the flock, ain't it?"

A muscle worked in Zane's jaw as he swallowed his anger.

Kathleen glanced from her father to her husband and back again as the tension in the room went up a notch. Rising, she said, "I'm a little tired. I think I'll go to bed. Zane, are you coming?"

Nodding, he followed her up the stairs.

"This is never going to work," he said after she closed the door. "Your mother's not bad, but your old man ..." Zane shook his head. "He's never going to trust me. Or forgive me for marrying you."

Not knowing what to say, Kathleen put her arms around him and rested her cheek on his chest. "Maybe moving into town is a good idea," she said quietly.

"Are you sure?"

When she nodded, he wrapped his arms around her. 'I love you. You know that, don't you?"

"I know."

Cupping her face in his palms, he kissed her lightly, tenderly.

"Can I ask one favor?"

"Anything," he said.

"Would it be all right if my mother came and stayed with us for a few days after the baby's born?"

"Sure, darlin'." Holding her close, feeling their child moving within her, he would have promised her anything.

In the next few days, Zane and Taggart managed to keep out of each other's way. Zane left for town early and came home late. He'd spoken with Nephi Landon, the man who owned the rental. At first, it had been touch and go.

"I don't have much love for Injuns," the man said. "But, seeing as how you're the sheriff, and married to Miz Taggart, I reckon you'll be all right."

"Much obliged," Zane said dryly.

Langdon grinned a crooked grin. "I reckon you can move in on the first."

"Fine."

"I'll be needin' the first month's rent when you move in."

Zane nodded. "Nice doing business with you."

Helen Taggart stared at her daughter across the breakfast table. Zane had already left for work. Tobias had gone down to discuss the day's work with the cowhands. "What do you mean, you're moving into town?"

Kathleen took a deep breath. She had put off telling her mother as long as she could. "You know as well as I do that Zane and Dad don't get along at all. He … we thought it would be best for all of us if we moved out."

"Well, I disagree! I've only been home a short time, and now you want to move into town? I forbid it." Seeing the stubborn look in Kathleen's eyes, Helen softened her tone. Reaching for her daughter's hand, she said, "At least wait until the baby is born. Let me share this time with you."

Kathleen worried her lower lip between her teeth.

Giving Kathleen's hand a squeeze, Helen said, "I'll speak to your father."

What do you mean, you've changed your mind?" Zane asked as they got ready for bed later that night. "I thought we'd agreed moving was the right thing to do."

"We did. I do, but I just couldn't tell my mother no."

"Dammit."

"She said she'd talk to my father and ask him to stop being so critical."

Zane snorted.

"Please, Zane? The baby will be here in a few months. Can't we stay until then?"

Mouth set in a grim line, he nodded. Giving Kathleen her way was almost worth it, he decided, as she threw her arms around his neck and kissed him, her hot, pink tongue sweeping over his lower lip before delving inside.

With a low groan, he swung her into his arms and carried her to bed, all his qualms about staying forgotten as she poured her love over him.

Zane blew out a sigh of relief as he rode into town a few days later. He didn't know which was worse, living with Taggart's dislike or putting up with his efforts to be congenial. He thought he preferred the old man's gruffness to his fake joviality. Still, it kept peace in the family and made the women happy.

Kathleen seemed to grow more beautiful with each passing day. There was a sparkle in her eyes when she talked about the baby, a kind of glow about her as she sat beside the fireplace knitting baby booties or tiny bonnets. Day by day, the reality of impending fatherhood grew stronger and, he had to admit, more worrisome. The only father figure in his life had been a drunk who beat his wife and son. And while he wasn't afraid that he'd haul off and slug Kathleen, the fear that such behavior might be in his blood bothered the hell out of him.

For all the animosity between himself and Taggart, the old man was a good father zand, as far as Zane could tell, a good husband, as well. Whatever had driven Helen to leave the ranch, it hadn't been her husband. And Kathleen loved the old man.

Shit. He had never made any secret of his past, he mused. Kathleen had known what she was getting when she married him. So, he wasn't a well-bred gentleman like Oliver Plotkin. Zane grinned. Even knowing about his past, she had still chosen him.

He was smiling when he reined up in front of the jail. Dismounting, he tossed the buckskin's reins over the hitch rack, settled his holster on his hip, and stepped up on the boardwalk.

He was reaching for the latch when he felt a burning pain slice across his left arm, followed by the sound of a gunshot. Instinct took over. Without conscious thought, he turned as he drew his Colt, located the man who had fired at him, and pulled the trigger.

The bullet caught the man in the chest. He pitched forward, convulsed once, and lay still.

The sound of gunshots drew a half-dozen men, including Cosgrove. "What the hell happened?" the deputy asked.

Zane jerked his chin toward the dead man. "He took a shot at me."

"That's Cleve Ashby, one of the Triple E cowboys," Cosgrove said, kneeling beside the body. "He was one of the men at the hanging."

Zane muttered an oath, wondering if the whole outfit was going to come gunning for him. "Cosgrove, go get the coroner. I'll be at the doc's office if anybody needs me."

The doctor grunted as he examined Zane's wound. "You're lucky the bullet just grazed your arm, but you're going to need a few stitches," he said as he washed away the blood. "Didn't hit anything vital. You'll be sore for a week or so I reckon. Don't get the wound wet or lift anything heavy with that arm."

Zane nodded, his jaw clenched as the doctor put five stitches in his arm, then smeared some kind of smelly ointment over the injury and bound it up.

"That'll be two dollars," Doctor Joe said. "You can pay my wife on the way out."

"I can handle things here if you want to go home," Cosgrove said when Zane returned to the jail.

"I'm all right." After hanging his hat on the rack, Zane tossed his bloody shirt in the trash can, then pulled his extra shirt out of the bottom drawer of the desk. Slipping it on, he sank into the chair behind the desk. "Do you think Ashby was acting on his own? Or did Edling send him?"

"Hard to say. Ashby's been with the Triple E a long time. I guess he took Glancy's hanging pretty hard."

Zane grunted. "You think the rest will come in one by one?"

"Better than all at once," Cosgrove remarked.

Zane sat there, staring into the distance for a few minutes, then rose abruptly and reached for his hat.

"Where are you going?" Cosgrove asked.

"Out to the Triple E."

Cosgrove stared at him, wide-eyed. "Alone? Do you think that's a good idea? I mean, hell, I saw two of the Triple E cowboys ride out of town. No doubt Edling knows all about the shootin' by now."

Zane paused. Once, he would have ridden out alone without a second thought. But he was about to be a father.

Muttering, an oath, he jammed his hat on his hat. "Grab a couple of rifles and find Richards. I'll go round up Wade. One way or another, I intend to settle this once and for all."

Mark Edling's ranch looked to be about the size of the Taggart spread. According to Cosgrove, Edling had been a widower for the last five years and it was easy to see the lack of a woman's touch. It was there, in the little things. Unlike Taggart's place, no flowers grew in front of the house. The paint was fading, the curtains in the front window looked limp and unwashed. A hound dog barked at them when they pulled up in front of the place. Cosgrove. Richards, and Wade fanned out behind him. Zane didn't dismount.

A few minutes later, the screen door banged open and Mark Edling stepped out onto the porch, a rifle held loosely at his side. He was a big, raw-boned man, with shaggy black hair going gray, bushy brows, and deep frown lines.

"You've got a helluva nerve coming here after killing two of my men," he growled.

"One of them shot a man in the back right in front of me," Zane retorted. "The second one took a shot at me. What was I supposed to do?"

"If you've come looking for sympathy or an apology, forget it."

Zane shifted in the saddle. "I've come to warn you. The next time one of your hands take a pot shot at me or anybody else in town, I'll be back. And it won't be to talk. I'll drop you where you stand. You got that?"

Edling stared at him defiantly, but Zane didn't miss the fear in his eyes, or the tremor in his voice when he said, "Get the hell off my land."

"Remember what I said." Keeping his gaze on Edling's face, Zane backed away until he reached the gate, then he reined the buckskin around and lit out for home. Cosgrove, Richards, and Wade trailed after him.

Chapter Thirty-Three

Kathleen let out a startled cry when Zane rode into the yard. Dropping the skirt she'd been mending on the porch, she ran down the stairs, her eyes wide. "You've been hurt!"

"I'm fine," he said as he swung out of the saddle.

"What happened?"

"One of Edling's men took a shot at me earlier today. Bullet grazed my arm. Nothing to worry about."

"Nothing. To. Worry. About," she repeated. "A man shot at you and you tell me not to worry."

"Hey," he said, wrapping his uninjured arm around her. "It goes with the job."

"Maybe you should quit and go back to ranching."

"I don't think so," he muttered as they climbed the porch steps. To his surprise, he rather liked being on the right side of the law. It wasn't as profitable as bounty hunting, but at least it allowed him to stay in one place. And the pay wasn't half bad. "Where's your father?"

"He went into town to pick up the mail and a sack of sweet feed."

"And your mother?"

"She's making bread with Juanita. The first loaf just came out of the oven."

The scent of freshly baked bread reached his nostrils as soon as he stepped into the house. "How about bringing me a slice? And a cup of coffee?"

"All right. You sit down and rest."

With a nod, he dropped into one of the easy chairs and closed his eyes. In spite of assuring Kathleen that he was fine, his arm throbbed like a Cheyenne war drum.

The women of the house fussed over him the rest of the afternoon. Even Helen seemed genuinely concerned. Zane couldn't remember a time when he'd received so much attention. Rather than fight it, he sat back and enjoyed it.

It was nearing dinnertime when Taggart stormed into the house. Standing in front of Zane, his feet planted wide, he demanded, "What the hell's going on? All anyone in town could talk about was how you killed one of the Triple E cowhands." He frowned when he saw the bandage wrapped around Zane's arm. "Nobody said you'd been hurt."

"It's nothing."

Taggart grunted. "What are you trying to do, start a war with Edling? You've been responsible for the deaths of two of his men."

"I rode out today and had a talk with Edling. I don't think he'll be starting more trouble any time soon."

Brow furrowed, Taggart dropped down on the sofa. "What makes you say that?"

"I told him if anybody else came gunning for me, he'd be the one to pay for it. Glancy shot a man in the back while I was watching. That wasn't my fault. All I did was arrest him. A jury found him guilty. A judge declared his sentence. As for Ashby, he took a shot at me and I fired back. My aim was better."

Taggart regarded him for several moments, then a slow smile spread across his face. "I guess maybe hiring you was the right thing to do. You know, we'd had some trouble with Edling before you came along. I knew he was stealing some of our cattle, but we could never prove it or catch him at it. All that stopped once you started working for us." Slapping his hands on his thighs, he stood. "I need to wash up for dinner."

Zane stared after the old man as he walked briskly out of the room. What in holy hell had just happened?

He was still wondering when the family gathered at the table for dinner that night. It was the most amiable meal he had ever spent with Kathleen's parents, and although Zane didn't have much to say, they included him in the conversation, most of which was about Kathleen's pregnancy. The baby was due in a few weeks and Kathleen and her mother were mulling over names.

"If it's a boy," Helen mused, "you could name him after his grandparents. What was your father's name, Zane?"

"We're not naming any son of mine after that sonofa—" He clamped his mouth shut.

Silence fell over the table.

"We have chocolate cake for dessert," Helen said brightly. "Tobias, will you help me, please?"

They left the room as if their feet were on fire.

Tossing his napkin on the table, Zane muttered, "Sorry about that."

"You really do hate him, don't you?"

"Damn right." When he started to rise, Kathleen laid her hand on his arm. "Don't go. I'm sure my parents understand."

"I doubt it," he said, but he settled back in his chair.

Moments later, Helen and Taggart returned with dessert and Taggart started talking about the rising price of beef.

Later, alone in their room, Kathleen sat on the bed beside Zane. "We do need to talk about names, you know," she said, as she ran a brush through her hair.

"Anything you want is fine with me."

"We don't have to name him—or her—after anyone in the family," she remarked, then smiled as Zane took the brush from her hand and took over.

"That feels so good," she murmured, wondering why it felt so much better when he did it.

"I like the name Kathleen," he said, pausing to kiss her cheek.

"I like the name Zane," she replied. "Zane Tobias Two Shadows."

Tossing the brush aside, Zane drew her into his arms and held her close. He'd thought his need for her would wane after a while, that his desire might cool. But he had only to look at her to want her. He knew there were wives who considered bedding their husbands as nothing more than a duty. His Kathleen wasn't one of them. There was no need for words. He said it all in a kiss that stole her breath away and she responded by drawing him into her arms, warm and willing and eager for his touch.

Summer had given way to fall. The leaves changed colors, withered, and fell from the trees. Nights grew long and cold, with the wind blowing down out of the mountains.

Zane was filled with a sudden restlessness. The baby was due in early December, only a few weeks away. Taggart and the cowhands had moved the herd closer to home. In deep winter, it was necessary to haul hay out to the cattle. The chestnut mare was due to foal in early spring. The first dusting of snow sat on the distant mountains.

He couldn't believe how quickly time was passing, with one day quickly running into the next. New buildings were going up at the far end of town—Bitterman's Bootery, Tom's Cigars and Tobacco. There was also a dentist office. New houses were also being built. The schoolhouse was being enlarged as several new families had moved into the area.

The Cheyenne would be hunting often now. The women would be making pemmican and drying meat for winter, repairing lodges against the cold. He had a sudden yearning to turn his back on civilization and join his brothers, to hunt the buffalo, to sit around the campfire at night and listen as the medicine man related stories of *Wihio,* the spider trickster, and *Mehne,* the water monster, and *Nonomo,* the thunder spirit. He longed for the scent of roasting buffalo and sage, for the sweet music of the flute, the soft sound of the wind sighing through the cottonwoods …

"You look far away," Kathleen said, coming up behind him. Leaning down—no easy task with her expanding girth—she kissed his cheek.

He blew out a sigh. "I guess I was missing home."

She came around the sofa and eased down beside him. "You mean, with the Cheyenne?"

"Yeah."

A cold knot of fear settled in her heart. Was he bored with her? Thinking of leaving? She told herself she was being foolish, that he would never leave her, not with the baby coming …

He slipped his arm around her shoulders. "Just feeling restless," he said. "The People are getting ready for winter now. The men are hunting … been a long time since I hunted the buffalo."

She swallowed hard. "Are you thinking of going back to the Cheyenne?"

"Only if you go with me."

Her relief was palpable.

"Would you go with me? If I asked you to?"

"Not until the baby is weaned and walking." Taking a baby across country seemed like a really bad idea.

"I don't mean right away. And I don't mean to stay forever."

She snuggled against him. "I'll go wherever you want, Zane. Don't you know that?"

"I thought you would. But it's nice to hear." He kissed her then, a long, slow kiss filled with love and desire. They sat there, locked in each other's arms, until Helen called them to dinner.

Zane looked up from the wanted posters spread across his desk as Ed poked his head into the sheriff's office.

"Got a minute?" the bartender asked.

"Sure. Come on in. What's up?"

"Maybe nothing, but a couple of strangers came into the saloon a little while ago. I didn't catch their names, but they looked a lot like Glancy." Ed shoved his hands into his pockets and rocked back on his heels. "They had a few drinks and left. As soon as they were gone, Dan Clemons, the old guy who sweeps up over at the livery, came hurrying in. He said he overheard the two of them talkin'. Seems they think Glancy got a raw deal."

"Where are they now?"

"Clemons said they rode out of town."

"Did he say which way they went?"

"He wasn't sure, but he did hear Edling's name."

Zane swore softly. "All right. Thanks for the heads up. If you see them again …"

Ed nodded. "I'll be sure to let you know."

"Obliged."

"Come on down to the saloon later," the bartender said as he strode toward the door. "I'll buy you a drink"

Zane lifted a hand in farewell. Sitting back, he drummed his fingers on the desk top. He had no proof the strangers were kin to Glancy, yet he felt an old familiar tightening in his gut that warned him trouble was heading his way.

Chapter Thirty-Four

Kathleen pressed a hand to her back. It seemed to hurt a lot these days, although she wasn't sure why. Her mother and Juanita wouldn't let her do anything more strenuous than fold the laundry. They insisted she nap in the afternoon and put her feet up when she sat down.

At the moment, her father was out on the range with the cowhands, Zane had left for work early, her mother and Old Mort had gone into town, and Juanita was at her home babysitting one of her grandchildren. For the first time in weeks, she was blessedly alone.

And bored.

Annie had told her walking was good for pregnant women and with that in mind, she decided to take a short stroll around the yard. She slipped on a warm jacket, a fur-lined hat and gloves and stepped out onto the porch. There was a decided chill in the air. The trees, stripped on their leaves, looked sad somehow. She saw a couple of their cowhands away off in the distance.

She smiled as the baby gave a lusty kick. The doctor had assured her that everything was fine and that she shouldn't have any trouble delivering a healthy child. Still, the thought of childbirth was daunting. She told herself it couldn't be too bad. If it was, women wouldn't have so many children.

Tucking her fears away, she walked through the narrow path that led into a clump of trees, pausing now and then to admire the last of the fall flowers. She glanced over her shoulder at the sound of hoofbeats, felt her blood go cold as two strangers rode into view. One of them led a saddled horse. She told herself there was nothing to worry about, they were probably just lost.

"Howdy, ma'am," the older man said. "We were looking for the Taggart place. A fella in town said they were hiring."

Kathleen forced a smile. "That's true. If you come back later, you can speak to my father."

The two men exchanged glances, and then the younger one dismounted.

When he took a step toward her, she turned and ran, but it was useless. He caught her easily.

Pummeling his chest, she shrieked, "Let me go!"

"We ain't gonna hurt you," the man said as he pinned her arms to her sides. "But you might hurt that baby if you keep fightin' me."

She stilled instantly.

"That's better." He lifted her onto the back of the third horse, handed the reins to his companion, then swung onto the back of his own mount.

Terror was a cold lump in her throat as they left the ranch behind.

Zane huffed a sigh as he hustled a couple of drunk cowhands into the jail and locked them up. He didn't ordinarily come in so early, but Ed had sent a man out to the ranch to say he was needed in town and there was no one at the jail. Cosgrove had broken his arm in a bar fight and was recovering at home. His two temporary deputies were unavailable.

Charlie Richards had eloped with Jensen's daughter and wouldn't be back for a few days, and Bob Wade had left town.

Tossing his hat on the rack, he dropped into his chair, stared blankly at the wanted posters on the wall across from his desk, and thought about Kathleen. It had been a while since they'd made love and although he could still hold her and caress her, he missed the intimacy of feeling her body writhing beneath him, the warmth of burying himself deep within her, the sense of oneness that he'd never felt before.

Muttering an oath, he was reaching for his hat when the door opened and a boy of maybe thirteen darted inside. "You the sheriff?"

Zane nodded. "How can I help you?"

"A man give me two-bits to give ya this," he said, pulling a wrinkled sheet of paper out of his pants' pocket. Thrusting it into Zane's hand, he turned to leave.

"Hold on," Zane said as he scanned the note. "Who gave this to you?"

The kid shrugged. "Never saw him before."

"Where is he now?"

"I dunno know. He rode out of town soon as he give it to me."

Zane swore under his breath.

"Can I go now?"

"Can you describe him?"

The kid scrunched up his face as he thought about it. "He was kinda tall with brown hair and his eyes were funny. One was blue and the other was brown."

"Obliged, kid."

With a nod, the boy ran out the door.

Zane felt a cold knot of dread in the pit of his stomach as he read the note again. *We have your woman. We'll exchange her for you. Tonight. Six o'clock, at the shack by Turner's Pond. Come unarmed, on foot, and alone. If you try anything, she's dead.*

Fear for Kathleen's life coalesced into rage and a burning desire for vengeance. Checking his Colt, he grabbed a rifle and left the office.

Kathleen huddled on the floor, shivering not only from the cold, but the icy fear that engulfed her. From the snippets of conversation she overheard, she realized the two men were related to the man who had killed Austin. The taller one was his brother, the one with the mismatched eyes was a cousin. They intended to kill Zane, and she was the bait in the trap.

She had to get out of here before Zane showed up, but it seemed hopeless. She struggled against the rope that bound her hands together, but doing so only seemed to make the knots tighter.

She blinked back her tears. Crying wouldn't help. But the tears came anyway, and with it the sense of time passing, each minute putting Zane that much closer to danger.

Taggart was standing on the front porch when Helen and Mort pulled up in front of the house. He frowned when he didn't see Kathleen with her mother.

"Tobias." Helen smiled as he helped her from the buckboard. "I missed you."

"Where's Kathleen?"

Helen frowned. "Isn't she here?"

"No. Juanita has no idea where she is."

"Where can she be? She wouldn't ride into town alone. Maybe Zane picked her up."

Taggart shook his head. "She would have left a note, or let Juanita know she was leaving."

Helen stared at her husband, her brow etched with the same worry she saw on her husband's face. "Mort, please put the supplies away. Tobias, we need to go see Zane."

She had no sooner spoken the words than he rode into the yard, his horse lathered and breathing hard.

"Is Kathleen here?" he asked

"No. We were just going to ride into town to see if she was with you."

"Dammit!" He pulled the note from his pocket and thrust it at Taggart. "Someone's got her."

Helen clutched her husband's arm as her face paled.

"Where's Turner's Pond?" Zane asked as Taggart passed the note to his wife.

"It's about ten miles south of here, on the edge of Edling's property."

Helen crushed the note in her hand. "Why have they taken her?" she asked anxiously.

"They're looking for revenge," Zane said tersely.

"Revenge?" she exclaimed. "Against Kathleen? Why?"

"It's me they want," Zane said. "Glancy was their kin."

"It's not your fault he was hanged," Helen said, blinking back her tears.

"Near as I can figure, they aren't sure who was on the jury and they can't get their hands on the circuit judge, so they've decided to make me pay because I'm the one who arrested him."

Taggart muttered an oath. "What are you gonna do?"

"What the hell to do you think?"

Taggart snorted. "They'll shoot you on sight."

"Maybe, maybe not."

Taking a deep breath, Taggart said, "I'm going with you."

"No, you're not," Zane said.

"She's my daughter, dammit!"

"And if anything happens to me, she's gonna need you. Besides," Zane said, taking up his horse's reins. "I won't be alone."

Kathleen stared out the shack's dirty window. The sun was setting. It would be dark soon. The two men who had abducted her, both dressed in dark clothing and carrying rifles, had gone outside a few minutes earlier. She knew they were going out there to wait for Zane. Did they intend to shoot him on sight?

She stared into the gathering darkness, her heart pounding with fear for the man she loved.

She struggled against the rope again, twisting her wrists this way and that until she bled, but the ropes refused to give.

And then she heard Zane's voice.

Zane stopped riding when he reached the squat wooden building. There was no light inside. The night was unusually quiet. Nightbirds were silent. A sliver of moonlight broke through the drifting clouds, casting silver highlights on the pond. He tightened his hold on the reins when the buckskin moved restlessly beneath him.

"I'm here," he hollered, his gaze darting back and forth. "Let the woman go."

"Get off your horse." The command came from his left.

Moving cautiously, Zane dismounted.

"Hands up." This command came from a little behind him to his right.

Zane raised his hands to shoulder height. "The woman. Let her go."

"All in good time," the man at the left said, a leer in his voice.

They had no intention of letting her go, Zane thought, his gut tightening.

"Walk toward …" There was a high-pitched shriek, followed by an eerie silence.

Zane hit the ground when he heard the faint snick of a rifle being cocked. Rolling over, he waited for the unseen man at his right to fire, and shot at the muzzle blast.

There was a muffled cry.

Zane stayed where he was until a voice called, "Both are dead, *kola*."

Rising, Zane started toward the shack when Kathleen came running out the door. Tears streamed down her face as she threw her arms around his neck. Behind her, Teetonka grinned at him.

"Kathleen." A sigh shuddered through him as he realized how close he'd come to losing her. "Thank God you're all right." He held her close, the tension draining out of him as he assured himself that she was unhurt. "Don't cry, love," he murmured as he brushed a kiss across the top of her head. "Everything's all right now. I've got you."

Zane glanced to the left as a second warrior materialized out of the shadows. "Thank you, my brothers."

The second warrior let out a war cry as he waved a bloody scalp in the air.

Feeling the bile rise in her stomach, Kathleen buried her face in Zane's shoulder. When she looked up again, the Indians were gone.

"Come on, darlin'," Zane said. "Let's go home."

Later that night, after Kathleen's parents had assured themselves that their daughter was all right and heard the story of the rescue, Helen and Kathleen went up to bed. Zane started to follow them when Taggart asked him to wait.

Curious, Zane watched while Taggart filled two glasses with whiskey and then handed him one.

"How did you find the Indians so fast?" Taggart asked, taking a seat on the sofa.

Zane remained standing. "They're camped nearby."

Taggart's brows went up. "Why am I just hearing about this now?"

"I told Teetonka a while back that if things got rough, they could camp in the trees."

"And dine on my beef, I suppose," Taggart muttered.

"A small price to pay for your daughter's life, don't you think?"

"You could have been killed."

Zane shrugged. "That's a possibility every time I strap on my gun."

"I'm trying to thank you."

"All right, you've thanked me."

"You sure don't make it easy," Taggart muttered.

"Dammit, I don't want your thanks. If it wasn't for me, she wouldn't have been in danger in the first place."

Taggart stared at him, surprised by the guilt in his son-in-law's voice, the pain in his eyes. "You really love her, don't you?"

"More than my own life." Zane downed the whiskey in a single swallow, hurled the glass into the fireplace and stalked out of the house.

"Well, I'll be damned," Taggart muttered. "Maybe I've misjudged the boy all along."

CHAPTER THIRTY-FIVE

Fall turned to winter and the snow came. Great white drifts gathered against the fences. Dark clouds hovered low in the sky, punctuated by intermittent days of sunshine.

Regardless of the weather, Zane spent an hour or two outside every day, either riding the buckskin, or down at the barn cleaning the tack, or just enjoying the solitude. Helen and Taggart spent a lot of time reading or playing cards, or napping by the fire. Kathleen was also restless as the time for the baby's birth grew ever closer. Zane couldn't blame her. Impending fatherhood had him feeling a damned sight nervous himself.

Tonight, Helen and Taggart had gone up to bed early. Kathleen was reading a book. Every time she twitched or sighed, Zane held his breath. He glanced outside, thinking it would be a hell of a night for the baby to be born. It had been snowing since noon with no sign of stopping any time soon.

Damn, he hated waiting.

"I think I'll go to bed," she said as she closed the book and set it aside. "Are you coming?"

"Yeah."

Smiling, she pushed to her feet, and let out a cry as pain knifed through her.

Zane was on his feet and at her side in an instant. "Is it the baby?"

"I think so." She gasped as water pooled between her feet.

Zane muttered an oath as he grabbed a blanket and spread it over the sofa, then eased her down on it. "Don't move. I'll be right back."

Taking the stairs two at a time, he ran up the stairs and pounded on Taggart's bedroom door.

Taggart muttered, "What the hell's going on?" as he eased the door open.

"The baby's coming."

Taggart's eyes widened, but before he could say anything, Helen pushed past them both and hurried down the stairs, her nightgown flapping behind her.

Zane and Taggart followed her, only to pause in the doorway as Kathleen let out a low moan.

"This could take a while," Taggart remarked quietly. "And it's best left to the women."

Zane nodded, his gaze on Kathleen's face. He knew a little about childbirth. He had held his mother's hand while she delivered her last child. He clenched his fists as Kathleen let out another groan.

"Zane," she whimpered.

"I'm here." Moving to her side, he took her hand in his.

"We should get her upstairs to bed," Helen said, looking at Zane. "Tobias, go heat some water and bring me some clean sheets."

Bending down, Zane gathered Kathleen in his arms and carried her upstairs. He held her while Helen turned down the covers and spread a couple of towels over the mattress.

When she had everything fixed to her satisfaction, Zane eased Kathleen down on the bed.

"Don't leave me," she murmured, reaching for his hand.

"I won't."

Time seemed to slow, until it seemed he would stand beside her forever, watching her agony, hearing the heart-wrenching cries she made as she labored to expel their child. It had been hard, watching his mother give birth to his brother. It was harder, watching Kathleen, knowing he was the cause of her pain. He had seduced her, never thinking of the consequences. He called himself every name he could think of until, at last, the child was born.

Beaming, Helen said, "It's boy," as she wrapped the infant in a blanket. "Here," she said, passing the child to Zane, "hold him while I look after Kathleen."

Zane stared in wonder at the tiny scrap of humanity cradled in his arms, and in that moment, he loved Kathleen as he had never loved her before. "A son," he murmured. "I have a son." He wondered if his own father had felt such a sense of wonder, and if so, where it had gone.

He looked up as Taggart tiptoed into the room and saw the man as if seeing him for the first time. They had something in common now, he thought, something more than loving Kathleen. "Would you like to hold your grandson?" Zane asked, his voice thick with emotion.

Tears welled in Taggart's eyes. "Yes, son, I would."

Watching from her bed, Kathleen felt a sudden wetness in her own eyes as the two men she loved the most gazed in awe at the child they shared, all their previous antagonism washed away as if it had never existed.

She smiled when Zane returned to her bedside.

"I love you," he said quietly. "You've given me everything I ever wanted."

"And you've given me everything I've ever wanted. Everything except a little girl," she said with a grin. "Maybe we can work on that next year."

"Next year!" He shook his head. "I can't go through this again."

"*You* can't?" she exclaimed with mock ferocity. "I'm the one who did all the work, Mr. Two Shadows."

"My brave girl," he said, stifling a grin. "I guess if you can stand it, so can I. After all, getting there is half the fun."

Epilogue

Zane sat on the front porch, his son in his arms, listening to Kathleen and Helen as they prepared the mid-day meal. Hard to believe his son was almost a year old. Kathleen had had her way and they had named the boy Zane Tobias Two Shadows, but called him Toby for short.

In the spring, the chestnut mare had delivered twin foals—a filly and a colt. Both looked just like their dam.

With the help of Taggart, the cowhands, and some of the men from town, he had built a house for Kathleen a half-mile from the home place.

To everyone's surprise, Oliver Plotkin married Kathleen's best friend, Susannah. Zane managed to put his dislike of the man aside, partly for Kathleen's sake but mostly because Plotkin had once come to his defense.

With a sigh, he stroked a finger over his son's cheek. The boy looked just like him—same tawny skin, same black hair, same dark eyes. It was a miracle, he thought, and then he smiled. Who would have thought that hiring on to work for Taggart would bring him everything he had ever wanted?

Filled with a sense of peace he'd never known until he met Kathleen, he went inside and kissed the woman he loved.

Kathleen smiled inwardly as she looked forward to being alone with Zane later that night. Because she had a secret, she thought, as she placed her hand over her belly. A secret she was dying to share.

About the Author

Madeline Baker is one of those rare birds—a California native. She's lived in Southern California her whole life and loves it (except for the earthquakes). She and her husband share a home with a fluffy Pomeranian named Lady, a mischievous cat named Trouble, and a tortoise named Buddy.

Madeline and her alter ego, Amanda Ashley, have written over 90 books and short stories, many of which have appeared on various bestseller lists, including the New York Times Bestseller List, the Waldenbooks Bestseller list, and the USA Today list. Not bad for someone who started writing just for the fun of it.

Madeline loves to hear from her readers. You can contact her at darkwritr@aol.com.

For a list of all her books, including covers and chapter previews, visit her website at www.madelinebaker.net.